THE
SERPENT
IN
HEAVEN

ALSO BY CHARLAINE HARRIS

Gunnie Rose:

BOOK 4

THE SERPENT IN HEAVEN

CHARLAINE HARRIS

SAGA PRESS

LONDON SYDNEY **NEW YORK** TORONTO NEW DELHI

SAGA PRESS
AN IMPRINT OF SIMON & SCHUSTER, INC.

1230 AVENUE OF THE AMERICAS, NEW YORK, NEW YORK 10020

First Saga Press hardcover edition November 2022

SAGA PRESS and colophon are trademarks of Simon & Schuster, Inc.

For information about special discounts for bulk purchases, please contact Simon & Schuster Special Sales at 1-866-506-1949 or business@simonandschuster.com.

The Simon & Schuster Speakers Bureau can bring authors to your live event. For more information or to book an event, contact the Simon & Schuster Speakers Bureau at 1-866-248-3049 or visit our website at www.simonspeakers.com.

Interior design by Kathryn A. Kenney-Peterson

Manufactured in China

1   3   5   7   9   10   8   6   4   2

Library of Congress Cataloging-in-Publication Data has been applied for.

ISBN 978-1-9821-8249-6
ISBN 978-1-9821-8251-9 (ebook)

For the usual suspects: Hal, Patrick, Wade, and Julia;
Paula, Treva, Dana, and Toni; my literary agent,
Joshua Bilmes; my book-to-screen agents,
Debbie Deuble-Hill and Steve Fisher; and my editor,
Joe Monti. Thanks for being the best support group ever.

ACKNOWLEDGMENTS

I always thank the same people in the Acknowledgments. But these are the people who always, always, contribute to my life as a writer and a human being: my agent, Joshua Bilmes; my editor, Joe Monti; book-to-screen agents at APA (Debbie Deuble-Hill and Steve Fisher); my husband, my children, and my grandchildren; and my dear friends Paula Woldan, Treva Jackson, Dana Cameron, and Toni L.P. Kelner (aka Leigh Perry).

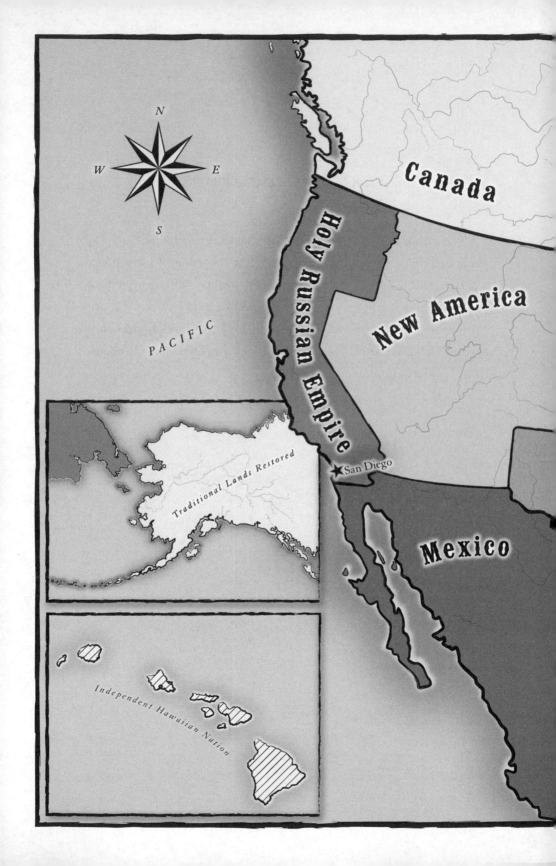

CHAPTER ONE

I stood with my back against the doorframe while Miss Priddy held the yardstick to it.

"You've grown again," Miss Priddy said. "You need new uniforms."

She really hadn't needed to measure me to see that my skirt was too short and my wrists stuck out of my sleeves, but the woman was a stickler. Priddy had been headmistress at a girls' school long ago, before America had dissolved into five countries. She resented being a house manager for the Grigori Rasputin School in San Diego, which not only didn't belong to her but was also mostly run by Russians—who, by the way, are hell on uniforms.

Students at the Grigori Rasputin School wear navy blue and yellow. I think it's so the general population can get away from us quickly in public, in case we try to practice magic, even the ones like me who aren't really supposed to have it.

I stepped away from the doorframe and waited. I wasn't going to apologize to Priddy for having grown. The old woman glared at me, the lines around her mouth deepening as she scowled.

I couldn't help growing now that Father had been dead for two years.

Father—Oleg Karkarov, a fair-skinned Russian—had decided I'd be safer in the slums of Ciudad Juárez if I was small and grubby and brown, indistinguishable from any other Mexican urchin. Or maybe both Father and my uncle were dismayed at the idea of coping with a maturing girl. Or both.

So my father spelled me to stay little. It was a clever spell, and it didn't have to be as potent since I never had enough food.

Since Father been killed, I'd grown—very slowly at first. When my half sister Lizbeth and her partner, Eli, had found me living with my uncle, they'd thought they were rescuing a skinny eleven-year-old. When I'd arrived in the Holy Russian Empire (formerly known as California and Oregon) with Eli, I'd looked that age or younger. I'd been placed in the lowest grade, naturally. Though I'd been insulted, that mistake had given me time to acclimate.

Now that I'd been attending the school for well more than a year, getting regular meals and rest and no doses of magic, my body had begun making up for lost time. I was beginning to have breasts. My hair was not dusty black anymore but dark brown. And my skin had grown several shades lighter since I spent so much time indoors.

Miss Priddy didn't like me or my skin, and she wasn't moving to help me.

"I do truly need new uniforms. I don't want to embarrass the school," I said. That should jolt her into action.

With great reluctance, Priddy turned away to rummage through the neatly stacked shelves, her hard white fingers flipping through the folded garments. She turned to hand me two bundles, each containing a skirt, a blouse, and a sweater. One of the blouses had a large faint stain on the front. The skirt in the other stack had a botched hem.

I glimpsed a familiar silhouette through the glass of the door. It began to open.

"I would prefer a blouse that wasn't stained and a skirt with a level hem, please." I made sure my voice was even and respectful as I pushed the clothes back across the counter.

"If wishes were horses, beggars would ride," Miss Priddy shot back with a sneer. "Be grateful for what you are given, Felicia. You're a charity girl. And you're not even a grigori!"

Thank you, Miss Priddy. I suppressed a smile.

"That's the way you treat this student? A blood relative of our founder?" Madame Semyonova, the headmistress, croaked from behind the housekeeper.

Priddy actually jumped.

"Madame—I didn't . . ." Priddy was so horrified that she could not go on.

"I assume you were going to say, 'Madame Semyonova, I didn't know you were standing there observing my rudeness.'"

Priddy glared at me with anger she could not express. She would not forgive me for this. But she hadn't liked me anyway.

It was worth it.

Madame leaned on her cane. She made it clear she was going to remain in the storeroom until I had proper clothes or Miss Priddy died of mortification.

Priddy turned back to the shelves, her shoulders rigid. I watched her ribs expand and fall as she took a deep breath. She reached up to gather another set of garments and swiveled to toss two brand-new uniforms to the counter between us, plus the beret and undergarments that went with them.

"Better give her a third set," Madame Semyonova said. "After all, we don't want her big sister to come calling, do we?" Madame's smile was grim.

My half sister, Lizbeth Rose, a gunnie by trade, is a great shot with both pistols and rifles. For all I know, she's good with a bow and arrow or a slingshot, too. She's killed many other gunnies. Also, she's married to a prince. She is a hard act to follow. To give her credit, Lizbeth doesn't seem to know that.

With a curtsy to Madame Semyonova and a "Thank you, Miss Priddy," to prove I was the better person, I carried my three sets of clothes out of the supply room on the ground floor of the dormitory.

My room is on the third floor. I bounded up the stairs to make my heart pump hard, since I didn't get as much exercise as I liked.

Our door was open, so I knew my roommate was in. Anna Feodorovna is a trainee grigori (magic user) from a Russian family. She had not liked being saddled with a charity case as a roommate, much less one who was only enrolled due to her Rasputin blood, not her grigori talent. But her room had the only empty bed, since Anna's first roommate had had to go home.

"I'm not rooming with a filthy Mexican null bastard," she'd said to one of her friends the day I'd arrived, her eyes on me and her voice loud so I'd be sure I knew where I stood. My father was the bastard, not me. He'd been one of Rasputin's by-blows, but he had been married to my mother. For sure.

Father's favorite life lesson to me was, "Never let *anyone* get away with *anything*."

That night, while Anna slept, I'd turned her hair darker than mine. Anna had burst into tears and refused to leave the room until I returned it to its original blond, shimmery straightness.

Now we get along much better. In fact, I sit with her and her coterie every morning at breakfast, even though I find their conversation insipid and boring. I am just that contrary.

Practicing magic on Anna wasn't without risk, since I was not supposed to have any magic to practice, as far as the instructors knew. But the result had been worth it.

I wanted to stay here, at the Rasputin School for Grigoris, with a passion that shook me sometimes. This place was a haven for a half-Mexican, half-Russian orphan.

I wanted to be a real grigori, not just a blood donor for Tsar Alexei, who has the bleeding disease that only Rasputin's blood can alleviate. When the raggedy Russian flotilla had finally landed in California after years of wandering, William Randolph Hearst had invited Tsar Nicholas and his wife, Alexandra, and their family to the compound he was building north of San Diego. It was heaven for the longtime fugitives whom no country would accept—and now their son ruled this new country.

It was heaven for me, too. I didn't have to steal, I wasn't in fear, I got to eat every meal. And there were books. I got to *learn*.

"Anna, I have new clothes," I called—in English, of course. No one else in residence spoke Spanish.

"Good for you, now you won't look like a scarecrow," she called back in Russian. "You have a visitor."

The students and teachers of Russian background spoke fluent Russian. The students and teachers from England, Ireland, and Scotland spoke English. Since the former State of California USA was now the Holy Russian Empire, classes were taught in American English.

Luckily, I had a great gift for languages.

I still had a lot to learn in San Diego.

The clothes and shoes were strange. (Not so bad.) I got to eat three times a day. (Wonderful.) I had my own bed to sleep in and indoor plumbing. (That was best of all.) I had to go to church, and that was boring, but boring didn't hurt.

My new life was a lot to adjust to. Since Eli and Lizbeth had left for Texoma (the former states of Texas and Oklahoma), I had no one to discuss all this with except Peter Savarov, Eli's younger brother.

I wasn't too surprised that Peter was my visitor. He was sitting in my desk chair looking at my class notes, while Anna pretended to read as though Peter wasn't there.

"New uniforms!" I told Peter, throwing the bundles onto my bed.

"Good," Peter said. "The one you're wearing is a scandal."

I shrugged. "Now I'll look better," I said.

"If you two are going to talk, can you do it somewhere else? I have to study." Anna held up her book to make sure I noticed it was a secondary text for spell-casting, the text for a class I wasn't offered as a mere blood source for the tsar. Even though Anna knows what I can do, she's also realized that for some reason, I don't want everyone to know. So she acts this way.

Peter is no favorite of hers, since his father and stepbrothers were staunch supporters of Grand Duke Alexander in his attempt to stage a coup. She fears contamination by association.

"Of course, dear," I said, and kissed Anna on the cheek. She gaped at me. Peter and I left the room before she could recover.

"Does Anna bend that way?" Peter whispered as we went down the stairs side by side.

"You didn't ask me if I do!"

"Oh, who the hell knows what you will do?" he said, sounding twenty years older. "I've given up. You could kiss a bear, it wouldn't surprise me."

Good! I smiled at him.

"But I am keeping an eye on you, just so you know. My brother and your sister have charged me with watching out for you, and I will do that." He stood proud and tall, his grigori vest still new and unstained.

"Is that why you were waiting in my room? To find out what I was doing?"

"I don't hang around where I'm not wanted, even by such a nobody as Anna, unless I have a reason."

We reached the covered walkway that led from the dormitory to the school. Instead of walking along it, Peter stepped onto the grass and went over to the Founder's tomb, elevated and white and topped with the Russian Orthodox cross. Rasputin's tomb was situated between the school and the high iron palings of the fence enclosing the school grounds, visible but not accessible to passersby. I shrugged and followed him.

Peter looked over his shoulder. "My mother wants to know if you will come to dinner with my family tomorrow night. Felix is invited, too, and he'll stop by to pick you up and return you to the school after, if you can come." Peter, now a full-fledged grigori, was living at home until he got his first job or assignment. Peter hadn't yet gotten either.

"I'd be glad to come," I said. "Unless the tsar needs me, of course."

Any slip or fall, any accidental cut, and the tsar would bleed. Then he'd need me or one of the other remaining Rasputin-descended bastards whose blood kept Alexei alive. There weren't many of us left, but at least the rate of attrition had slowed down since the tsar's uncle had been shot. Alexander had been devious enough to start picking off Alexei's blood donors. He would have gotten to me in time.

"Of course," Peter said. He looked self-conscious, and I could tell he was boosting himself up to say something. "Since you gave Anna a kiss, will you give me one?"

"No," I said, astonished. "Why do you ask?"

"Just wanted to see what you'd say. Why Anna but not me?" Peter cocked his head.

"Because Anna is not important in my life, and your family is," I said.

"You sound like I should have known that." Peter was half smiling.

"If the shoe fits," I said, tossing my head. I was proud of working in that adage. I wheeled and walked into the school building at a brisk rate. I didn't actually have a reason to go into the school, but I needed to walk away from Peter, and I didn't want to go back to face Anna yet. Let her simmer for a while.

This kissing people was a new thing and had popped up along with the appearance of my breasts.

Tom O'Day was on door duty in the lobby. Tom was the only grigori I knew of who came from Texoma, like Lizbeth. I felt it formed a bond between us, though Tom did not share that opinion. Many of the girls were interested in Tom, though he was at least ten years older than most of them, surly, and (as far as I could tell) humorless. Good-looking, though.

"Tom," I said, to get him to look up from *Great English Wizards*.

"Um?" He marked his place with an envelope and shut the book. His face did not change at all when he looked at me. *Hell*.

"I'm invited out tomorrow," I said. "The Savarovs. Felix will fetch me and return me."

Tom's broad face turned even grimmer. "Felix," he said. He might as well have spat.

"You know Felix is engaged to Lucy," I said.

Tom looked blank.

"Peter and Eli's sister."

"Felix isn't interested in women," Tom said, his sandy eyebrows shooting up like caterpillars.

A breakthrough in our relationship! Tom had volunteered an opinion.

"He and Lucy seem quite pleased about the engagement," I told him, sounding prim.

Tom shook his head and reopened his book. I was dismissed.

"Aren't you going to enter it in the log?" I said, just to aggravate him.

Tom didn't make any effort to keep his own sigh silent. He laid his book aside and took up a pen to write in the logbook.

"Thank you, Tom," I said, just to stay there for a moment more.

The fire grigori did not look up. "Girl, get yourself some new uniforms."

"Just got them," I said.

"Then for God's sake, go change."

So I left.

CHAPTER TWO

Master Franklin tapped the tip of his long pointer on the map. "And this used to be?" he asked, his bushy eyebrows going up as he waited for the answer. Since History was the second class after lunch, we were drowsy.

"Texas," Cyril said. The rest couldn't be bothered.

"And this?" *Tap, tap.*

"Oklahoma," Cyril told him.

"And now they are?"

"Texoma!" the whole class chorused, getting into the moment.

"But this part of Texas . . ." Franklin tapped the southern part. "Now belongs to?"

"Mexico," I said, to end the long silence.

"Ah! And you used to live there, did you not, Felicia?"

"Yes, sir." He knew that. They all knew that.

"Show us where."

I got up from my desk and marched to the map hanging down over the blackboard. I touched my finger to Ciudad Juárez, suddenly remembering the people and the smells and the heat. I felt a sharp pang of homesickness. "My sister lives here, west of Dallas," I said, touching the approximate location of Segundo Mexia. I remembered her curly dark hair, her wiry build, the smell of gun oil. To hide the surge of water in my eyes, I resumed my seat.

"So your family is Mexican?" Master Franklin seemed determined to mark me out.

"My father was Russian, my mother was Mexican, and my family is dead," I said flatly. Master Franklin knew this. My last name was Karkarova.

I stiffened my back and stared into his deep brown eyes, bracketed with wrinkles.

To my surprise, just for a second, I could tell he felt sorry for me.

"Do any of the rest of you have parents who are of different nations?" Master Franklin said, turning away to survey my classmates.

Three hands shot up. I was surprised. Maybe the history teacher wasn't trying to make me feel like a mongrel . . . or maybe at least he wanted to show me I had a pack?

Bobby Gaynor was half-Irish, half-Britannian. Karen Olmsted was half-Norwegian, half-Holy Russian. Susan Kwan had a half-Chinese father and a mother from the HRE.

They were all at the Rasputin School because they'd shown a talent for magic at an early age. Their families had put together enough money to send them here to develop that talent and go into the service of the HRE, the only government I knew of that employed grigoris. Or they might go into private service, which was more lucrative but chancier.

I was at the school solely because of my valuable blood. Always in a unique position. Always the odd one out. Now that I'd started growing at such a rate, it was going to become obvious I had some secrets.

The chime sounded to tell us to change classes. I gave Master Franklin a nod as I left by way of a thank-you, though I was glad to leave. Next was Basic Elements, the only grigori class I was in. That was because it fit the gap in my schedule, not because the teachers supposed I could practice magic.

I was the oldest one in the class, but at least until now I hadn't looked it.

I liked Madame Lubinova, the teacher. She had been astonished that I did well in the class, since none of the other Rasputin by-blows had. I hoped she would convince the others to move me into more grigori classes.

Today the hour went well. We were discussing what guided a grigori to pick a guild, how to discern what element was your primary affinity. I was prepared, my homework complete. I was sitting by Cyril again. He was smart and funny—but never at my expense, which made me fond of him. Cyril was eleven, the age I'd looked when I'd arrived at the school.

Though he'd looked all right in History, Cyril laid his head on his desk. His face was flushed.

"Is something wrong?" I asked.

"Not feeling very well," Cyril muttered. "It came on all of a sudden."

I remembered a rumor I'd heard in the refectory that morning. I felt a quiver of fear, but I tried to hide it. I touched Cyril's forehead with the back of my hand, snatched it away. I said, "Madame Lubinova!"

I'd interrupted her in taking roll. The gray-haired teacher looked at me over the top of her spectacles. "Excuse me, Madame. High fever," I said. I nodded toward Cyril.

Everything in the classroom seemed to halt. All eyes were on poor Cyril. Everyone feared the same thing; we all knew there'd been cases of Spanish influenza popping up in the city.

"Go wash your hands immediately," Madame Lubinova told me as she brushed past to crouch by Cyril's side. I left the room while she was asking him questions. When had he begun to feel ill? Had he gone anywhere public in the past few days—grocery store, shops?

Had he had visitors from home? Cyril mumbled his answers, his head still down.

I scrubbed my hands in the girls' bathroom. I'd seen how fast illness could spread. It would fly from person to person just as fast in San Diego as it had in Ciudad Juárez. What if Cyril had influenza? Every time the disease flared up in North America, it took souls away with it. I felt my shoulders tense at the thought, and I scrubbed harder before I returned to the classroom.

Cyril and Madame Lubinova were gone. "They went to the infirmary," Susan Kwan told me. She shivered. No matter what you looked like or how rich or poor you were, Spanish influenza was a scourge.

Tom O'Day, called off door duty, came in to lead the class. Though I was worried about Cyril, I hoped Tom would give me a special nod. He didn't.

When the class chime sounded again, I ran up the stairs to my room. I'd barely closed the door before I was stripping off my uniform. It was great good luck that I'd woken late and grabbed one of the old ones.

I pulled the navy dress and yellow sweater off and then the old panties and hose. I put the discarded clothes in my laundry bag with my name stenciled on the side. I attached a note saying *Burn these clothes* before I shoved the bag down the chute in the corridor. Then I hurried to the shower room with my dressing gown around me. (I hadn't known what a dressing gown was when I'd arrived here.)

I scrubbed my body and my hair and dried off quickly. I wrapped my towel around me while I rubbed some argon oil into my hair. This was one of the few pleasant things Anna had taught me in one of her fits of condescension. Now, instead of having a frizzy black mane, I had smooth curls of shiny dark brown.

Back in the room, I scrambled into one of my new uniforms. Since I was going to a dinner at a private home, it would be proper to wear other clothes, civilian clothes, but I didn't have any that fit. I hated to ask Lizbeth for money to buy more.

I also hated wearing my old shoes—they pinched—but it was either that or go barefoot.

I brushed my hair and put on my school beret at a jaunty angle. There was nothing left to do but stroll to the main building to wait for Felix. Tom was back on door duty. As usual, he was reading. He looked up and didn't immediately look back down at his book. *Yes!*

But the grigori didn't give me a compliment or comment on how pretty I looked. Instead, he glanced at the clock on the wall. "Another ten minutes before Felix is due," Tom commented.

"How is Cyril?"

Tom looked even more grim than usual. "Looks like influenza," he said briefly.

"I scrubbed down after I touched him." And I was wearing brand-new clothes.

"Was he coughing or sneezing?"

"Not in the classroom. But should I tell Eli's family I won't be coming?" I was really disappointed at the prospect of cancellation, but that was better than taking the flu with me. Lots of people still didn't believe that the air could carry disease, but air grigoris who had a talent for healing had confirmed it, so we were sure at the school.

"There've been cases in the city already. Cyril's our first. You might as well go. You seem to feel well. No fever?"

I shook my head. I felt fine.

"So if any of the Savarovs seem under the weather, walk right out."

Tom looked at me with a lot of intensity. For a second, I felt hope.

He said, "You have a loose hair on your collar."

I pressed my chin against my neck to look down at myself. It's not a good look for anyone. I spotted the long hair trailing across my clean new blouse. I twitched it off, looked up at Tom questioningly.

Tom scanned me, nodded, and returned to reading. But after a moment, he looked up as though he was looking at something specific. He nodded to himself and pressed a button on the desk. This was a new system, designed to let the doorkeepers see who was asking admittance to the school. I assumed the "looking" required magic, since no one could see through walls—at least, no one I knew of. Anyway, pressing the button would make the front gate open.

A few seconds later, Felix Drozdov pushed open the big front door and paused, looking from me to Tom. Felix's long dark hair was a tangled mess around his face and shoulders. To be fair, his short beard and mustache had been trimmed. He was scowling. Felix as usual.

"Ready?" he said, by way of greeting.

I twirled around.

"Good," Felix said. "New uniform. Your clothes fit."

"Oh, no, don't flatter me," I said emotionally, hoping Tom would pick up on my sarcasm.

Felix looked at me funny, and Tom returned to reading his book. *Oh, well.*

Without further comment, Felix turned to lead the way out of the school.

"Rude," Tom muttered behind me.

I didn't think Tom had much room to point fingers. At least Felix *could* be charming, from time to time. He could be a lot of things.

This evening, he was a silent chauffeur. He did open the car door for me, and he did wait until I'd gotten my skirt out of the way before he shut the door. For Felix, that was gallant.

"Do you and Lucy have a wedding date set?" I asked as the car pulled away from the curb. That seemed polite and social, the kind of question normal engaged people would be glad to answer.

Felix loved Eli, my half sister's husband, not Eli's little sister. I was sure Lucy was aware that Felix did not see women and think, *yum*. But both Felix and Lucy seemed determined to see the wedding through.

Felix didn't answer, didn't even look my way, for quite a while. Something was clearly on his mind besides navigating the crowded streets, though that was difficult enough. There were cars and pedestrians everywhere on this cool spring evening.

The Rasputin School was close to the waterfront. At this time in the afternoon, people were getting off work and coming to the wharf area to dine in one of the many restaurants or to stare across the water at the buildings on North Island, where the tsar's palace sat.

"There's influenza in the city," Felix said.

I'd decided he wasn't going to speak the whole way to the Savarovs'. I'd gotten lost in watching the faces and cars go by.

I said, "A boy in one of my classes got sick today. Before you ask, I feel fine."

Felix glanced over at me. "That's good. It would be a shame to take it to the Savarovs, if Peter hasn't already done that."

"He looked okay yesterday," I said. "He acted okay. Well, like Peter."

Felix grunted. "Lucy and Alice have never had it," he said after a moment.

"What does that mean?"

"Some people believe that if you've had it once, your chances of getting it again are less," Felix said. "I don't know if that's true."

"There's no spell that can make someone less likely to get it?" I looked longingly at the many pockets on Felix's well-worn grigori vest, wondering what was in them and how he'd decided which spell would go where.

"Not yet."

We'd gone three more blocks when something terrible happened. We'd stopped at a light, and among the crowd of pedestrians crossing was a dark-haired young woman in a blue jacket. Squarely in front of Felix's car, she crumpled to the ground. I heard a thud as she hit the bumper.

"Oh, no!" I said, and jumped out of the car.

Felix said something I didn't hear because I was rushing to her aid, as were others. Two men bent over her. I was hoping at least one was a doctor, but they looked awfully rough for professionals. I knelt beside the woman. Her eyes were closed, her body slack. I didn't see any blood, which was good.

"Did you check her pulse?" I asked as I reached for her wrist. She was dark enough to be Mexican or Chinese, something other than white.

A hand grabbed my own wrist in an iron grip. I looked up to meet the eyes of the smaller of the two men.

"Let go of me! I'm fine!" I yanked back as hard as I could. With my free hand, I tried to grab hold of the car. Did he think we had hit this woman on purpose?

"I don't think you're fine," said the other man. He grinned at me. "I think you're in trouble." He gripped my free arm and yanked hard enough to pull my hand from the car.

I screamed, "Felix!" as loudly as I could, which was pretty loudly. The other people gathering to help the woman (or gawk at her) jumped back in surprise. Unfortunately, this gave the two men the opportunity to yank me up to my feet and away.

They began to run with me, half dragging, half carrying. The crowd was staring at us with confusion, even embarrassment, of all things.

"Felix!" I shrieked again. "Help me!" I could not look back to see what happened to the woman or if Felix was following us, because I was being hurried along with great speed. We were going in the direction of an old sedan parked at the curb. Since screaming hadn't worked, I began to whisper a spell, one of the first my father had taught me after a man had tried to take me as we were shopping for fruit.

My assailants flinched at the pain in their hands, and one of them said, "Goddammit!" The pain spell had worked, but it seemed these two were used to magic. They weren't as shocked or startled as they should have been. And they were used to being hurt.

We were almost at the car.

Once inside it, I would be going somewhere I didn't want to go.

I let my legs collapse, hoping to bring the men down with me. It didn't work. They hauled me back up.

I tried to kick the shorter man on my right. It's hard to kick when you can't brace yourself, and my shoe landed weakly against his calf.

"Felix!" I turned my head and just glimpsed him, shoving against the crowd. Most of the onlookers were yelling, and none of them seemed to understand what was happening. Since Felix was ruthless and seldom polite, he was making progress. I had a flash of hope.

Just for a second, as the crowd was forced apart by Felix, I could see the hand of the woman on the ground. That hand shot out and gripped Felix's ankle just as he took a step. Felix went down hard.

I'd lost.

CHAPTER THREE

I was never unconscious. I wished I had been, though. The next few minutes were very unpleasant. The smaller man clamped his hand over my mouth, while the larger man, who had rough dark hair, held my own hands together. They began to try to stuff me into the backseat of the car.

I made it as hard as I could. I wanted to kill them and spit on their bodies. I bit the hand over my mouth, and its owner slapped the tar out of me with his free hand. It hurt, and it shocked me. It had been a long time since someone had used force against me.

Even my father and my uncle had seldom laid hands on me (though once my father had made me immobile for ten minutes).

I had a reaction to this violence that scared me, though the strength of it felt almost . . . divine.

I went crazy. I fought like a tiger, and when my attacker pulled away his bitten hand, I screamed with every bit of air in my lungs.

A policeman came running toward us. I saw a glimpse of his uniform approaching, even through the increasing crowd.

I yelled, "Help me! Help me!"

I saw the "hurt" woman straightening to her feet, and I begged the crowd to stop her. A burly man in a construction uniform grabbed the woman's arm, but the policeman swung around to confront him instead of pursuing me. The bitten man had time to heave me into the back of the car. His accomplice was already in the driver's seat. Before the door shut on the manhandler, we were pulling out into traffic. The people around us seemed to have finally caught on, because several of them pounded on the car as we went by. In a second, the car was moving too fast for me to unlock the door and throw myself out.

I'd been kidnapped.

I was pretty scared.

I worried about Felix for a second, but Felix was well able to take care of himself . . . if he hadn't been injured too badly by his fall to the street.

The smaller man twisted in his seat to give me a glare. He was cradling his hand. "Don't you scream anymore or try to get out," he warned me. "If you do, I'll belt you, and I won't hold back."

I was fairly sure he hadn't held back the last time, but I didn't point that out. After I weighed the value of fighting against the pain of being hit in the face, I made the decision to cower.

I would have taken the chance to fight—at least, I hope so—but the car had picked up speed and was in a neighborhood of homes: no stores, no help in sight. The pedestrians were fewer, and most of them were very old or very young. None of them was a grigori.

With my eyes closed and my face slack, I thought hard. When Felix was able to talk to the policeman, he would say plenty. I knew he'd be enraged that I'd been taken while I was in his company. Not only did Felix have a very high opinion of himself, but he was a man. Maybe the two were synonymous.

I kept my lips pressed together so I wouldn't shriek or cry. I had to keep myself together. Inside was another state of affairs. I screamed in my head for everyone I knew: Felix, my sister, her husband, Peter, even Tom O'Day and Madame Semyonova. As far as I could tell, this internal screaming for help did about as much good as nothing. So I tried something else.

I looked hard at the men in the front seat, trying to fix their faces in my head, which was still ringing from the blow. Just then, Man Two, the larger one, turned to give me a glare. Seeing my eyes fixed on him, he stretched over the seat and belted me again. That was all I knew for a bit.

When I could think again, I was being dragged into a shabby house in a run-down neighborhood. The front yard was tiny. The paint was peeling, and the front porch sagged. That was all I had time to notice, because the men were moving so fast. As Man One and Man Two hauled me along, each gripping one of my upper arms, they argued.

"You should not have hit the girl," Man One was saying. "She'll come unglued."

He wasn't talking about me; maybe "she" was the woman in the blue coat.

"As long as the girl's alive, we'll get paid," snarled Man Two.

"Didn't think of that." Man One sounded impressed with the reasoning.

But I knew *no one* with money. My sister and her husband didn't have cash at the ransom level, for sure. And they were my only family.

These idiots had snatched the wrong girl.

I started to tell them so, but just at the last second, I realized that was the worst thing I could do. If they had meant to grab Lucy or Alice Savarova (which made much more sense) and they found they didn't have her, these two goons might kill me out of hand. As they shoved me up the stairs, I couldn't think of a single way to get information without cluing them in on my worthlessness as a kidnap victim. Until I knew what to say, I wasn't going to speak. When they shoved me into a room and shut the door, it was a real relief.

Now I couldn't say the wrong thing.

Now I could have time for my head to stop hurting.

Now I could figure out how to kill them.

CHAPTER FOUR

I had more than enough time, as it turned out, because I didn't see M1 or M2 for twenty-four hours.

The room was real familiar by then.

There was a bucket in the corner. There was a bottle of soda and a wrapped sandwich and a pickle. There was a cot. There was a small empty closet (not even a left-behind coat hanger). Mouse droppings. Dust.

And dark. The window had been boarded up.

From time to time—through the remaining afternoon and during the night—I stood with my ear to the door. I never heard a peep. Even if my abductors weren't talking to each other, it stood to reason they'd move around, get a drink, go to the bathroom, something.

They'd left me here alone.

At least I could make as much noise as I wanted.

There was one window in the room. It was covered with fresh plywood, which had been nailed to the sash. The wood felt sound, and my searching fingers found that the nails had been pounded in flat.

The sheet of plywood was bigger than the window, so there was a ledge all the way around. I tried gripping the bottom and pulling back. Nothing. I jumped up to grab the top of the plywood. I got splinters in my fingers . . . but I thought I'd felt the wood shift a little.

So I did that fifty more times, until my fingers began bleeding and my legs got weak.

I sat on the edge of the cot to rest for a while and to think. Who would look for me?

Felix, if he had lived. His pride would demand that he retrieve me.

The Savarovs, because I was the sister of Eli's wife. Also, I had helped defend their home during the previous winter's coup attempt. Also, Lada and Alyona (Lucy and Alice) liked me. I'd worked hard on building that.

The staffers at the Rasputin School, because I was in their charge and because the tsar might need my blood.

Though a voice in my head whispered that no one would care if I were missing forever, I recited all this over and over in my head.

Then I made myself catalog the worst that could happen. *You don't want to be taken by surprise, do you?* The men were expecting money for grabbing me, but when that did not come, they'd kill me—or they'd try to.

They might decide to rape me first, of course. I'd almost gone through that in Ciudad Juárez (the time I simply hadn't run fast enough). Thanks to my father's random training, I'd survived it. I could survive it again.

On the other hand. On the bright side. In the morning, they would probably bring me more food. If they hadn't given up on payment, in which case . . . well . . .

If they brought me food, they'd open the door.

An open door would give me my only chance.

I wasted about one minute of the long night regretting that I didn't have any of my explosive spells loaded in my pockets. I was really good at making explosives, thanks to Father. In my defense, I hadn't imagined needing to blow up anything while I was at dinner with the Savarovs.

I realized it was a waste of time regretting what I *didn't* have.

What did I know that might help? I took off my painful shoes to lie flat on the cot, ignoring the pain in my bloody fingers. I set my mind to looking back at the things Father had taught me when he'd been in the mood. Mostly, he'd thought of spells I could use to defend myself or spells to help me get away with stealing when we were short of food.

When it had occurred to Father, or when he was drunk and wanted to amuse himself and his brother, I'd learned things. That was what I'd craved from the moment I'd found myself at the Rasputin School, because those times were my good memories, when my father had seen me, recognized my budding power.

My inventory was sketchy. I could be invisible for five minutes; Father had taught me that one when he'd found me bruised and bloody after I'd been accused of stealing a chicken (I had, I was hungry). I'd hoped my father would track down the women who'd beaten me and beat them to a bloody pulp. *You will die for laying hands on my beloved daughter.* Instead, he'd taught me to become invisible so they couldn't catch me.

I could make someone sprout cat whiskers. Man One and Man Two might laugh at each other real hard if I tried that one. I could run then.

Hold on a minute, said my brain.

If I could make hair grow, could I make other things grow? When I'd made whiskers appear on my uncle, I'd gotten some hairs from a stray cat as my father had directed (not an easy process). I'd imagined them as whiskers and then thrust some power into my will. *Voilà!* as my father had been fond of saying.

So probably, yes, I could. But how could I be sure of the origins of any hair I picked up from this floor?

I needed to shock Man One and Man Two. I needed to startle

them so much that they'd leave the door open for a few seconds. In that brief time, I'd have to get past them and down the stairs. (But what if only one of them came upstairs—to bring me food or shoot me or rape me?)

Assuming I got past the men and out of the house, what then? I didn't have any money to call a cab or catch a bus. I was wearing a distinctive uniform, so I was easy to spot. I could feel my thoughts skittering off in all directions and panic setting in.

I told myself, *Get out first. Step one.*

I might have slept for a couple of hours before I sat up. After a long think, I'd gotten as far as I could with so many variables.

I wondered how Felix was. I wondered if the school knew yet, if Felix had called and Tom O'Day had answered the phone. *Not Felicia!* Tom would say. He would be aghast at my awful fate. He would think, *She's so young, but I see now what she means to me. I will get her to safety, no matter what the cost.*

I was being silly. Of course, Tom wouldn't think that. Imagining that was weakness on my part. I was in charge of my own rescue. My sister Lizbeth would never spin dreams if she should be planning. That was why she was so good at what she did.

I remembered how Lizbeth had tried to spare me after the siege of the Savarov house, when I'd gotten close to the bodies of the men and women I had killed. Those were my first adult spells: a mixture of herbs in small packets infused with my will to give the result I wanted, like real grigoris did. They'd worked better than I could ever have foreseen.

I shuddered. I allowed myself a few seconds to wish with all my heart that Lizbeth and her guns were here. Then I dragged myself back to the lonely here and now.

I was ready, if only the men would come. I was hungry and thirsty. I knew it was morning—a little light was showing around the edges of the damn plywood. I ate and drank just a little bit more of the sandwich and the water. And then, at what I thought was noon, the same. And then in the middle of the afternoon. This was stretching out much longer than I'd imagined.

Maybe the men had died! And I would die here, since no one would be able to find me.

I had just figured it must be about five o'clock, twenty-four hours after Felix had picked me up at the school, when the front door opened downstairs.

They'd returned.

CHAPTER FIVE

When I heard two pairs of big feet clomping up the bare wooden stairs, I started the spell. It was simple, a repeated phrase from a children's rhyme: *My little girl, she is so sweet. My little princess, prim and neat. My little daisy, in full bloom. My little lady in a palace room.* I'd timed it on my fingers during the night, imagining the rhythm of those footsteps.

I'd cut it too close. If I hadn't been standing behind the door, they would have seen me the second before I became invisible.

For the two men, who looked even rougher today, the sun from the landing was streaming into an empty room.

Man One and Man Two asked themselves a lot of futile questions, like "Where did she go?" and "Is she hiding somewhere?"

And then, finally, they did what I'd wanted. They stepped inside, leaving the landing empty.

I had taken my pinching shoes off hours ago. I was holding them in my left hand.

As the two men moved toward the closed closet, the only possible place of concealment, I began to edge around the open landing door. Man One was staring at the closet door as if he expected me to jump out and shout *Boo!* Man Two, perhaps a bit smarter, was looking around the room, quick little glances. They hadn't panicked yet.

They'd find out the closet was empty in seconds. I had to get the hell out of this house. Quietly, quickly, I eased around the door and stepped silently out onto the landing.

I froze when I saw a padlock hanging from the door. I could pull the door to, click the lock shut, and run! I started to put my shoes down so I could use both hands.

I had second thoughts.

If I fumbled! If they barged out before I could get it done! I'd be back in the room, and they'd be very angry. I clamped down on myself and made my feet move down the stairs. Quietly, steadily. I could hear their voices rising behind me as I concentrated. They were angry with each other.

I reached the bottom. Right opposite me was the front door and freedom.

I turned the knob quietly.

They'd locked it when they'd come in.

Now my hands were shaking, because any minute, they'd come out . . .

And I saw the deadbolt above the doorknob, turned it, and the door was open. I stepped outside. I closed the door behind me as silently as ever a door had been shut.

I spared one quick glance around me. As I'd glimpsed the day before, I was in a poor neighborhood. Houses needed paint, had dirt yards. There were a few ancient cars parked here and there, and the pavement was cracked and had potholes.

I'd been right about the time of day, too. It was late in the afternoon. But this was not a busy street, with men coming home from work and kids playing in the cool evening. There was one woman in sight, sweeping her porch across the street. She hesitated as I began running, her broom stilling, looking around her. It was obvious she couldn't see me, but somehow she could sense me. At least, she didn't shout.

My instinct told me to go left, so that was the way I ran. After I'd gone a block, I turned right. Just halfway down that second block, I could hear shouting from the house. I needed to put my shoes on, but I couldn't stop. I had to get as far as possible while I held the precious advantage of being unseen.

My eyes darted everywhere, trying to pick out hazards: the broken sidewalk, activity in the houses around me, cars in the street, the choices in the route ahead. I went past two children skipping rope in a bare-dirt yard. They didn't pause their game. I didn't fall, though clutching the shoes was throwing me off-balance. A lumbering bus stopped at the next corner, and some scruffy people got off. If I timed it right . . . I threw my shoes into some bushes so I could run faster. What the hell, they pinched anyway.

I leaped on at the last possible second. Of course, all the seats nearest the door were full. I caught my breath as quietly as I could while I stood looking for a seat at the back. An empty one. I glanced at the driver to be sure he hadn't sensed me. His name patch read HACKEN-FUSS.

I could hear a man yelling, "Wait, wait!" I turned my head, and here came Man One, running to the bus.

Oh, hell.

Quickly, quickly, I began to move down the aisle, moving my feet carefully. I forced myself to breathe lightly.

"What the heck does he want?" Hackenfuss grumbled.

"Forgot his supper?" a thin woman offered, and there was a little chuckling.

By the time Man One had put a foot inside the bus to make sure the driver didn't take off, I'd gotten to the back seat. I sat down as lightly as I could, hunched over, even though I knew I was still not visible.

"Listen, my daughter ran away, and I think she may have caught your bus," Man One said, panting.

I'd never looked at him when he wasn't threatening me directly. He was swarthy and brown-haired, his hair greased into place. He needed to shave, and his suit was rumpled. He was in a towering rage, trying hard to keep his temper in check. He did not impress the driver.

"No little girls on this bus," Mr. Hackenfuss said.

"You sure? She's wearing a school uniform, she's a brunette, about yea tall." Man One held his hand at my height.

"Look for yourself. But be quick about it." Mr. Hackenfuss was not sympathetic.

Man One did not quite go to the lengths of walking down the whole aisle, which was lucky. I had all I could do to control my panicked breathing. I looked down. Somehow I felt that if I looked into Man One's eyes, he'd know I was there.

I was disgusted to find I was shaking.

After a few moments, Mr. Hackenfuss said, "You've had your look. Off the bus, now! I have a route to finish."

Man One glared at the bus driver, but he couldn't very well demand to do a more thorough search of the bus. None of the passengers expressed any sympathy for his search for his runaway daughter, either. The fact was, One just didn't look like a father worried about his daughter. He looked like an angry thug who wanted to beat someone up. "If you see her," he snarled, and put a scrap of paper in Hackenfuss's hand.

The last glimpse I had of him, Man One was standing on the sidewalk, looking this way and that, trying to figure out what to do next.

When the bus pulled away, it was one of the best moments of my life.

However, all the passengers now knew a young girl was a fugitive. I could not afford to let them see me. The moment was growing near when I would pop into their view. I bent over in my seat, waiting. The second I could see a bit of my hand, I said the spell again.

I'd never done that. It felt like I was stretching thin, somehow. Like another grigori could see through me. I was afraid. But after a few moments, I hadn't collapsed or had a fit.

I breathed a little easier. I was going to be all right, though I'd used a lot of magic (energy? power?) in just a few minutes. But I could feel there was more inside me. I felt proud, which gave me a pump of energy. I needed it so badly. I was exhausted and unfed, and I had realized during the bus ride that my feet were in bad shape. My socks had been as worn as my shoes and provided almost no protection for my feet in my running on bad pavement, littered with gravel and less pleasant trash.

At least my fingers had stopped bleeding.

I leaned my cheek against the window and tried not to think about my hurts. They were small compared to what could have happened to me at the hands of Man One and Man Two.

The next time the bus stopped, it was on a busier street, still not one I recognized but a bit more prosperous. There were nicer houses and larger shops . . . and phone booths. If only I had money! I looked at the dirty floor of the bus, hoping someone had dropped a nickel, but in the neighborhood where I'd gotten on, that was an important coin.

Off we lurched again. I'd been afraid the bus would get so crowded someone would need to share my seat. I was a little puzzled that people mostly got off, and very few had gotten on.

I found out why at the next stop.

"Holcombe Street, end of the line!" Mr. Hackenfuss called, as he pulled in to the curb again.

Everyone but me had already gathered up purses and paper bags of groceries. They stood to begin shuffling forward. I fell in last.

The passenger ahead of me stepped off, and the driver reached to close the door. I would be trapped! I'd have to go wherever buses were parked when they'd finished their day's route.

Wait . . . would that be so bad? It would probably be in the central, older part of San Diego, closer to the waterfront where the school was.

I slid into the fourth seat from the front.

Now that he thought he was alone, Mr. Hackenfuss began to sing to himself. His voice wasn't bad. I listened to his version of a popular ballad of the dissolution, "No More Miss America." I bent over and pushed myself down as far as I could go between the seats, just in case. The small space felt oddly safe. Despite my many aches and pains, I fell asleep.

I was completely shocked when my eyes flew open to see a broad face right in front of mine. I was upright, pulled into position by a big hand grasping my shoulder.

"Oh!" I gasped, strangling back a shriek.

"What are you doing, girlie?" Mr. Hackenfuss growled. "You might have been shut in the bus all night if I hadn't seen the top of your head. How'd you get in here without me seeing you? You need to doctor them feet. No shoes? What were you thinking?"

"I'm so sorry!" I said, letting my eyes open wide. "I didn't mean to fall asleep. I don't even know where I am."

"The city bus barn, Florida and Adams," Mr. Hackenfuss said, sounding a little less angry. He sighed, a big and gusty sound. "Girl, I thought you were dead."

"I'm sorry," I said again, and I was.

"I'll call your dad from the phone in the office and tell him you're here after all," the bus driver said, turning to leave. "He gave me a phone number. He can come pick you up. Come along, now."

"No!" I said, so sharply he turned back to me with raised eyebrows. "Mister, my real father is dead. I'm trying to get away from a man who's been hurting me. That man who told you he's my father, he's a liar. He means me harm."

I could see the reluctance in the way Mr. Hackenfuss's shoulders set. He didn't want to get involved in my troubles, but he didn't want to give me back to someone who'd abused me, either. He sat in the seat opposite mine to ponder.

"If you'll just give me directions to get back to the Rasputin School, I'll be safe." I hated to sound so pitiful.

"I didn't recognize the uniform. That's where you're in school?"

I nodded.

"You'll be one of them magicians?"

"I hope so," I said, and that was honest.

"It's a long way to the waterfront." Mr. Hackenfuss wanted to be persuaded.

"I'll be safe," I repeated. Hoping.

The driver debated with himself for a minute or two. He sighed again. "I've got girls at home younger than you. Listen, I'll go out of my way to get you a bit closer. Then you take yourself where you want to go. That's the best I can do."

Well, it wasn't the best he could do, but it was the best he would do. I could only be grateful for that bit of help. It was more than I'd gotten from anyone else.

Mr. Hackenfuss was as good as his word. He had an ancient Ford, and I climbed in with only a few misgivings.

We went west and south, which felt right to me. And gradually, I was on streets that seemed familiar.

By then, it was getting dark. Cars had their lights on, streetlights were glowing, and workers were on their way home. The bay area was emptying out. Only the cafés looked busy.

Mr. Hackenfuss pulled to the curb, my signal to get out and walk. I had to squelch my impulse to beg him to take me to the gate of the school. It wasn't that I was scared, I told myself. It was that my feet hurt, and my hands hurt, and I was so tired and hungry.

I climbed out with my lips clamped together from the pain. It was a huge effort to bend down to say, "Thank you so much. You've really helped me."

"You be careful, you." I couldn't see his face clearly by the streetlight, but I thought he looked embarrassed. He might well feel he could have helped me a little more. "Listen, girlie, you walk four or five blocks south, and you'll be there."

"Thanks," I said. "From here, I know my way."

To his credit, the bus driver watched me until a left turn took me out of sight.

The dusk was gathering thicker by the minute—which was good, since everyone I passed gave me a second look. I was dirty and shoeless, with bloodstains on my hands and feet. There was no telling what my hair was doing. I kept to the shadows. I didn't have enough energy to make myself invisible again. I needed to keep hold of the magic I had left. Besides, my socks had ripped away, and I was leaving bloody spots with every step. Nothing would hide those.

I was pretty close to the end of my rope when I could see a back corner of the gleaming white wall surrounding the school, just a couple of blocks distant. My feet began moving faster, despite the pain. Almost safe!

Suddenly, I froze in my bloody tracks. A big thing I hadn't considered loomed in my fears.

If my abduction had not been a mistake, if I was indeed the chosen target, anyone who wanted to get me back would be waiting close to the school to spy me returning.

Where else would I go?

CHAPTER SIX

I'm not the kind of person who imagines things—okay, I am, but not this time. I felt badness in the evening air, and it was looking for me, Felicia Karkarova.

I stopped, pressing myself into the recessed front of a stationery store. The shop windows were still lit, but there wasn't a light over the door. The niche felt safer than standing out on the street. It was a good place to ponder my choices.

Break into a run, make a mad dash two blocks, and turn left to reach the front gate, the only way into the school? My feet could stand that much, I figured. Maybe. I'd have to wait while someone noticed me and let me in, for the gate was locked at night. Once through the gate, I was safe. No one would dare attack a student on the grounds of the school where Grigori Rasputin himself was buried. No one!

I stuck my head out of the recess to scan the narrow street. There was some light traffic and a few people walking. None of them looked in my direction. My muscles tensed. I prepared to make the run, even on my battered feet. But I hesitated one more second, and that saved me.

The woman who'd pretended to get hit by Felix's car emerged from an alley on the other side of the street. Though she was wearing a full skirt and a sweater instead of a suit and hat, I knew her. She didn't see me, but that could change at any moment.

I'd been right—they were watching.

Maybe I could make the dash. I was lighter and younger. I should be faster. I might make it. But she had shoes, and I didn't. She probably had help, maybe the same two men . . . and I didn't.

I just didn't have the nerve to risk getting caught again.

With no thought at all, I reached behind me to turn the doorknob of the stationery store and stepped inside. It was warm, and there was a rug on the floor. It felt like heaven under my feet. I did feel a bit guilty about the blood but only for a moment. I looked around me.

I was surrounded by shelves holding all kinds of paper, from stationery with flowers, to sketch pads and invitations, many shades of white and cream and pink, all pretty, squared up, in order.

There was no salesclerk in the room, and there was a telephone sitting on the counter in plain sight. Quick as a wink, I was dialing the number of the school. The sound of the dial was awfully loud. *Please answer*, I thought. *Please please please*.

"Rasputin School," Tom O'Day said.

"It's Felicia. I'm at the stationery store behind the school," I said, pushing the words out as fast as I could. I kept my voice very low. For no reason.

"You're free?"

"Free but pursued. Come quick." I hung up and put my hands behind my back to look like I hadn't picked up anything. Maybe I'd just heard a step, for at that moment, the door behind the counter opened. A woman who might be thirty stepped through from the back room. Her eyes got wide behind her glasses when she saw me. She'd expected to see someone, and that someone was not me.

Filthy, bloodstained girls in school uniforms probably didn't come into the stationery store very often.

Wait till she spotted my bloody footprints on her nice wooden floor and wool rug.

"Can I help you?" she said, politely enough. She had her keys in her hand. Perhaps she'd just been going to lock up.

Maybe it was because of the day I'd had. Maybe it was growing up where the good poor were tossed like a salad with the violently criminal. But I had one of my bad feelings about the way this woman was looking at me. If I'd been a dog, the hair on my back would be rising.

"I'm sorry." I hoped I sounded just as pleasant. "I hope it's okay if I use your telephone, lady?" I reached for the receiver.

"Of course," the woman said pleasantly. "As long as it's not long distance." She had tight waves in her short brown hair, red lipstick, little gold earrings, a conservative dress. She looked like Nelly Normal, though she was wearing a lot of makeup for a woman who sold stationery.

"I wouldn't do that," I lied. "Thanks, I really appreciate it." I dialed the school again and got no answer. It rang and rang. *Oh, thank God.* That meant Tom was on the way or gathering reinforcements, or at least, I hoped that was what it meant.

"I was sure my dad would be home," I said, giving her what I hoped was a rueful look. "My name's Felicia, by the way."

"You seem to have had a hard day, Felicia," she prompted me, still with the little smile.

Just to see what would happen, I leaned across the counter to lift the telephone receiver again. Dialed again. Got no answer again. I kept my eyes on her. The more I leaned over, the more I could smell her perfume; it was strong and was supposed to be flowery, but I'd never smelled flowers like that.

The woman smiled at me, leaning over the counter toward me in turn. Her teeth were big and white, snowy against the red lipstick.

"I'm Gwen," she said, and decked me.

CHAPTER SEVEN

When I woke up in a new room, my first thought was, *Lizbeth would never have been caught by surprise.*

My second thought was, *I am going to hit that bitch so hard.*

I was angry at my failures. First, I'd gotten grabbed. True, I'd gotten away by myself, but then I'd fallen asleep on the bus and missed what remained of the daylight. And now I'd gotten grabbed . . . again.

I wanted to do something way more drastic than go invisible. I hoped the chance would come my way. I could feel the power coiling around me. When I felt like that, I didn't need a grigori vest or spells I'd learned by rote—or any damn thing.

My dad might have been a low-level grigori who made a living by putting on magic shows in rural towns, but my mother's family had been very different, he'd always told me. Though he'd never explained how.

I hadn't heard anyone else breathing or moving while I thought about what I'd do. I opened my eyes. I was lying on a couple of pallets in what must have been the storage room in the back of the stationery store, judging from the boxes of paper and the stacks of envelopes and racks of pens.

It would burn *great*. I smiled. But of course, I thought twice.

I hadn't tried to get up and walk yet, and there wasn't a door in sight from where I lay. It would be supremely stupid to set a fire in a room I couldn't escape. The windows were too high for me to access. There had to be doors in here. It only made sense that there would be two, one leading into the public part of the store, one out to the delivery area behind.

I pushed myself up to a sitting position. I was sore all over, and my feet were throbbing. I looked down at my bloody fingertips and shook my head. But I had to move. I set my teeth together and stretched my arms . . . which I could do because my wrists weren't tied. Neither were my ankles.

That was interesting.

I pulled myself up with the help of a heavy set of shelves. They didn't come crashing down on me, so maybe my luck was turning.

A day of being afraid, running, and not eating had reduced me to weak and wobbly, but after a few seconds, I was standing. Holding on to a higher shelf, I looked to my left and right. I spotted one door. It had to lead outside. I was going to escape again!

When I turned the knob silently and eased the door open a crack, I saw a toilet and a sink. I growled under my breath.

Now what should I do?

First of all, I used the toilet.

I was just about to wash my hands and face when a door—the one I hadn't found yet—opened, letting in a shaft of light from the store.

"She's back here. I knocked her out," said Gwen, trying to sound casual. I could tell she was proud.

"You tie her up good? She's very strong and crafty." Another woman's voice, one I didn't recognize, with a Spanish accent.

"Nah, she's out of it. I couldn't find any string."

"String?" said the other voice. "Miss Manley, the girl got away from David and Halsey. They're twice as old and twice as big."

"And twice as stupid," Gwen Manley said. "I warned you they had limitations."

"They were the best I could do on such short notice. I could hardly hire someone off the street corner," the accented voice said. It was the equivalent of a shrug.

I could hear two sets of feet on the wooden floor, and I could tell when they saw the cot was empty. The second woman blistered Gwen in no uncertain terms. I was impressed. I hadn't heard (or used) some of those words since I'd come to San Diego.

"We'll find her," Gwen said, sounding certain enough to make me clench my teeth. "I'll hit her again, this time with magic. She won't wake up."

"Right," said the other woman. She didn't believe that for a second. "You had better leave that to me."

I touched my swollen jaw. *We'll just see who doesn't wake up*, I thought. I heard high heels tapping on the planks of the floor as Gwen came over. "The back door is still padlocked," Gwen said. "So I guess our little fugitive is in *here*!"

Gwen flung open the door to the bathroom with a broad smile on her face. I socked her as hard as I could.

It was my turn to smile as she staggered and fell.

CHAPTER EIGHT

Slowing only to stomp on Gwen's arm as hard as I could, I leaped into the air to come down on the newcomer, who flung her hands up to defend herself. Sure enough, it was the dark-haired woman who'd pretended to be hit by Felix's car. I landed on top of her and bore her down to the floor, bumping one of the shelves hard enough to make a big box of stationery fly open. The paper fluttered around us like flat snow.

This woman knew how to fight back, and she was bigger. But she was surprised, and I wasn't. I broke her nose right quick, because that hurts a lot and the pain would distract her. I grabbed hold of her left wrist. With a heave, I got hold of her right. She began to bring her knees up to pummel me, and I realized that I, too, was trapped, now that I had her arms pinned. I was considering what my next move might be when I saw a man's foot in a heavy shoe press on the woman's neck.

She began to gargle and tried to thrash. But I didn't let her hands go.

I saw the air wriggle a little. The owner of the foot had cast a spell. The woman went limp.

I was able to let go. I rolled off my enemy and over onto my back.

"Tom," I said in an awfully weak voice. "You came."

Tom O'Day stared down at me. "You look like hell."

"I defended myself," I said, trying to keep the whine out of my voice. "This is Gwen Manley," and I pointed. "She knocked me out and put me back here. Then she came in with this woman, the one you stepped on. She's the woman who pretended to be hit by Felix's car. You know about that?"

"Every grigori in San Diego knows about that. We've all been out looking for you. Felix is out of his mind." Tom seemed pleased about that. "I'd just come back to get my coat when I answered the phone."

"Took you long enough to get here," I said, trying to sound hard. "But thanks for coming," I added politely.

Tom almost smiled. "I had to tell someone where I was going in case I didn't come back. I had to put my coat and my vest back on. I had to find out where this shop is. Then I had to break in the front door."

He'd broken down the door to get to me.

I felt foolish lying on the floor.

I held out my hand, and Tom took it, pulling me up easily.

Then two instructors from the school, Master Rostov and Madame Rostova, and Molly Foster, the disciplinarian, hurried into the back room, their hands at the ready to cast spells.

I had to go over the whole story again.

It surprised me that they questioned me as closely as they did, Miss Foster especially. She was a muscular wind wizard in her forties who wore her hair in a long graying braid. I'd always thought Miss Foster would look just right with a longbow in her hand and a quiver slung across her back. She was a serious fighter. It was easy to see she felt keeping a school full of kids in line was a paltry use of her talents. But she did a good job of it.

Miss Foster was very fair in her judgments, and she never believed a sob story. Since I had to report to her often, we were getting to know each other.

"Again, Felicia?" she said. But I also thought Miss Foster was relieved to see me whole. "Is 'trouble' your middle name?"

"No, ma'am. It's Maria. How is Felix?" I should have asked first thing.

"He hit his head on the pavement pretty hard. And he's angry, of course. But he'll recover."

"This is the one who tripped him," I said, pointing at the dark-haired woman, who was moaning but unconscious. "She's the one who had me abducted."

Gwen Manley was beginning to look around her and assess the situation, though the pain of her arm must have been considerable.

I pointed at Gwen. "And she helped her."

"I believe your arm is broken," Miss Foster said to Gwen. "What's your friend's name?"

Sweat had broken out on Gwen's forehead. She didn't look so crisp and put together now. And look at the mess in her orderly white store! *Ha!*

Madame Rostova said, "Shall I heal her?" in a voice that was completely indifferent.

Her husband squatted by Gwen and looked at her arm without touching it. "It should at least be set if she's to keep the use of it," he remarked.

"Who broke her arm?" Tom said.

"Ah . . . I did." When the two teachers looked up at me, I said, "Master Rostov, Madame Rostova, thank you for coming." (Terms of address at the school were all over the place. Some in English, some in Russian, some in combinations of languages. The teachers required courtesy and respect in any language.)

"How?" Miss Foster said. She'd come to the school from Britannia, and she sounded it.

"Stomped on it after I knocked her down," I said, looking at a box of stationery.

Madame Rostova shook her head sadly. "You are a blunt instrument, young lady," she said. "You need to learn to be a scalpel."

As long as I got the job done, I couldn't see it made much difference, but I nodded obediently. Scalpel it was.

"Look at Felicia's feet and hands," Tom said.

The Rostovs and Miss Foster had a good gander. Miss Foster gave a short, sharp nod.

"We need to take Felicia back to the infirmary," Tom said. "And these two should go into the guesthouse. We need to talk to them."

The guesthouse was a separate building in the rear of the school, a pretty cottage everyone said was used for housing visiting lecturers or parents traveling from other parts of the country. I'd noticed some odd things about the cottage. For one thing, most guests stayed in a dedicated room on the ground floor of the dormitory. Even when there were enough guests to overflow to the cottage, you couldn't hear them move around inside. And the curtains were always drawn.

"Of course," Miss Foster said. Suddenly, she smiled. It was a scary thing. "Gwen Manley! I remember you. You were expelled from the first class at the school."

Gwen made the mistake of spitting at Miss Foster, who slapped her just where I'd hit her jaw. Gwen howled. A slap from Miss Foster was a slap indeed.

"We wouldn't put up with it then, we won't put up with it now," Miss Foster said.

A lot of people would have hesitated to hit someone whose arm was broken. Not Miss Foster.

Abruptly, we were on the move. Gwen Manley and the black-haired woman—who was still limp—were wrapped in invisible air blankets by the Rostovs. The two women floated along in the center of a loose circle we formed around them. When the lights were out in the store (Tom took care of that), we all went out the back door, the captives floating through one by one, which made me want to giggle.

I needed the distraction. Standing and walking on my cut feet made me bite my lip. I couldn't hold back a gasp.

"Keep your mouth shut," Miss Foster said, her voice just above a whisper.

I nodded. It was taking everything I had to put one foot in front of the other. The pain was sharp and unrelenting.

We drifted down the alley behind the shops, which were all closed now. There were a few security lights shining over alley doors. There was no one else in sight, not a soul to witness this strange procession: two women floating in the center of a widely spaced circle of four grigoris and one limping girl.

But after a moment, I noticed all the grigoris had their hands at the ready as they looked around them—up, down, every direction. The tension jumped to me.

Now that I was afraid again, I was burning up my last reserve of energy. I hummed like a motor about to go out. All of a sudden, that motor seized. I stumbled and would have fallen to the dirty pavement, but Miss Foster grabbed my upper right arm and kept me on my painful feet.

"What's happening?" Tom said.

"She needs food and sleep and medical treatment," Madame Rostova said. "Her feet are bleeding more."

"Fifteen more minutes, Felicia, and you can have food and sleep and take care of your feet," Tom said.

I knew it was a bribe, but having a time limit did help. I kept moving, with Miss Foster's assistance. (I was going to have her finger marks on my arm, in addition to all my other scrapes and bruises.) I was filthy, too, and I had a creepy-crawly feeling inside from having too many emotions in one day.

It felt like a very long time before we reached the high white brick wall around the school grounds. (I thought it was way more than fifteen minutes.) I expected us to walk around to the front of the school to enter by the front gate. The back wall was—had always been—solid.

But it wasn't.

Madame Rostova muttered a few things, tossed a pinch of something into the air, and an iron-banded wooden gate appeared. And swung open. Silently.

This was not creepy at all, right? I was delighted.

We went through the brand-new gate onto the back lawn. The grass felt cool and pleasant against my feet. I glanced behind me to see a solid white wall.

Without any consultation, our little party split apart. The Rostovs and Miss Foster veered left toward the cottage, the prisoners floating along. A curtained window showed light. Someone was waiting for them.

Tom took over from Miss Foster to help me walk. I wanted to lean against him in the worst possible way, but I'm not a leaner.

We went in through the back door of the dormitory, which normally was locked at dusk. I expected to be steered to the staircase that would take me to my shared dormitory room. But for what seemed like the hundredth time that day, I was surprised. Tom went down the corridor on the ground floor and stopped at the door labeled INFIRMARY. I'd never had cause to visit it.

Tom pushed the door open, and the school nurse, a water

grigori named Galina Benton, gave me a sharp look. She pointed to the examining table. I couldn't manage climbing onto it, even with the stool Benton shoved over. Tom helped me as impersonally as he would have positioned a dog for grooming, which I appreciated.

I hadn't known how much my feet hurt until I got off them. I bit my lip to keep from moaning.

Mrs. Benton began running her hands over me, about an inch above my skin. This method of treatment seemed mighty odd, but I kept my mouth shut. For all I knew, it was the grigori norm. As a student, Benton (or Galina Ostrova, as she was then) had worked her way through this school by serving in the infirmary. So she must have been good.

My stomach growled. I refused to be embarrassed.

Tom's face didn't change. Mrs. Benton smirked. I hate people who smirk, especially at me. I refused to be embarrassed.

"So we know she's hungry," the nurse said. Her starched white apron, which doubled as a grigori vest, made a crinkly sound as she bent over me. "Even more, she needs water." Tom filled a glass at the sink and handed it to me.

By then, Benton had given an examination to my fingers, sore and torn and flecked with dried blood. She pulled up my skirt and scanned my legs, while I looked anywhere but at Tom.

When Mrs. Benton reached my feet, her lips tucked in as she looked them over. She got a very unmagical basin of water, a bar of soap, some tweezers, some washcloths, and a towel, rolling everything over on a little cart. Tom patted my hand in an awkward way. I tried to think of something to talk about.

"How could it have been me they wanted?" I asked Tom. "Do you think they mistook me for one of the Savarov girls?"

"I don't see how they could. You don't look anything like either one. You're wearing a school uniform, and neither of them has attended the school. You weren't coming from the Savarov house, you were coming from the school."

I'd thought about this over and over during the long night. "There's no reason in hell anyone should kidnap *me*. The only people who'd pay ransom are Eli and Lizbeth. They don't have much money. And they're far away." I sucked in my breath as the nurse began to wash the dirt and blood off my feet. I couldn't talk anymore because this really, really hurt.

I have to admit Mrs. Benton's hands were as gentle as possible cleaning the scrapes and cuts and bruises, and it was necessary to get the glass and other trash out of the cuts, but the procedure was pretty awful. Sometimes I gripped Tom's hand hard. He never protested.

Finally, the ordeal was over. Mrs. Benton threw the towel onto the cart. The water she'd squeezed out of the washcloths was dark. In fact, all the cloths were dirty.

"Almost done," Mrs. Benton said. "Now comes the hard part."

Now? Like the other part had been pleasant?

Mrs. Benton opened a bottle, put a cotton ball on the top, inverted the bottle, and put it down. Then she applied the antiseptic. She was right. This was the hard part. Tears rolled down my cheeks.

"Next, I'm going to apply balm. Your feet need to be wrapped for a few days. I'll rewrap them tomorrow morning and tomorrow night. Maybe one more time after that. You must stay off your feet completely for at least four days. You have to be rolled in a wheelchair or carried to the toilet and back." Benton proceeded with the balming and wrapping, and the end result was quite neat. It was a relief not to see my feet. In fact, I dozed off.

Then I was lifted from the examining table and carried into a narrow room with a high bed with rails. It looked amazingly clean and comfortable. And somehow I was on the bed, the rail pulled up to keep me safe, and I was covered with clean sheets, and Mrs. Benton gave me another long drink of water and told me to have a good night.

Tom said, "Go to sleep. You're safe."

And I did.

CHAPTER NINE

I woke up to the sound of coughing from the next room.

The curtains had been opened on my own small window. It was a beautiful day. I struggled to remember where I was, why I smelled so bad, why my feet were bandaged.

I heard the coughing again. It sounded strange, as if whoever was coughing had lungs full of water. Whoever it was in the next room, they were very ill. Was it Cyril?

When Mrs. Benton brought me a breakfast tray, my mouth watered so much I had to remember to use a fork to eat. But after I swallowed the first bite, I asked about my classmate.

"His family will arrive this morning," Mrs. Benton said. I could tell she was trying to tell me something without spelling it out, but I wasn't sure what her silent statement was, exactly. And I was too busy stuffing my face to ask.

One of the healing students came in thirty minutes later. To the embarrassment of both of us, she helped me with a sponge bath and into a clean gown, then lifted me into the wheelchair to take a trip to the bathroom, where I stayed while she whipped off my sheets and tucked in new ones. Then she maneuvered me into the wheelchair again. With the help of another nursing student, I was placed back in the bed. "I may not be in to help again," my nurse's aide said, sounding halfway apologetic and halfway relieved.

"Oh?" I didn't know what to make of this.

"Yes, my parents are coming to get me. Best of luck with your recovery." She nodded and left.

I stared at the door she had closed after her. It wasn't term time or a holiday. Why would her parents come? After listening to the coughing—coming from more than one chest—all morning, I finally understood that there was a crisis going on that had nothing to do with me. It had to do with the Spanish influenza.

Also, there was something weird going on. Around nine o'clock, one of the grigori-skills teachers stuck his head into my room, looked at me as if I were a giraffe, and left.

Next to pop in was my roommate, Anna. She'd skipped a class to brighten my day.

"Is it true you got away from bad men all by yourself?" she said.

"Yes," I said.

"Tell me all about it."

"No, I can't," I told Anna. It was hard to say no, since she looked like a pretty storybook picture, with her gleaming blond hair falling around her and her wide blue eyes focused on my face. But Tom O'Day had told me the night before not to talk to other students about my adventure.

Anna pouted—she even looked pretty pouting—and pleaded, but I stuck to my resolve. I'd sat up and hung my legs over the side of the bed when she entered, and Anna noticed my heavily bandaged feet. Her eyes got big.

"Oh, my God, did you walk on glass? They must hurt horribly!"

I nodded.

"Can I unwrap the bandages to see?" There was something avid and hungry in the curve of her mouth. All of a sudden, Anna did not look so pretty.

"Absolutely not," I said firmly.

This was a side of Anna I'd never seen before, and it made me wonder what kind of grigori she aspired to be.

"Have you found your element?" I asked her. I should have asked before.

"Oh, I think maybe I'm fire," she said casually. "My parents want me to marry a fire grigori, to strengthen the talent. They're so in demand now, for construction jobs and metalwork."

"You're not here to get married," I chided her, but I thought I might be mistaken in saying that. "Aren't you here to find out what you yourself can do?"

"Silly Felicia," Anna said, with an appearance of fondness. "Sooner or later, I'll find out what knack I have, though what I'd truly like to do . . ." And there she stopped, just when I thought I might have an interesting conversation with her.

Another teacher looked in, gave me an interested gaze, nodded, and left.

What the hell?

"Are they all bloody and raw?" Anna was again staring at my feet.

"Absolutely horrible," I said. I was getting bored.

Madame Semyonova stepped in, and Anna leaped to her feet. But Madame did not even glance her way. She was giving me a full-on eye scan.

"Are you healing?" she said, as if she were forcing herself to be polite.

"Yes, ma'am. Mrs. Benton is taking good care of me."

The old lady nodded, a sharp jerk of her chin, and left the room.

"That was strange," I muttered.

"When are you going to come back to the dormitory?"

"Tomorrow or the next day," I said. But that was only my guess.

"Well, I'll see the scars when I come back," Anna said, as if satisfying herself of a treat in store.

Come back from where? But I was thinking about all my morning visitors, and I didn't ask.

I was doubly glad to see Felix come in. Over Anna's gleaming blond head, I gave him a wide-eyed look.

"Feodorovna, take a hike," Felix told her, with his usual charm.

Anna looked up at him, shocked. "You have no call to speak to me in that tone!"

"You're sitting in my chair," Felix said. "Get up, or get dumped on the floor."

Anna left.

"You shouldn't encourage that girl," Felix said, settling into the guest seat.

My brother-in-law's friend was very fond of giving advice, even when none had been asked for. I brushed that aside. I could not see how I was encouraging Anna—to what end, anyway?

"How are you?" I said.

Felix looked irritable and rubbed his head. Well, his dark hair couldn't look any messier. "Better," he said, but not as if he were happy about it.

"Have you seen her? The woman who tripped you?"

"Yes," Felix said, smiling for the first time.

"What was her name? How did she become involved in such a stupid plan? What *was* the plan?"

Felix wore his favorite much-put-upon look. "I'm not here to answer your questions."

"Sure you are." Otherwise, why would he have come?

Felix shrugged. "She told us her name is Rosa. But she's not saying anything more than that. There are a million women named Rosa. She says she stepped in front of my car because she is not used to big cities, being only a humble woman from Texoma. She grabbed my ankle in an attempt to get my help. She knows nothing of any kidnapping."

"Hah! Then why did she pop up at the stationery store last night? Between me and the school! Where someone who wanted to grab me again might be expected to lurk!"

Felix's mouth twisted. "Because dear Gwen is the only woman she knows in San Diego, and Rosa needed her help after her terrifying accident. Being hit by my car."

"That's total and utter . . . bushwa."

"I agree."

"She has a base. She'd changed into fresh clothes somewhere. And I don't believe she could be in the wrong place at the right time two days in a row. Gwen was so pleased when she was telling Rosa she'd hit me and put me in the back room . . . so proud to tell Rosa she had me in custody. They know each other, you're right, but not in a long-term-friendship way."

"You walked right into their trap."

"How was I supposed to know?" I was very indignant. "It was the only place still open, and it had a recessed door, and I was hiding. I started to run for the school, and then I saw this Rosa woman, so I had to get out of sight. There was a telephone on the counter when I went into the shop. And that's how I got saved!"

Felix said, "It's weirdly coincidental. Are you sure you didn't feel strangely drawn to that shop?"

I gave it some thought, though I was quite angry. "It was lit and open and the only one that offered me a place to hide," I said slowly. "And no one in the outer room and a visible telephone. So . . . maybe."

Felix nodded. That didn't mean the subject was closed, but it meant we wouldn't talk about it any more right now. "Gwen said she believed Rosa was an agent of Iron Hand, in this city on a secret mission. Gwen believed Rosa contacted her because she'd heard Gwen was a former student at the school and therefore would know about how things worked here."

So Gwen had talked. "That kind of makes sense, if you knew Gwen had gotten expelled and would help because she held a grudge."

Iron Hand was the biggest security company on the continent. It was based in Britannia in a city called Boston, but the company had operatives everywhere: Dixie, Texoma, New America, the Holy Russian Empire.

A memory stirred. "Didn't you and Lizbeth meet some people who worked for them? When you were in Dixie?" I asked.

"Yes. The man died, but the woman lived. Her name's Harriet Ritter."

"Maybe you can get in touch with her? Ask her about this Rosa? I always thought Iron Hand was more of a law-enforcement-type company. You think they'd be part of a kidnapping?"

"I have no idea," Felix said. "It's a money-making company, so they might go to some lengths if they were convinced they were act-ing legally. If someone, for example, told them you'd been abducted, they would help to snatch you back."

"But who would pay a big company like that money for me?"

We stared at each other blankly. Felix just shook his head.

"My father and my uncle are dead. When they were alive, they had to scrabble for every penny . . . when they were sober. My sister doesn't need to kidnap me. If she knew anything about this, she'd be here now. I've got no one else."

"True." Felix's head gave a little jerk. That was Felix's way of saying, *I am listening to you, go on.*

"Iron Hand is supposed to be so professional, right? So what sense does it make that they'd hire two idiots like the goons who grabbed me?"

"Well, those goons managed to get it done. And they scared you." Felix was scowling. It was going to take him a long time to get over that.

"Yes, they did," I said. "But think. If Rosa hadn't lain out in the road, caught hold of you . . ." (Brought him down flat on his ass.) "You'd have blasted those goons with some magic, and I would have been saved."

"Yes." Felix nodded. We both believed that.

"So this Rosa is clearly the brains, for sure. Why would she need to hire local idiots to help her? Why not bring trained Iron Hand muscle with her?"

"That's a very good point." For the first time, Felix looked impressed.

"So maybe Rosa telling Gwen she worked for Iron Hand was total rubbish."

Felix rolled his eyes in my direction. "May have been, but Gwen Manley believed it. Gwen had to tell me the truth." There was no doubt in his voice at all.

"Did Rosa have to tell you the truth?"

"Rosa is a tougher nut to crack," Felix said, angry all over again. "I don't even know her last name."

"It would make more sense if she was trying to take me because I have the Rasputin blood. That's the only thing valuable about me."

"How many of you are left?" Felix ran his fingers through his beard. It was already a mess, and the finger-combing didn't help.

"Living descendants of Rasputin? There's—let's see—one actual child, in his fifties, named Arkady. The searchers just tracked him down. There are three of us grandchildren living at the palace or school. A man in his early twenties, soft in the head, named Nestor. Ruslan, he's about sixteen, he has some little job at the palace. They're hoping . . ." And I realized I couldn't finish the sentence.

"Hoping what?"

I took a deep breath. He'd find out sometime. "I overheard

the chief steward say they wanted to, uh, breed Ruslan to me so they'd . . ."

Felix flung up a hand. "Not another word," he said through clenched teeth.

I wanted to say that I understood the tsar was more important than either Ruslan or me. On the other hand, if I let someone "breed" me, I wasn't any better than a dog or a horse.

I was sure Felix knew all this, and more, but we'd never talked about it frankly.

In a few moments, he'd calmed himself. "Look at it this way," Felix said. "Out of the remaining descendants of our glorious founder, how many have as much magic as you?"

The answer was easy. "None."

"You're unique. Maybe that's the way."

The way to keep me from being bred. God, I hoped so. Lizbeth would shoot people right and left if she knew anything about this plan.

Both Master Rostov and Madame Rostova stuck their heads in to ask how I was. They gave Felix quick nods, and then they were gone.

The strange behavior of the teachers was beginning to make me very nervous. The staff found me an object of interest now. While I'd wanted that before, now it made me uneasy. When Master Rostov said good-bye, he closed the door behind him.

That was odd. But Felix didn't look surprised.

"What's happening?" I wanted an answer.

"Nothing, yet."

Worst answer ever. "Felix, tell me."

"Where is he?" a woman's shrill voice demanded from the hall outside.

Mrs. Benton answered in a low voice. I couldn't make out what she was saying.

Felix must have heard this exchange, too, but he ignored it. "Eli and I both recognize your potential. Tom O'Day, too. Anyone must, who saw you fight in the battle at the Savarovs' house."

Tsar Alexei had been penned up in their house during a last-ditch attempt of Grand Duke Alexander's son to carry out his father's plot. The Savarovs had defended the tsar, and I had helped. Quite a lot.

"I thought the school would change its attitude after that," I confessed. "I thought I'd be in all the grigori classes. Maybe get a medal, though I don't care about that." I almost meant it.

Felix said, "Here are the reasons that didn't happen. First, maybe the faculty members don't know the extent of your help. Peter wasn't in the house the whole time and perhaps didn't know what you were doing, and Eli left San Diego right after the wedding."

"But you were there." I tried not to sound questioning.

"Yes, off and on, I was there. But no one likes me." Felix didn't seem bothered by this. "I think their attitude has changed since you told them about your escape. You went invisible, I understand?"

I nodded.

"They're obviously talking about you now. I think they'll put you to the test when you are better. Then you'll get the education you need."

"Did you explain to the Savarovs why we didn't make it there that evening?" I didn't want to offend Lizbeth's in-laws.

"I told them there was influenza in the school, and you were anxious not to bring it to their house."

I could hear a lot of weeping next door in Cyril's room. And hoarse, wet coughing. Poor fellow. Cyril was coughing so hard.

And then he wasn't. The coughing stopped as if scissors had snipped it off.

And the woman who had asked "Where is he?" began screaming, "No, no no!"

Tears began to run down my own face.

"I'm sorry, Felicia," Felix said, and we sat without words. After a while, he returned to his mysterious job.

I spent the rest of the day listening to the tramping of shoes on the bare boards as the healers moved up and down the corridor and families arrived to remove their children from the dormitory or the sick rooms. Late in the afternoon, there was a different kind of step, the shuffle of men carrying a burden. I knew it was the undertakers taking Cyril away.

CHAPTER TEN

I need your bed," Mrs. Benton said the next morning. She was standing in the doorway, and she looked even grimmer than usual.

"Sure," I said, and swung my feet over the side, trying to figure out how I'd get up the stairs to my room on the third floor. I knew there was already another student in Cyril's former bed next door—I could hear the coughing.

"Wait." She sat on a stool and put one of my feet in her lap, unwinding the bandages quickly. She scowled at my foot. "You can't go upstairs yet," she told me. After dabbing on more ointment, she rewrapped my foot in seconds. "All right, stay there for a minute."

I really didn't have a choice.

Mrs. Benton whisked out of the room. I could hear a lot of conversation out in the hall, but I couldn't tell who was doing the talking. The Rasputin School was in turmoil.

Callista Roper rushed in. She'd just graduated, and she was a journeyman in the water guild. I hardly knew her, but I'd heard she was sharp and a reliable healer.

"Here we go," she said briskly. "I'm putting my arm under yours . . . there, put yours around my neck." She scattered a pinch of herbs with her free hand. "I'm sliding my other arm under your knees. Bend them, please? Good. And then I'm lifting you."

Callista's face tightened a little, and I was being carried against her as if it were easy.

Granted, I was not heavy, but the ease of Callista's lift was amazing. Maybe someday I could do this, too? If I was allowed to take all the grigori courses?

Callista, tall and sturdy and redheaded, toted me down the hall as if I were no heavier than a breakfast tray. She'd waited for a moment when the passage was empty. Every door I passed was shut, though I could hear coughing, movement, or voices behind each one. Then Callista shoved a partially open door with her hip, carrying me into a room adjacent to the back door. A glance told me this was not a regular infirmary room. The bed was lower and wider, there was no rail, and there was a carpet on the floor.

Once I was deposited on the bed, Callista said, "You all right now?" Scarcely waiting for me to nod, she was gone.

"Please leave the door open," I called after her, and she did.

I had hated the feeling I'd had the day before—that big secret things were happening around me while I was ignorant.

I'd heard the school kept a spare room for overflow in case the cottage was occupied, but naturally, I'd never been in it. This was larger and much homier than an infirmary room. A little table and a chair, a wardrobe, a screen almost hiding a sink and a toilet, and an easy chair made up the furniture. And I was lying on a double bed!

It was the nicest room I had ever had in my life. A far cry from the dirt-floored shack I'd lived in with my father and uncle in Ciudad Juárez, even better than the room I shared with Anna.

As soon as I'd thought of her, she poked her head in. "I found you!" she said, beaming. "I wanted to tell you my parents have come to get me. I'm leaving for home. My brother, too."

Anna's little brother was almost as pretty as she was. I'd never seen her older brother. She didn't talk about him.

"Anna, what's the situation?"

Anna's smile vanished. "I guess you know Cyril passed? Three other kids are very sick, another one possibly has it, and the janitor, too. Madame sent out a call for all students to be picked up by relatives, to stop the spread."

I wondered if they weren't carrying the disease home with them, but who was to know?

"Of course, you don't have anyone to come to get you," Anna observed with casual cruelty. "Too bad, Felicia. Good luck!" And she gave me a finger wave and left, in answer to a male voice calling her from the other end of the corridor.

I thought I might be forgotten in the agitation and speed of the departures of the day. I was relieved when Callista came in to help me over to the toilet behind the screen and to bring me a lunch tray. I got to sit at the little table to eat, resting my heels on a stool. I ate every bite of the sandwich and soup and drank every bit of the tea. Callista returned as I was finishing. She sank into the armchair with a sigh of relief. Her red hair was coming loose, and her apron was stained.

"How come you're not going home?" I asked.

"I'm somewhat in the same position as you are. I know you have a sister in Texoma, but she can't very well run over here to get you, and you couldn't catch the train by yourself."

I bet I could! I'd get there just fine. But I didn't have any money to pay for a ticket, so I let that go.

"Where do you come from, Callista?"

"I come from New America, a little town smack dab in the middle." She spotted a brush on the sink, stretched out to grab it to work on her hair. "Besides, I might not survive going home. I'm lucky I didn't get stoned as a witch before my folks shipped me over here. When Pa found out Mr. Eaker was traveling to San Diego to see his new grandson, he sent me here along with him."

"How'd your parents know about the school?"

"Thank God my dad reads the papers. There was an article about the school. I was scared, but I figured coming out here, learning how to do something, was better than dying from our neighbors' rocks and so forth."

"They didn't think you were a witch, your folks?"

"No, they ain't that stupid. I can't say they were too crazy about the idea of me learning magic skills, neither. But they didn't want me to die that way. I was good with my brothers and sisters, and I worked hard on the farm. Ma and Pa figured I'd earned my escape."

"You're the oldest?"

"Yeah. Got two little sisters and three brothers. You?"

"Just the half sister. But she's quite a character."

"I heard. Well, let me take your tray. Maybe you can try walking tomorrow. We just don't want the cuts to reopen. Since you're down here by yourself, I brought you this." She pulled a penny whistle from her pocket and put it on my bedside table. "If you need me and I ain't come in a while, use it."

"You're such a good nurse. And we're all grigoris. Why can't we heal people of the Spanish influenza?"

"Our power is more useful on wounds and other injuries," Callista said. "Broken legs and the like. Sicknesses . . . we can help a bit, but magic just isn't as effective. One reason the tsar has a regular doctor in addition to healers and blood donors."

"Are you taking care of the sick ones all by yourself?"

"Miss Priddy and Madame Semyonova are helping, and Felix shows up sometimes," Callista said. "Mrs. Benton isn't feeling so well the past couple of hours."

"When I'm better, I'll help," I offered. "I can at least change bedding and empty bedpans. It doesn't disgust me."

"When you're better, I'll take you up on that." Callista smiled at me. Her blue eyes scrunched up at the corners, and little curves appeared on either side of her mouth. "Let me take you behind the screen before I go."

That was a welcome relief.

Callista got me back to the bed with her helpful magic. It felt strong but not well controlled, as if she'd been using it too frequently. She shut my door on her way out, before I could call to stop her.

I spent the afternoon with one of the books that had been on the bedside table, *Red Harvest*. When I looked at the picture of the author, Dashiell Hammett, on the book jacket, I was surprised to learn he'd worked for Iron Hand, the same detective agency Rosa claimed as her employer, before he became a writer.

I'm not much of a reader. Books didn't come my way often in my childhood. The cover was kind of battered, and the pages had been turned a lot, so at least I knew other people had enjoyed it.

Red Harvest was pretty great. I understood the people. The next time I wrote Lizbeth, I'd tell her to find a copy. Or maybe I'd send her this one. I figured a previous guest at the Rasputin School had left it behind. I could imagine Lizbeth doing all the things the unnamed man did in Personville. Other kids had made reading novels sound boring. This one was anything but.

After a couple of hours, I heard a lot of coughing down the hall. I concentrated harder on the book. I didn't want to think about another student, someone my age, dying like Cyril had.

Miss Priddy cried out, "Hurry up!" To Callista? I heard lots of movement, lots of footsteps, doors opening and slamming shut. Part of me wanted to be up and helping, but part of me was scared. I'd seen people die a lot in Ciudad Juárez. Since I'd moved here, I'd come to expect the people I knew would live.

That was dumb.

I wondered about Rosa, the so-called Iron Hand operative in the guest cottage. Was anyone taking her food? Or had everyone forgotten about her in the influenza crisis? Why did I care?

After a couple more hours, I would have been glad to see Felix, even.

By late afternoon, I was feeling sleepy from sheer boredom, and I'd finished the book.

Suddenly, my eyes flew open. The sounds had changed.

Footsteps weren't walking fast, they were running. Voices weren't calling, they were screaming. I smelled magic use, not the herbal healing smell but the combat smell I remembered from the siege of the Savarovs' house.

Callista screamed, "Get away, you assholes! Sick children!" Then she made a sound that I knew, the sound of someone who'd been wounded.

I was out of bed before I knew it. I got to the door on my own two feet, too agitated to register the pain. I opened it just an inch.

There were two strangers in the hall. They must have come in by the door next to my room, because their backs were to me: a dark-haired man in a handsome suit and shiny shoes and a woman in a smart hat and expensive street clothes. Their hands were up to focus their magic, and they were firing spells down the hall as they advanced. The school staff blocked their way.

They were trying to kill Miss Priddy, Callista, and Mr. Van Peebles, the janitor, who was holding himself up against the wall with one hand because he was weak from influenza. He was striking out with a mop handle with the other. Felix popped out of the kitchen, looking surprised. Peter erupted from another door, a pinch of something flying from his hand to land on the woman in a puff of green smoke. She let fly her own magic at him, and he wavered but stayed up. Then he fell. *Peter!*

I was *very angry*, shaking with it, and I could feel the power rise in me. But Callista and Miss Priddy and Peter Savarov might get hit if I was careless. At the same time, I was going to burst if I didn't use this power. In my white nightgown, I stepped out into the hall. In my hardest voice, I yelled, "Rasputins, *down*!"

It was a miracle they obeyed, but they did, even Felix.

Then it was just me facing the intruders, who'd whirled at the sound of my voice. My hair was floating around my head. There was a high-pitched hum in my ears.

I held out my hands, palms facing the strangers. Both of them were staring at me with their mouths open.

"It's her!" the woman said in a choked voice.

I screamed, "*Die!*"

My power flew out and blasted them backward. I still remember how the woman's skirt flared around her legs.

And then they were on the floor in heaps.

After a second to make sure they were down for good, so was I.

CHAPTER ELEVEN

Felicia? Can you hear me?"

The voice, good, familiar, coaxed me back into myself.

I managed to move my head.

"That's a good girl. Can you open your eyes?"

Well . . . that was harder. I struggled. I opened them a bit. Saw a face I liked. A young woman, red-haired. Her shoulder was bandaged. Couldn't recall the name. We were still in the hall.

"Remember me? Callista? Thanks for saving us. I was scared they'd kill everyone, even the sick kids."

"Why?" I croaked.

That was my big question. Why would two grigoris, trained God knows where, invade the Rasputin School to attack sick students and a few low-power to no-power staff?

"We're all wondering, too." Callista had an arm under my shoulders. The rest of me was still on the floor. As I opened my eyes a bit wider, I could see blood on the wall. I didn't think it was mine.

"Miss Priddy told me she heard some grigoris on the back lawn a couple of nights ago," Callista said. "She looked out her window and saw the Rostovs and Tom O'Day and Miss Foster. You, too. And two women she didn't know, who seemed to be prisoners. And then they vanished. Can this be connected?"

I trusted Callista as far as I knew her, but that wasn't very well. "Maybe," I said. "Is Miss Priddy okay?"

"She was hit by their first blast," Callista told me. "That was her blood on the wall. She didn't make it. But that would have been all of us, if not for you." Callista managed a smile. "Didn't know you had it in you, girl."

"I got so mad." I tried to smile back.

"Then I know to watch out when you begin getting peeved."

"Who's hurt?" I said instead.

Callista looked away. "The Savarov boy, Peter, he landed too hard, and he's all over bruised. Mishka, one of the kids in here with the sickness . . . he's dead. They looked in his room first. Mr. Van Peebles has a broken arm and leg. The healers are with him now."

I couldn't remember what Mishka looked like, and now he was gone. He must have been one of the younger boys.

"Where is Tom? Where are the Rostovs?" Where was *anyone* who should have been here to protect our school?

"I don't know," Callista said. She looked tired and sad. "I tried, but I'm not . . . that much of a grigori."

"I heard you yell," I said. "Sounded ferocious."

She managed a fleeting smile. Then she looked up sharply. "Someone's coming," she said.

I hadn't been listening, but now I heard the footsteps, too. Coming from the direction of the school building, at first walking, then running. Tom O'Day must have smelled the magic. I knew it was him.

Tom swore, long and loud. Callista gasped, but I'd heard much worse.

"What happened?" he said. "I'm gone for two hours, and . . . what *happened*?" He was looking at the two bodies on the floor. They lay as they had fallen.

"Felicia saved us," Callista said. She sounded numb. "Or we would all be dead."

"You're bleeding," Tom said to Callista. The bandage on her shoulder was spotted with red.

"I think it's not too bad," Callista said. "I was worried about this one. She killed them, and then she collapsed."

"Then let's get you fixed up while Felicia gets back to herself," Tom said. "And while I'm looking at your shoulder, you can tell me exactly what happened. First, let me contact the guild and get some people here to guard the place."

I think I went to sleep for a few minutes. The next thing I knew, Tom was picking me up and putting me back in the guest room at the end of the hall.

"You're a barrel full of tricks," he muttered. I thought he didn't know I could hear him. "Were they after you?"

It was hard to make my lips work, but I said, "Maybe they were looking for the women in the cottage. But they said they recognized me."

I felt Tom start. Then he said, "That's not good."

And that was all I remember. I'd used up everything inside me.

I dreamed. My dreams were full of horrible moments. Callista's injury. The death of Mishka, when I hadn't even been present at his passage. Sour, nasty Miss Priddy, gone forever. And Madame Semyonova? Where was she? She was so old, and her body was so fragile.

Had I really killed the two intruders? I'd meant to get rid of them, stop them, but I hadn't exactly intended to kill them. Shouldn't I feel bad about that?

Over and over, I relived stepping out into the hall in my nightgown, my hands extended—like I was pressing the intruders back with my palms. But I hadn't said a spell. I'd just exploded at them, with my will. Telling them to die.

I was frightened, more than a bit. At the same time, I knew this power was something that was mine. I'd gotten glimpses of it inside me. I could feel it quivering in moments of danger or stress. Now it had broken loose. It showed I was a real grigori, not some runty girl out of the slums who'd been often neglected.

It also proved how dangerous I was.

And the woman had said, "It's her!" Like she knew me.

Sometime later, I woke up to see Felix sitting beside the bed.

"Good," he said. Felix's cheeks were covered with stubble, and his clothes were even more rumpled than usual. He got up and went to the door. "Madame!" he called.

Madame Semyonova was almost as disheveled as Felix, within her own limits. Her dress was bloodstained, and the braid wound on top of her head was beginning to loosen from its careful pinning. She sat in the chair Felix had vacated.

I waited for the questions to begin. Madame stared at me, her small brown eyes set deep in the papery wrinkles.

"Who was your mother?" she said.

I hesitated. And then I decided I would not tell the whole story. In fact, I would lie.

CHAPTER TWELVE

I don't remember her much," I said slowly. "She died when I was maybe four." That was the truth.

Behind Madame, where he had propped himself against the wall, Felix gestured for me to go on.

This was something that hurt to talk about, so . . . not easy.

"My mother was from a well-to-do family in Ciudad Juárez," I said. "At least, they had way more than us. Maybe not really rich." I shrugged.

"What was their source of income?" Madame said crisply.

"Father told me they were merchants."

Madame didn't call me on the lie. She wasn't testing me. She really didn't know.

Neither Felix nor Madame spoke. I stumbled on. This was my most hated memory.

I had never shared it. I might not, even now.

"When my mother met my father, and I don't know how that happened, she decided she would marry him, and her father was very upset and angry. She did it anyway. After she died, he didn't come to the funeral. I think some of her sisters did." I went on slowly. "My father drank a lot after she died. And we had next to nothing as far as money or food. My uncle taught English to some wealthy people. After a few weeks, Father took me across town to this nice neighborhood. The streets were clean. There were lampposts." I had not known it was possible for streets to be lit and safe at night. I had been in awe that people could live in such luxury.

"We went to a house with a high wall built around it. I could hear a fountain inside." I remembered the splashing even now, how cool and rich it had sounded, how much I wanted to put my hands in it—to go inside. Belong.

"Father said, 'This is where your mother grew up.' I couldn't believe it."

"What was her name?" Madame asked.

"My father just called her 'your mother.'" That was true, as far as it went. "She'd been the favored daughter of the family before she eloped with my father—an unaffiliated grigori *and* a bastard."

"A bastard of our founder," Felix said.

I shrugged. *A bastard.* "Father knocked at the door. A young man opened it. Father told me later that this man was my uncle." I shrugged again. Might have been true, might not.

"Did they let you in?" Madame said, after a long time had passed.

"No." I met her eyes, daring her to make me feel bad about it. "My father said, 'This is your niece, Felicia. Now that my wife has died, her daughter should be with your family. She would be safer.'"

"What did he mean?" Madame said.

"I think he meant I would be safe from people who wanted to use my blood because I am Rasputin's granddaughter." No point beating around the bush.

Felix winced, and Madame's lips pressed together in a thin line. I decided I'd better move on with the story before they decided to argue about Father's prediction.

"I was hurt that Father would give me away to strangers." Even if we seldom had money and my father usually ignored me, I knew him. And I was afraid of my aunts, who had looked at me with such scorn at my mother's funeral. "But I could hear that fountain. I liked the high wall." I had loved the idea of being safe. Where we lived, I was always watchful, always on guard.

"My uncle said it was not up to him. He looked at me hard. He said he could see the likeness. Then he went away to get someone else."

"Your grandfather or grandmother?" Madame said.

"It was an older man. My father told me later it was my grand-father."

"Did you talk to him?" Madame said.

"No. He looked at me for a while. At least, it seemed like it. I looked back at him. Then he shut the door."

There was another long pause, as Madame and Felix looked away from me.

"But more happened," Madame said at last.

"Father leaned against the wall and just stared at nothing for a while. I think he was ill, maybe with the fever that took my mother. Then another door opened, a . . . humble door, further down the wall. A woman, really a girl, kind of hissed at Father. We went to her."

"Did she help?" Felix said. You could tell he wanted to hear a yes.

"Yes." I sighed, tried to keep it silent. "She was my youngest aunt, I think. She gave Father money and her own necklace to sell. I could hardly understand her, she talked so fast. Didn't want my grandfather to catch her helping us, I guess. My father was . . ." *Sick, proud, angry.* "He couldn't say he was grateful. But he nodded. She said she would try to help, but he must never come to the house again. She shut the door. We left."

"No more contact after that?" Felix said.

"Not that he told me." I shrugged. "But we did seem to do a little better. I think she sent us money. We had more to eat. My father got a headstone for my mother's grave. He said he owed her that. But nothing else changed, except my father decided he didn't want me to grow. That is, until my sister and Eli found me."

"How old are you, really?" Madame asked.

"Fifteen?" I shrugged.

The two grigoris stared at me like they were trying to memorize me.

"Your father was strong enough to cast a spell to keep you looking younger. Why?" Madame asked. "And if he was that strong, why didn't he do better financially?"

"Father thought I would be safer if I looked like a little child. There were one or two men who would harm a little child—not many. But a girl who'd started bleeding? Fair game to a lot more." Then I answered the second question. "And he didn't want to give his blood to anyone, much less the tsar. He'd gotten a letter from one of the other bastards. A few of them kept track of one another. He'd been warned. All his fund-raising trips—that's what he called them—were far away from home."

Felix looked disgusted. "I don't know whether to applaud his ingenuity or dig him up and kill him again." So I wasn't the one who disgusted him, it was my father.

"He was not a very good man in a lot of ways," I said. "But he was my father. He taught me some things that kept me alive." *When he'd felt like it.*

Felix nodded stiffly, and that was as much concession as he was able to give.

Madame said, "Including the spell you used in the hall?"

"No, Madame Semyonova. That was myself." I could not lie about that.

"Not a spell you were taught?" It wasn't like Madame to ask something a second time.

"No, Madame. I was so angry, it gathered me up and aimed me at the intruders." That was the best I could explain it.

"What, *exactly*, did Oleg Karkarov teach you?" This from Felix.

"Father taught me how to stay invisible for a few minutes. That was how I got away from my kidnappers. During a period of political unrest in Ciudad Juárez, he taught me how to make explosive spells."

Madame said, "Holy Father, have mercy."

"Well, he was drunk when he did that," I said. "I was too scared to try it for real until we were besieged in the Savarov house. But Eli could tell you, I'm really good at explosions." I smiled with pride. "Also, my father taught me how to change people's features for a while, like the time I gave Anna brown hair. But that was Father funning. He'd take whims when he was bored." *Or drunk*.

Madame closed her eyes. It was like watching a turtle blink. "When he was bored." She opened them again. "In my opinion, if he had had training and discipline, Oleg Karkarov might have been a notable, but erratic, grigori. As it was, the man wasted all the opportunities in his life, except persuading a woman of means to marry him and therefore having you. I must rest. We will talk later."

She got up and left the room, Felix in her wake. I wondered if that had been a compliment.

I got up and padded to the door to listen.

Madame said, "Now we know how she did it. More or less. But we still don't know who the two grigoris were and why they came here, what they wanted to achieve."

"If it hadn't been for Felicia, I think everyone—perhaps including you, Madame—would be dead."

"Was this the second attempt to kidnap Felicia? Or did they want to kill her? Or were they here to rescue the women in the guesthouse? Thank God I put it out of sight yesterday."

"Whatever they were after, Felicia stopped them. We can only be grateful for that." Felix was doing his best for me, and that touched me more than he would ever know.

"Yes. Probably."

And I heard Madame's cane *thunk* on the floor as she moved away, so I padded back to bed and climbed in. My feet were hurting, of course.

Felix gave a quick knock and entered, looking at me steadily. His face was blank. He was thinking.

Finally, he said, "Food?"

I nodded with so much enthusiasm that Felix smiled a little bit. It took him thirty minutes to return with a tray. He put my tea on the bedside table, the tray across my knees on its little legs. He'd brought me breakfast: pancakes and bacon and eggs. He could have brought me lunch, or dinner. Didn't make any difference to me.

I had a long drink of tea and then launched into the food.

"Are you chewing?" Felix said. "I've heard that's a good thing."

With an effort, I slowed down.

I'd learned languages very easily. Manners were harder.

My stomach could not hold as much as I'd imagined. I stopped eating.

"Please tell me exactly what happened," I said. "I came to the party late."

"There were only a few people in the building. A good thing," Felix said. "The two grigoris came into the dormitory from the door by your room."

It was seldom used. The door opening to the covered walkway leading to the school building was the primary access door. Like Madame, I wondered if they'd been looking for the woman Rosa, the one in the (now) invisible guesthouse.

"Madame had stepped outside, thank God. Miss Priddy, Callista, and I were here tending to the sick. I don't tend too well, but I have been running errands for those who do." Felix looked wry. But I thought it was surprising and good that he'd done that. "Peter had come by to see how you were, on instructions from his mother. Mrs. Benton has come down with the influenza, and so has her husband. They're at their apartment, doing as best they can. The rest of the patients are students, from Cyril's class. And Mr. Van Peebles. And then you."

"So there were just two grigoris? And they came in blasting?"

"Yes. They were casting stunning spells. Miss Priddy was old, and her skull was thin. That was enough to kill her when she hit the wall."

Miss Priddy had been awful to me. I tried to feel sad about her death, but the most I could manage was regret that I had not been able to save her.

"I was in the staff kitchen unloading groceries. I was not prepared when I ran into the hall." Felix was scowling. He was angry with himself. "I was about to fight back when you came into the hall and told us all to get down." Suddenly, his scowl turned into a smile. "I'm really glad I did what you told me."

"I killed them." My voice cracked a little.

"You did."

"Peter? What about Peter?"

"That boy." Felix shook his head. "He'd gone to the lavatory."

"That's where he was coming from."

"He heard the screaming and stepped out without any idea of what was going on. He got a spell off, because there was a char mark on the woman's left shoulder. But her counterspell knocked Peter down directly after."

"He's okay?"

"You really care?" This was Felix at his worst, sarcastic, cold.

"Yes, Felix, I do. Peter is Eli's brother, so he's related to my sister. I know Peter can be a lot to put up with, but he's always tried to do well by me. He may be rash, but he's brave. And he's good to his sisters, and you're engaged to one of them!"

Felix looked sulky. "You're right. Peter's resting on the couch in the nurse's office."

"You're not fair to Peter." I wasn't, either.

"Maybe I compare him to Eli at that age," Felix admitted. "Eli was so sharp, so aware, so full of promise."

No one would say that about Peter. But Peter was good-natured, agreeable, and lighthearted. I didn't think Eli would ever be described as lighthearted.

Felix loved Eli. Peter would never measure up to his older brother in Felix's eyes.

Was that what people thought about me? That I would never measure up to my brilliant sister? Lizbeth was not showy or boastful. She was rock-solid, reliable, and very, very good at what she did. And she was even (also) pretty.

I'd forgotten Felix was there until he said, "What are you thinking, young woman?"

"I was thinking I'm going to give Peter more chances," I said.

Felix looked at me a little oddly. "Do you like him?"

"I wish I could talk to Lizbeth," I said, dodging his question.

"Does she have a telephone?"

"Nearest one is at her stepdad's hotel. They'd have to find her, get her there, it would be expensive." I dismissed the idea. I'd like to be sitting under a tree with her. I remembered when we'd sat on a bench together, watching people go by, here in San Diego. We'd had a good talk. I'd known she cared about me. That was a new feeling.

"I need to go home," Felix said abruptly, rising and taking my tray. "Sleep. Think."

"Are there still prisoners in the guesthouse?"

"As far as I know."

"Someone's taking them food and water, right?"

Felix looked surprised. "I don't know. The Rostovs left."

"Maybe before you go home, you could check." I made myself not sound angry, and when I really thought about it, I didn't know why I was. She'd done me wrong and intended to do more. Why did I care if she starved or not?

"Yes," Felix said. "I will." And he left. That was Felix.

CHAPTER THIRTEEN

While Callista was examining my feet to see what damage I'd done when I'd hurried into the hall, Peter came to see me. He was supporting himself with one hand against the wall, propelling himself along. He collapsed into the armchair with a relieved grunt.

"How are you doing?" Peter asked, waving a hand at my unbandaged feet. He got high marks for asking about me. I was pretty sure Peter felt worse than I did.

"Nothing split open," Callista said, sounding surprised. "She's healing well. I've put some more salve on, and if she can stay off her feet today, I'll try to work a little magic on it tomorrow. I'm all tapped out now, after Mr. Van Peebles."

"How are the sick kids?" I said.

Callista shook her head. "I'm real worried about two of them," she said. Her shoulders were weighed down with worry. "I've done my best."

I remembered what she'd said about broken bones and wounds being easier to heal than infectious diseases.

"Mrs. Benton should be here," I said. I was angry about Callista's burden.

"She's not only got the influenza, she's pregnant. She shouldn't be anywhere but her bed at her place."

I hadn't known about the pregnancy, and I'd forgotten about the influenza. "I'm sorry," I muttered. Not something I was good at saying.

"It's okay," Callista said. "There's too much for me to handle, I admit, especially with this sore shoulder. I have to keep running." She left, and I saw she was practically staggering with exhaustion.

To my astonishment, Peter pushed the armchair closer to the bed and took my hand. I almost snatched mine back, but I could tell he was building up to say something.

"You saved us all," Peter said. "Even hearing the screams, I wasn't ready when I came out of the bathroom. You were ready."

At that moment, I thought more highly of Peter than I ever had. Not many males can make such an admission. I would have had a hard time saying that myself.

"It triggered something in me," I said. I was trying to be as honest as he'd been. "I couldn't not go out there and fight. I didn't think about it."

Peter nodded as if he understood. "For just a second, I wanted to stay in the men's room, but I couldn't do that. I'm glad you weren't hurt further, on top of your feet and hands."

I didn't know where to look. Finally, I mumbled, "Oh. Well, my feet are healing, and my hands are a lot better. I think I'm keeping all my fingernails. I wondered . . . have you talked to your brother recently? Since the influenza closed the school, say?"

"He and Lizbeth know there's influenza in San Diego. Or they will soon. My mother wrote them. But they don't know about you getting snatched, because Mother mailed the letter the day you were coming to dinner."

It was my turn to nod. "I don't know whether to try to call Lizbeth at the hotel or not. They might be out of Segundo Mexia on a job, for all I know."

"Do you think they're making ends meet?"

I had never thought about it. "I guess so," I said. "My sister worked pretty steadily before, and gunnies can make good money." If they survive. "Plus, she owns the house she lives in, and she can hunt for meat."

"I hope Eli is finding plenty to keep him busy. People in Texoma aren't too used to grigoris and their ways."

I'd never thought of that, either. But I'd seen grigoris giving help in building projects, excavation projects, and heavy lifting. And there was the occasional gift of healing. Grigoris—we—could be useful in everyday ways as well as combat.

"I'd like to talk to Lizbeth," I said. "I'd like to ask her about that." Since it had never occurred to me to do so before.

"Maybe this summer," Peter said, giving me a sideways look, "we could travel out there. And we could find out what their life is like."

"You know we're at the age where people will raise their eyebrows at us going alone together," I said, simply because the thought had crossed my mind.

Peter turned red. "I would never try . . ." He sputtered to a stop.

"Of course not," I said, a bit hurt. "And I don't care what people say. But the school kids will talk."

"Let them," Peter said stoutly.

"Your mother might have a few thoughts about it."

I was surprised and impressed when Peter retorted, "My mother knows me better than that."

I guess my allure was simply not enough to combat Peter's virtue. I tried not to mind.

"We can ask and see if they'll agree," I said. "And I'd be so glad to see Lizbeth and where she lives. But right now, we have things to worry about, close at hand."

Peter said, "The influenza is spreading all over the city. The hospitals and infirmaries are filling up. People are dying."

That was worse than I'd imagined. But that wasn't what I'd been thinking of. I was embarrassed. "I wonder what they did with the bodies. I assume Felix and Tom took care of them."

Peter looked blank for a second. "Which bodies?"

"The two trespassers?" I inclined my head toward the hall.

"Tom called a couple of grigoris from the Residence to help him and Felix carry them out."

The large apartment building for unwed grigoris was only a block away. Peter had told me the apartments were small and plain. But each had its own bathroom, and there was a cafeteria and cleaning service, and you could have your laundry done.

"And took them where?"

"I have no idea. Tom wanted to get the bodies out of here before any of the children saw them. Felix wanted to search them. Tom didn't seem very enthusiastic about the idea."

"We should search them," I said.

"What? Us?"

"If they haven't done it, or did it in a hurry, they might have missed something. We need to check."

"They'll smell by now," Peter protested.

"Then we need to hurry."

Peter's mouth hung open for a moment, but then he rallied. "All right," he said. "Hold on." He left for a moment and returned with some crutches. I thought he'd gotten them for himself, but he handed them to me. "I'm doing better," he insisted. "You need to keep your weight off your feet."

I nodded. I'd never used crutches, but I would try. "I don't think they'd have left the bodies in the dormitory. Do you agree?"

Peter thought for a moment. "Yes, that's true."

The crutches took some adjusting and some practice. But before too long, we were in the hall and turned right to the side door leading to the covered walkway. One pale child returning from the bathroom saw us and lifted a hand. We lifted ours in return.

When we were outside on the grass, I took a moment to drink in the sky and the clean air. After that, we looked around.

"If you were going to stow bodies somewhere no one would stumble across them, where would you go?" I asked.

"The chapel," Peter said right away. He'd been thinking about it, and I liked that.

It was true that with the school closed and most of the teachers gone, too, no one would think of going to the chapel. It was at the back of the ground floor of the school building, next to the refectory. It was only used once a week, and the priest was not a resident.

We walked under the arched roof, Peter walking pretty steadily and me rather jerkily. I didn't like crutches at all. I'd wrapped a dressing gown over my nightgown, but it felt odd to be outside without real clothes on.

We reached the side door to the larger building after what seemed like a very long time. It was unlocked, which was a relief. Of course, Madame Semyonova was probably in residence in her apartment.

The school building was too quiet. I'd never experienced it so empty of life. That struck Peter, too. I could tell by the way his eyes widened. No other footsteps sounded, no telephone rang, no teachers' voices, no Mr. Van Peebles cleaning the floors. No children.

"This is creepy," Peter said, his voice almost a whisper.

I stiffened my back. "Nothing here but us, and we are dangerous," I said stoutly.

Peter smiled at me. "You are, anyway," he said.

We sort of stumped along. I disliked the thumping of the crutches on the wooden floors, and I tried to keep to the worn-thin carpet runner from the front to the end of the long hall. We passed all the empty classrooms, some with books still on the desks. If anyone was in the building, they for sure knew we were there. But I didn't hear any movement from anywhere, and no one challenged our presence. There had been no one on duty in the reception room. Since the school was shut down, that made sense.

The doors to the chapel were closed, so I knew Peter had been right. Ordinarily, they were open in welcome, as Madame Semyonova had decreed.

The dead grigoris lay on the back pews. They'd been stored there hastily. The man's arm was hanging down in a limp and awful way, and the woman's mouth was open.

"Good God," Peter said. It was clear he wanted to say something much worse.

For the first time, I got a good look at the people I had killed.

They were both in their early thirties, and they were black-haired and olive-complexioned—like the woman who'd said her name was Rosa, who was (I assumed) still imprisoned in the guest-house behind the school. Something stirred deep in my memory, something I didn't want to look at.

"Let's search them and get out of here," I said.

Nothing I could have said would have galvanized Peter more. He took the man, I took the woman, and we were both thorough. I helped Peter roll the man over, an awkward business on the narrow pew. He helped me with the woman. All I found was a slip of paper with *The Rasputin School* written on it and the street address. I took off her shoes and even pulled at her underwear, but she had nothing else on her. She'd come prepared to be captured or die.

I'd been holding my breath, but eventually, I had to let air in and out. It wasn't bad. I suspected Felix or Tom had gotten an air wizard to help with the inevitable smell.

"I found something," Peter said.

I was at his side in an instant. He'd withdrawn something from the man's right hip pocket, a piece of yellow paper that had been folded and refolded until it was a tiny square. Peter unfolded it carefully. Together, we peered at it in the dim light of the chapel.

It was a receipt from the Claiborne Hotel, detailing breakfast charges for two from the day before. The signature was an unreadable scribble, but the room number was 613.

That had probably been the final meal for these two.

But I pushed that thought aside. Maudlin. Morbid.

"So that's where we go," I said.

Peter looked at me. "You don't think we ought to take this to Tom or Felix?"

"Maybe we ought to, but I want to go myself."

"Your feet," he protested.

I wanted to do *something*. I was not used to sitting idle. "I'll get back in bed the rest of the day, and we'll go tomorrow."

Peter's face was serious. It was a good look for him. When he wasn't being aggravating, he was much more like his older brother. I'd always liked Eli, who'd been unfailingly kind to me.

"What about shoes?" he said.

For a second, I didn't understand. Then I remembered I'd thrown away my only pair of shoes. They were in a hedge miles from here.

He'd remembered, not me.

"I don't have any," I confessed.

"All right. What size do you wear?"

I told him the size I thought I should be wearing, and I added, "I think some thick socks would be good, too."

Peter nodded. "Let's get you back to your room, and then I'll go shopping," he said. "Maybe I'll ask my sisters for advice."

I agreed without giving Peter any more trouble. I was tired already. Back in the guest room, I took a nap. I'd left my door open, so when I saw Callista hurrying through the hallway—and looking like hell on wheels—I made myself get up to help. I wasn't much good tending the sick, but I could change a bed, wash sheets, hang them out to dry, and fold laundry. I did help one little girl to the bathroom and gave her a sponge bath afterward. I don't know which one of us was more relieved when that was over.

When Callista had prepared grilled cheese sandwiches and salads, I made sure I ate it all. I wanted to be strong. I carried my own dishes back to the little infirmary kitchen and washed them along with all the other dirty dishes, which took quite a while.

Late that evening, a healer came to the school after Callista had called the Residence. This healer was an odd-looking geezer calling himself Talbot Lackland. He had an English accent and crazy pale blue eyes.

I could tell Callista was uncertain about this grigori's ability, but she brought him to my room to work on my feet. I think she wanted to watch him in action on something that wasn't crucial. Then she would be sure he could help the more desperately ill children.

"Oh, I recognize you," Lackland said, kind of crooning. "I know the look of your family."

"I don't have any family, except for a half sister," I said.

"I must be mistaken," Lackland said politely, after giving me a long look. "Now, let me have a peek at your hands and feet. Ah, they just need a bit more work." And his thin, pale fingers began to dance over the surface of my feet. They felt like cold fairy hands and made me shiver, but after a moment, I knew he was the real thing. After Lackland agreed to visit Mr. Van Peebles, I turned my feet up as much as I could and bent myself to have a look. Oh, they were so much better! No scabs any longer. I couldn't run, but I could walk without the crutches if I were reasonable. And my hands were just about back to normal.

I slept much better that night, for at least twelve hours. I felt like a new person when I woke the next morning.

Peter arrived carrying two shopping bags. He was smiling, but I could tell he was really nervous. "This is what I've brought," he said, brandishing the bags at me. "I hope it all fits."

I stared at the bags. "That's more than a pair of socks and a pair of shoes," I said.

"I knew you wouldn't want to wear your uniform if we're going out in public," Peter said. He was overdoing the matter-of-fact tone.

"I couldn't ask Lizbeth for extra money, not knowing how they were fixed," I said, trying not to sound stiff or affronted.

"If Lizbeth were here, she would have done this for you," Peter said. "Remember, you and I are in-laws. And I had the advice of my sisters."

Somehow that made a gift of much-needed clothing far more acceptable. We could stop tiptoeing around each other.

"Thank you," I said. "If you'll go out and close the door, I'll try them on."

Peter looked vastly relieved.

I emptied the bags on my bed the second the door shut. There were two pairs of shoes, saddle shoes and black Mary Janes. And socks. And several pairs of underwear and a bra, which I scarcely needed (but coveted). And navy trousers—I'd never worn trousers!—and a white and blue blouse and a navy cardigan. And a dress, a green dress. It was so pretty!

Though I should hand the bags back to Peter and tell him "No thank you," I knew there was no question of that.

Maybe most girls would have flinched at the idea of Peter having seen the underthings, but that just seemed silly to me. The boy had two sisters, and underwear was not any giant female mystery.

I sat down to try on the shoes. As I buckled the straps of the Mary Janes, I realized it was weird that I was too proud (or too afraid of asking for something she couldn't provide) to ask my sister for clothes money. But accepting free clothes from Peter felt quite all right.

But that was something to think about later, not now.

Everything fit, more or less. The trousers were a little long, but I'd grow. The blouse was a little loose, but my bosom would some-day be bigger, I hoped. The socks were just the right cushion for my feet, and the shoes were nice and flat.

I brushed my hair until it looked respectable and put two clips in it to hold it out of my face. Those were my own.

Peter was waiting outside, and he beamed when he saw me. "You look so nice," he said. "Did the dress fit also?"

"Yes," I said. I'd put it on first. I'd found I looked very good in green. "How did you know I . . . had run out of clothes?"

"That bitch Anna," Peter said. "She was trying to impress me while I was waiting for you in your room to invite you to dinner. She thought I would dislike you if I knew you didn't have a closet full of clothes." Peter looked disgusted.

So she'd showed him my almost-empty closet. Well! I would have to settle with Anna when she returned. I smiled, just a little.

"Don't turn her into a frog or anything," Peter said, reading me correctly. "She's just stupid."

That was the truth. Anna might go around being all blond and flirtatious . . . but she was stupid.

There was no one to watch us leave, no one manning the sign-out book. Madame Semyonova was helping Callista. I was suppos-edly still in bed, but I could walk some, so neither of them would be popping in to check on me with the smaller children so sick and Mr. Van Peebles laid up. (Miss Priddy's body had been taken to a funeral home for shipment to her family in Los Angeles, Callista had said.)

I figured Callista might wonder where I'd gone but only for a second. After all, she was run off her feet. I promised myself that when I returned, I would help her. For now, I needed to find out why I'd been targeted.

Peter had already figured out our route to the Claiborne Hotel, and he'd brought a map with him. All this foresight made me a little wary. It was like the previous Peter had been kidnapped and a more mature Peter left in his place.

We got on a cable car first. It was not too crowded, so we were able to sit. We had a longish ride, while Peter told me that Felix and Lucy had set a wedding date. They'd be married in three months.

"Is your mother happy about the marriage?" It was possible Peter would tell me that was none of my business, but he answered me.

"In some ways, yes. They both seem determined to get married, and frankly, the prospects for Lucy and Alice are dim now that Father proved to be a traitor."

Though Prince Savarov's second family had nothing to do with the treason, they'd been tarred with the same brush. Peter and Eli's (and Lucy and Alice's) mom was not exactly greeted warmly at court, though her house had been nearly destroyed protecting the tsar. Eli had been thanked for his services and requested to go live somewhere else.

"Your mom is managing okay?" I felt a pang of guilt. My new clothes had been paid for with Savarov money.

"Mother says as long as we're not extravagant, we'll be fine." My guilt vanished. "And since she's *never* been extravagant, the money will last. I'll be earning money soon, so that will help. It's a huge relief Bogdan and Dagmar can't come by any longer, trying to pressure Mother into loaning them money."

"Do their wives try to cuddle up to your mother?"

"They tried." Peter smiled. "Mother's begun to be very frank, when the occasion calls for it."

As long as he was open to talking about sensitive topics, I asked one more question. "What about her and McMurtry?"

Peter smiled even more broadly. "I think I'm going to have to ask him to spell out his intentions, he's around so often."

"That's good news."

Captain Ford McMurtry was in good favor at the court, and he seemed smitten with Veronika. If they married, not only would Veronika be happy, but the family's financial base would be solid.

"Here's our stop," Peter said, and off we clambered.

This street was all hotels and shops. We were at our destination after one block. The Claiborne was very nice. If I hadn't had new clothes, I would have been doubtful about going inside.

"How are we going to do this?" Peter asked me.

I'd thought of nothing else the night before, but I still had no solid plan. "We need to see the register," I said. "If they had anything to do with my abduction, they came here at least five days ago. Maybe they shared a room. There's a chance their bags will still be waiting in that room. From their looks and the appearance of the woman Rosa, they're Central or South American. So we should look for those names."

"Can you make yourself invisible to get a look at the register while I distract the desk clerk?"

"That makes more sense than anything else I can think of," I said.

"Let's see what the setup is. Be ready."

We went into the lobby through the revolving door. Peter

stepped to one side by one of the pillars. I joined him. There was a long line of guests checking out. The influenza was going to empty San Diego. Everyone I could see in a hotel uniform was almost running, especially the bellboys and the doormen. The two clerks behind the marble counter were equally distracted, accepting keys and payment, filling out receipts like the one we'd found in the dead man's pocket.

Peter smiled. "This may be easier than I'd figured."

"Wait," I said.

One of the guests, an old man sitting in an easy chair with a drink on the table beside him, beckoned to one of the bellboys who'd been fast-walking to the checkout desk. The boy, who might have been my age, bent to listen to the old man's question.

The boy straightened. He was not discreet. "No, Mr. Dominguez, I haven't seen them yet. As soon as I do, I'll come direct to tell you." And with that, the boy bustled away.

"What?" Peter was looking around the lobby, trying to spot the source of my agitation. Because there wasn't any doubt about it, I was on full alert.

"The old man." I said it so quietly I thought it was a miracle Peter heard me.

"The dark man with the big nose and white hair? The shriveled one?"

"Exactly."

"He has power." Peter looked grim.

"Yes." I stepped behind the pillar. "He mustn't see me."

"Why? Do you know him?"

"Hush, hush!"

Because the old man's small dark eyes were watching everything in the lobby, and his hands were gripping the silver-headed cane in front of him as though he were going to strike someone with it. I pressed my back to the marble, hoping he could not see any part of me. I couldn't explain the dread I felt. I couldn't voice the fear.

"He's waiting for them to come back," I whispered. Peter had to lean close to hear me.

"Them who?" he said, almost as quietly as I had.

"The ones I killed," I said.

Peter looked almost as frightened as I was, until he gathered himself together. "He doesn't know *me*," Peter said. "But you seem to think he knows *you*."

"Yes," I said. I shivered. I remembered the dead woman saying, "It's her!" "Dominguez was my mother's name. Chances are good that's a blood relative of mine."

So much for keeping it secret.

CHAPTER FOURTEEN

Peter looked at me for a long, long minute. "Stay hidden," he said. There were a thousand questions he wasn't asking.

"He must not know we're here," I said. I gripped Peter's hand to make sure he knew how serious I was.

"I understand," he said, holding on to his patience. He detached my hand. "Back in a minute." He made gentling motions with his hands, as if he was telling a half-trained dog to stay.

Peter strolled to the desk. He managed to look calm and Peter-as-usual. I watched from the far side of the pillar, the one that kept marble between me and the old man.

Part of me found that really reasonable.

Peter leaned over the marble counter, having stepped in front of the whole line, and whispered to the younger man who was busy counting change. The clerk was torn between being polite and saying what he really wanted to say, his expression caught somewhere between snarling and smiling. It was an interesting look.

After a moment of listening, the young man swiveled to retrieve a key from its little slot. He handed it to Peter, who slid him a bill, and removed himself from the view of the increasingly angry people in line.

He went directly to the elevators.

The elevators were in clear view of Mr. Dominguez. Peter stood calmly in front of the three elevator doors. He turned his head

slightly to catch my eyes and nodded his head to the left. In that corner, there was a door marked STAIRS, and it wasn't in the old man's
line of sight. I nodded. Peter lowered his left hand to his side, his fist
clenched with two fingers extended. *Okay, I got it.* I nodded again.

After Peter stepped into the next open elevator door, I walked
quickly to the STAIRS door and went up as swiftly as I could. I had not
glanced behind me to check if the old man had been watching. If I
didn't turn and look, he was not, I told myself.

I went through the door marked ELEVATORS where the stairs
turned, and there was Peter, holding open the elevator doors with
some effort. Once I had stepped in with him, he let them close and
pressed the button for the sixth floor.

"What did you say to the clerk?" I was eaten up with curiosity.

"I said all I needed was the key to my cousin's room, to retrieve
his luggage. He and his sister had missed their train and asked me to
pick it up. They had paid their bill the morning before."

"And he gave it to you?"

"You saw him."

"Why would he do that?"

"I gave him a big tip and a push with my will. I counted on the
desk clerks being very busy, since everyone is trying to leave San
Diego. Since there are plenty of empty rooms, the maids wouldn't
have been quick to clean the rooms of two people who'd checked out
but were coming back to get their luggage."

Peter was surprising me all over the place.

"How did you know they'd left it here?"

"Otherwise, they'd have had to take it to the train station and
stow it in a locker or with the stationmaster or something. Or leave
it with the bell captain. This was safer and easier. The old man was
expecting them, too. They would have wondered if they'd need to
change their clothes."

Of course they would, since they were going to attack a school for magical adepts.

The doors opened again, and we left the elevator, consulting the sign on the wall before we turned left. Room 613 was one of the first ones after the STAIRS door. Peter unlocked it, and we scooted inside before anyone could spot us.

The curtains were still drawn, and I went to the window to open them.

"No!" Peter almost rose in the air with urgency.

I froze.

"What if there's some kind of spell on them?" he said. "So if you throw them open, an alarm sounds somewhere? With someone?"

Why would the two grigoris take the time to set such a trap? They planned to return to fetch their things. But I turned away from the window and instead found a light switch.

I hadn't been in many hotel rooms, but this one seemed very pleasant. There was a thick carpet with a gold and rust pattern, and a partially open door revealed a white-tiled bathroom. There were two beds, which had been pulled into a bit of order, and a suitcase on the rack at the foot of each one. The suitcases, one brown and one blue, were shut and maybe locked. Peter put his hand on the brown one and closed his eyes. The locks popped open.

I knew I'd read Peter all wrong.

Because he was rash and emotional, I'd never believed him capable of deep magic. He was. I had underestimated Peter in a serious way.

"I'm sorry," I said, because my mouth opened and words came out. I could have bitten off my tongue after I said it.

Peter said, "Don't worry about it."

That was the most amazing thing of all.

He opened the blue suitcase without another word. While I searched that one, he returned to the brown one.

We were turning over the clothes of dead people, but I recognized that thought was stupid the instant it popped into my head. *So what?* The blue suitcase was the woman's. I tried to forget her limp body lying on the pew in the chapel. Instead, I picked up each garment and shook it. She had two changes of clothes, a nightgown, the necessary underwear, a comb and brush, and an extra pair of shoes and hose. The toiletry case held a toothbrush and toothpaste, tweezers, some rouge, and a lipstick. The lipstick was too dark for me, so I dropped it back into the case. There was also a Catholic devotional in Spanish.

From the pocket at the back of the suitcase, I pulled a little square bundle wrapped in plain paper and tied with a ribbon.

I sat down on the bed to open the wrapping. The enclosed items were photographs.

Peter sat beside me to look. The top photo was no one I knew, a young woman in clothes more than a decade out of date. She was very pretty in a dramatic way. I didn't recognize her. The next picture was . . .

"That's my father," I said. My voice sounded funny to my ears.

"Listen," said Peter, so sharply that I paid attention. "We need to get out of here now. Now!"

I stared at the little photograph for a few precious seconds before the words soaked in. "Yes!" I said. "Right now!"

We went for the door, hearing the hum of the elevator as we did. We scooted out of the room, Peter locked it, and we ran for the stairs. That door had no sooner closed behind us than we heard the elevator doors open. Through a glass pane in the stairway door, we watched the old man, supported by his cane, make his way to the room. He knocked on the door with the silver cane head.

"Diego? Bernarda?" he said.

If they'd been in the room instead of lying dead in the school chapel, they would have opened the door, willing or not. The old man's voice was full of command. When no one answered him, he turned away and unlocked the room across the hall. When that door shut behind him, I could breathe again.

"We need to get the hell out of here," Peter whispered.

So we did. We went down the flights of stairs as if my feet had never been hurt. In the lobby, we hid behind a pillar until we'd checked every single person in eyeshot.

Peter started to turn in the key, but I said, "No, keep it. Maybe he can track whoever touched it last. We can mail it in later." I didn't need to specify who "he" was.

We walked out of the Claiborne as eagerly as we'd walked in. We kept going for four blocks. We turned right and went another two. We found a bench in Balboa Park with a view of what Peter told me was the Botanical Building, constructed for the World's Fair. Whatever that was.

I unwrapped the paper again and stared at the picture of my father. I hadn't had a picture of him, ever. In fact, I'd never seen one until now. We'd never had anything as expensive as a camera. In this photograph, Father was talking to a woman in a street near our hovel. I recalled her the minute I saw the picture. She'd sold tamales from a cart. Though the picture was black-and-white, I could remember her bright yellow dress and the red of her cart.

But the memory of Bonita was nothing compared to seeing my father again. I was flooded with memories.

A lot of them were bad. But he was my father. And he'd had no idea he was being photographed.

Seeing Father with some perspective, I realized he was a handsome man. I could remember the shade of his hair, between blond and brown, and his fair skin. I could hear his voice, harsh when he spoke Russian or English, which he did to me and to his brother.

He had sounded like a better man when he spoke Spanish—kinder, gentler.

"And this next picture?" Peter asked.

"That's my uncle. Sergei. That's who I was living with when Eli and Lizbeth found me." In this picture, Oleg and Sergei were having some kind of discussion. Their faces were animated and their hands moving. They were both smiling a little.

"He's dead now?" Peter asked, careful to make his voice neutral.

I nodded. "Next picture," I said, handing them to him. I couldn't bear to hold them any longer. Peter slid the picture of Uncle Sergei to the bottom of the stack.

The next picture was of me.

It had been taken at least two years ago, maybe longer. I looked to be about ten; my father had started keeping me young by then. My hair was darker and snarled. In fact, I looked darker altogether from being in the sun almost continually. My feet were bare. My clothes were worn almost through. Like my father and my uncle, I had not known I was being photographed. I was running down a packed-dirt path. It had zigzagged through the collection of shanties we'd called our neighborhood.

"That's you?" Peter said. He sounded like he could scarcely believe it.

"That's what my father did," I said. "He thought it would keep me safer if I looked younger and darker, like everyone else."

Peter didn't comment on that, which was wise. After a long moment, he touched the back of my hand and said, "This is the real you, now?"

"My hair may get a little lighter," I said. "And in a month or two, at the current rate, I should look my age."

"And what would that be?"

"Fifteen? I think?"

I could feel the struggle. Peter was trying so hard to keep from asking if it was truly possible I didn't know how old I was. Since part of my father's "protection" was making my natural aging slow down, I had lost track of my birthdays—it was that simple.

Peter said, "Why do you think they had these pictures?"

"I can't imagine. My father and uncle have been dead for . . . let's see, my dad for at least two years, my uncle for . . . ?"

He'd died in front of my eyes; you'd think I'd remember the date. Right before Eli had brought me to the school. That had been in the late spring. "More than a year. Maybe Mr. Dominguez hired them to watch us. But who is Rosa, then? Why are they all trying to capture me or kill me? It seems they knew where I was all along, from these pictures. They could have *helped* me." My voice cracked on that.

Peter put his arm around me. I admit it: I, who never leaned on people, leaned against him and felt glad he was there. A nursemaid wheeling a baby carriage beamed at us. I closed my eyes so I couldn't see her smile.

"Would you have rather stayed in Mexico?" Peter said after a while.

I sat up and sighed. "It's hard to say now. When Eli and Lizbeth showed up, I'd been staying with my uncle because I didn't have anywhere else to be and no one else to stay with. He just returned one day from one of their trips. He said my father was dead. But he never explained what had happened, no matter how I begged."

"Not the means of his death? Or where he died?"

I shook my head. "I think that means Uncle Sergei ran away and left my father."

"Shit," said Peter, with feeling.

"Exactly."

CHAPTER FIFTEEN

We got back to the school around lunchtime.

"Where have you been? Madame was looking all over for you," Callista said. "She wanted to meet with you and some of the guardians from the Residence."

"I'm sorry. We went for a walk and to shop a bit," I said, pointing down at my new shoes.

"What do you need us to do?" Peter said, and that was the perfect diversion.

Callista gave us tasks immediately. The good part of her being so overworked was that she didn't question how we'd gotten out and back into the school, when the front gate had been locked with magic. (When Peter had told Felix he was visiting me this morning, Felix had given Peter the spell to enter and the counterspell to leave. He wasn't supposed to.)

While I chopped vegetables and boiled chicken for the broth (Callista had given me very clear instructions), Peter carried the soiled linens and nightgowns to the laundry. I figured a man had designed the blueprints of the school, because (of course) the laundry room should have been in the dormitory. Instead, it was in the main school building and had its own outside door to facilitate hanging the wet linen on the clotheslines.

Peter had very clear instructions, too.

While the vegetables were simmering in the broth, I helped him peg up the contents of the basket he'd carried out.

"I've never used a washing machine," I admitted. "Is it hard?"

"I used the one at our house when—you remember—our maid died."

Their maid had been a spy for the party wanting a different tsar, and she had died while trying to kill the Savarov family. My sister had had a great deal to do with that.

"You wash the clothes with soap powder, then put them through the wringer," Peter explained. "If you've done it once, you can do it forever."

"You have a lot of talents I never suspected." I hung up another sheet. The sun was bright and the temperature perfect if you had sleeves or a sweater. As I put on the last clothes peg, the wind whipped the white sheet out of my hands. It snapped as it blew, trying to free itself to fly.

Though we were in the middle of a flu epidemic, though my evil grandfather was in town and trying to kill me or kidnap me, I felt a moment of pure happiness. I was with someone I liked, the day was lovely, my feet didn't hurt.

When the basket was empty, I said, "You know what we should do?"

"What is that?" Peter smiled down at me.

"We should go see the woman in the guesthouse. The prisoner." The guesthouse was visible today, which was strange.

The smile vanished. "Why should we do that?"

"Because I'm betting her last name is Dominguez, and I'm betting she's my aunt."

"It's a day for doing forbidden things," Peter said, and off we went.

Though the guesthouse, now visible, belonged to the real world, it seemed to sit in its own little pocket of darkness. Even on this glorious day, the air around it felt still and unwelcoming.

"Probably a spell," I muttered.

Peter knocked on the door. (I would never have done that.)

And it swung open.

If my eyes were as wide as Peter's, we both looked a sight.

To my surprise, I found we were holding hands. I had no recollection of reaching for his.

I didn't expect Rosa to be in the house. I expected she had escaped.

I expected to find an injured person, but I thought it would be whoever had been guarding Rosa.

I had not expected to find Rosa herself sprawled on the floor at our feet, dead.

Peter said, "Don't scream."

"I am not going to scream." I bit out each word between my teeth. "Are you?"

"I don't think so," Peter said. "But don't give up hope. I may yet."

I looked up to see him trying his best to smile.

"So who do we tell?" I said.

"If we can find Madame, we should tell her," Peter said slowly. "I'll call her office. If I can't find her, Tom O'Day, I guess. At the Residence."

There was a telephone on a desk in the living room of the guesthouse, a little directory sitting right by it. While Peter made the first call, I pulled open the curtains. That only showed me how dusty the place was—and how dead my maybe-relative was. She wasn't newly dead, either. I figured it had been at least twelve hours.

Rosa lay on her back. She was still wearing the outfit she'd had on when I'd seen her in the stationery shop. I wondered where Gwen Manley was. Upstairs?

Peter hung up the phone and dialed again. He reached Tom O'Day, apparently, because from Peter's end there was a lot of "Yes" and "No" and "We don't know."

I decided to have a look around the house. There was the living room we stood in, two small bedrooms, a bathroom, and a very basic kitchen. The stairs were steep and narrow. At the top was an open area, just big enough for another bedroom. There was a let-down ladder in the ceiling. I pulled the cord. The steps seemed sturdy, so I climbed them to look into the tiny attic, which held nothing but the body of Gwen Manley.

I walked over to look at her. If I'd been given to gloating, I'd have had a good moment, but as it was, there was no point. I was living, and she was dead. Whatever I could have learned from her, it was lost knowledge now. I could imagine that Gwen had stayed so close to the school that had thrown her out because she was attracted to the learning of magic, the practice of magic, and the proximity to other people who had the gift. But that was just a guess. For all I knew, she could have gotten the job at the stationery store because she loved paper or because she could walk by the school and curse it every day.

Maybe when I remembered how she'd punched me, I did feel a little good.

Gwen Manley, at least, had been properly taken care of by a spell that would keep her body as it was for quite some time.

Peter's face became visible as he got near the top of the ladder.

"What's in there?" he called. "Tell me it's not another body."

"It's another body."

"Well, hell. Whose?"

"Gwen Manley's. The woman who hit me at the stationery store."

"I heard about that." He came into the attic room. "Thank God she's been spelled. The woman downstairs is beginning to smell."

I nodded. "Tom coming?"

"He said a few curse words, but he's on his way. The influenza has gotten into the Residence. He's been helping isolate those who are already sick."

"I guess my problems don't seem like much in the current situation."

"They do to me. When I said she smelled and we didn't know how to cast the preserving spell, he said he'd be on his way. I offered to dig a hole in the schoolyard and dump her in, but he wouldn't go for it."

"I bet Madame wouldn't, either." I had to smile at the thought. But I felt the smile slip away. "What happens to students who die on the school grounds? Are any buried here?"

Peter said, "Mostly, the families have them sent home. But there are some students who came here from England and Ireland whose families had disowned them or couldn't afford to ship the bodies back."

I hadn't seen any headstones or any gated area, as I'd expect. "So where are they?"

"They'd signed the permission," he said, as if that should explain everything.

"I don't know what you mean."

"Did you not have to sign a permission form when you became a student here? Or since Eli brought you, maybe he told them he'd assume responsibility if you died while you were enrolled."

"Peter, I don't remember any such thing. What are you saying?"

"I'm saying that if you don't have anyone who agrees to pay for your burial, the school is free to use your bones and so on as teaching materials."

"What . . . the . . . hell." I could not believe what I was hearing.

"I can tell you're upset."

I nodded. "You got that right."

"But it's a fair trade," Peter said, and I could tell he was serious. "Most of the students who fled from England—or Scotland, Ireland, and Wales—were disowned by their families for being magic practitioners, like kids in New America or Britannia."

"So they didn't pay any tuition. Is that your point?"

"That's my point. So they didn't mind signing a paper saying that if they died here, their bones and tissue might be used for teaching other kids spells."

"Dead man's bone," I said.

"Yes, dead man's bone. The powder is in so many spells, yet it's not that easy to get unless you're a grave robber. This system is so much better."

I made a mental note to ask Madame what was in my file. Lizbeth would guarantee my burial, I was sure. That was much more important than an extra set of clothes. I wouldn't mind asking Lizbeth about this. I did not want to end up being a pinch of powder in Anna's pocket. Or anyone else's, for that matter.

"Are you all right?" Peter was eyeing me as though I was a horse about to bolt.

"I'm getting used to the idea," I said. "I was wondering if we could bury the woman downstairs among the students who'd died. But I see that's not something we could do. Let me ask one more question."

Peter nodded, but I could tell he was reluctant. He didn't like being the bearer of shocking news.

"Are there *any* students buried here?"

"As I understand it, yes. Maybe not a hundred percent, but in the northeast corner, there are . . . I guess you would say remains."

"No markers?"

"There's a chart in Madame's office to detect the locations.

Unless you're looking for them with a spell, it's unlikely you'd notice in the ordinary way of things."

I nodded in turn. It seemed the dead grigoris, though they might not term themselves that, would be with me at the school forever. That was deeply weird.

We heard the downstairs door open. We looked at each other.

"If it's Tom, he'll call out," I whispered.

There was silence. We waited.

There was more silence.

Peter raised his hands, after getting a pinch of something from his vest. I noted the pocket, in case . . . just in case.

Footsteps, crossing to the body.

And then, to our complete surprise, we heard a woman begin to cry.

Peter lowered his hands and relaxed, but I reached out to take his arm, and I shook my head violently. Now was not the time to assume a weeping woman was harmless.

He looked unhappy, but he nodded.

If there's anything I can't stand, it's waiting for something to happen, and it seemed I'd had a bowl full of that lately. But I also knew it was better to outwait someone than it was to go into action too soon. So we waited some more, and I closed my eyes, taking careful breaths in and out, calming myself.

And the next sounds we heard were much brisker. There were a couple of grunting noises and then the sound of a body being dragged across a wooden floor. Once heard, never forgotten. The head bumps.

So Rosa was going on a short journey, pulled by someone unknown.

I took off my shoes—gosh, this felt familiar, and not in a good way—and took a careful step onto the ladder. I crept down very slowly, without making a sound. I heard Peter right behind me. You could hear us moving, but I thought the sounds of the body being dragged would cover that.

I peeked around the bend in the stairs. Madame Rostova—whom I'd last seen escorting this very woman she was pulling by the feet, who had supposedly left the school because she feared the influenza—was very much here, puffing and panting to haul Rosa's body out of the college. And I saw Tom O'Day pause outside the open door.

"What are you doing with her?" Tom O'Day asked.

His presence was a complete shock to Madame Rostova. She shrieked for real, threw her hands up (abandoning the corpse), and whirled around to attack Tom.

"Duck," Peter said. From behind me, he threw the powder in Rostova's direction and said a few words that sounded right in my ear. It was a good thing I'd ducked. The spell Peter threw at Rostova knocked the woman right down onto the ground.

Tom looked through the doorway at us, said a very choice word, and then knelt by Rostova, whose eyes were wide open. I could see them from where I was, and I could also see that they were blank and unmoving.

"She's not dead," Tom said. "But she's somewhere else. Would you two like to tell me what happened here?"

"We were hanging out the laundry to help Callista," I said, to underline how virtuous we'd been. "We saw the cottage didn't look quite the same, so we came over and knocked on the door. No one answered, but we thought we smelled something, so Peter turned the knob, and we came in. She was lying right there, in the middle of the room." I pointed at the spot. "Until Madame Rostova came in." I looked at Peter.

He obligingly took up the narrative. "We wondered what had

happened, since she'd been left in a natural state. No preservation spell," Peter explained, in case Tom was missing his point. "So while I called you, Felicia went upstairs to make sure all was well up there, and she found the second body. I went up there, too. And while we were up there . . ."

"This is the body, and it's downstairs," Tom said. He pointed down at Rosa's corpse.

"No, the *other* body," I said, with an elaborate patience to match his.

Tom covered his face with one hand. "There's another body upstairs?"

"We thought you knew." Peter looked at me.

"We really did," I said. And that was the truth. "We thought you'd stored her there. Gwen Manley."

Tom went past us and up the stairs. I heard a string of curses. I kept my eyes on Rostova. So far, she hadn't shown any sign of coming out of the spell. *Good one, Peter!*

"Well, we did tell him," Peter said. "It's almost like he didn't believe us."

"He knows better now."

"Should we leave or something?" Peter sounded hopeful. He looked out the doorway . . . the door was still open. Rosa's body and Madame Rostova were spoiling the view.

The day outside looked just as beautiful as it had before, maybe even more so, since right in this house, we'd looked at two women who'd never see any day, ever again. We could not guess what would happen to Rostova, who had clearly had some tie to the enemy.

Tom came down the stairs even more heavily than he'd gone up. He looked exhausted. I wondered if he'd been tending to sick people or disposing of their bodies, calling their families, things like that. If I apologized, it wouldn't help matters, since we would have done the same thing (called someone who knew what to do) whether or not we'd been eyewitnesses to every bit of his possible hard work.

"I realize my problems are not the most important thing going on right now," I said. "But they are problems, and I don't know what to do about them."

Peter looked at me like I'd betrayed him, and I fumbled around with the thought that I had, indeed, almost told Tom something that had belonged to Peter until now.

"What do you mean?" Tom said, and all of a sudden, he looked very cautious.

Suspiciously cautious.

As if he already knew what I was going to say.

I changed my mind as if I'd spun on a dime. "Those guys who grabbed me," I said, doing my best to sound tearful and frightened. "I'm afraid. I don't know why they took me or who they work for. I asked Peter to stick around today. They might try again."

Peter shrugged, looking embarrassed at being caught out as a gallant grigori. "My mother agreed the school needed my help more," he said. "After all, given the flu situation, no one's going in and out of our house except me. Even the maid is staying at home."

Tom nodded. "How is Callista doing, handling the infirmary single-handed?"

That hit me out of the blue. "Callista is doing a hero's job," I said honestly. "I've helped a little now that my feet are better, but she needs more hands."

If Tom's idea of an interesting woman was Callista, I had definitely been barking up the wrong tree. It was good I had gotten wiser.

"Are you going to call Master Rostov?" Peter said.

"Have you seen Felix today?" Tom asked casually.

"No," Peter said. "We haven't. I wondered at his not being here to guard Felicia. And to ask this woman more questions." We all looked down at Rosa. "After all, she's the woman who caused him to miss rescuing Felicia on the street."

And look at what's happened to her, I thought. I was sure all of us were thinking this at the same moment.

Felix did have a temper.

But as soon as the thought crept into my mind, I banished it. Felix wasn't *sneaky*. This was a sneaky thing to do, leaving a rotting corpse where anyone might find it, simply for convenience's sake. If Felix decided Rosa should die, he'd be proud enough to do a good job of it.

I thought of the powerful old man, Dominguez, waiting to hear from the two grigoris (I doubted they'd called themselves that) he'd sent to find Rosa. (At least, that was my guess about why they'd come to the school.) He'd been so angry, so restless. Way too late, I realized I should be hoping the two I'd killed hadn't called back to the hotel to say something like, "Hey, Evil Ancient Guy, we tracked her down, and we're about to go into the Rasputin School to get her."

I couldn't disguise the shock that spread through me when I understood what might happen. I wouldn't need to hide from my grandfather. He'd come right here to me. He'd kill everyone in the school. He'd take me so he could take his time about killing me.

"What is it?" Tom said, but not like he really could tell I was very, very worried. It was more like, *Gee, she looks anxious, maybe I'd better be nice to her, calm her down a little.*

"You need to get the bodies out of here, right now," I said. "And I mean *right now*."

"And where am I supposed to take them?" Tom said.

Any other time, I would have seen this as a reasonable query, and I would have understood, but not today.

"If you don't get them out of here, everyone in this school will die," I said.

The only thing keeping Tom from *pish-posh*ing me was the fact that I was serious. Dead serious.

"You clearly know something you haven't told me," Tom said, but he'd already begun preparations. He'd gotten a pinch of this and that out of his vest pockets, and he began saying words under his breath, words with power.

Rosa's body began to shrink and shrivel.

Peter and I took a step back. This was the most disgusting thing I'd ever seen. It was like someone had put the body on a drying rack out in the desert sun and advanced the time.

"I'm going to take care of the one upstairs," Tom said, and vanished.

Without me realizing we'd done it, Peter and I were outside, and the door to the guesthouse was closed.

"I've never seen anything so awful," I said, very quietly.

"I've seen worse." Peter was not being boastful or trying to outmanly me. He meant it.

"I hope it works. I really don't want to see my grandfather again. Ever."

"You sure Señor Dominguez is your grandfather?"

"I can't understand any of this otherwise. I just don't know why he's so determined to find me, after ignoring me all the years I was right at his hand."

"He didn't want you until you were here," Peter said, as if he was mulling that over. "So what changed?"

"Here I give my blood to the tsar," I said. "Here maybe I can learn how to be a grigori, now that the teachers know I have power. Here I am growing into my real size and age."

"There—there's something about that!" Peter looked as if he were concentrating hard. "Something about that idea." Then his face fell. "I almost had it, but it ran away," he said.

"It'll come back."

Since Tom hadn't come out yet, and it wasn't likely he'd be glad to see us if he did, we checked the laundry we'd hung. The wind had helped a lot, but it still wasn't quite dry. So we went inside and were model citizens the rest of the day, helping Callista and the just-graduated wind grigori Maurice Culpepper, who'd come in answer to Callista's appeal to the Residence. Maurice was reedy and had hair like dandelion floss. Though I was doubtful about him at first, he proved to have a wicked sense of humor. The day was not all grim work. Callista seemed to enjoy the lighter atmosphere more than anyone. And the help was definitely welcome.

When the working day seemed to be done, Maurice and Peter headed out to get some food at the Residence. I was left cooking in the tiny infirmary kitchen. There was a less-than-tender piece of beef, carrots, an onion or two, and a potato that tried to hide from me. I put in some of the beef, water, tomatoes that were about to go bad, and some seasoning. When the beef flaked apart, I added the vegetables and simmered the pot. That evening, we were able to feed it to the sickest patients. Those who were less ill were glad to feed themselves.

After I climbed into bed in the room I'd been using, I slept better than I had in days. I did not dream of my grandfather or the two grigoris I had killed, and I did not dream of the dead women in the guesthouse.

I did hear Tom O'Day's voice in the middle of the night when I woke to use the toilet, and I felt sure I heard Callista giggling.

She deserved to have some fun.

CHAPTER SIXTEEN

The next morning, I went to hang more laundry—by myself this time—and I saw a group of air grigoris standing in a circle around the guesthouse. They were working some magic. They ignored me.

I was very curious, but I knew better than to stand around gawking. I hung up the wet clothes and went inside to help Callista change more beds and bathe and feed the weakest children. Mr. Van Peebles was on the mend, thankfully, and he insisted on bathing himself. He made an awful mess of it. Modesty certainly got in the way of efficiency sometimes.

A few of the grigoris who'd been doing a ritual around the guesthouse came into the dormitory when they'd finished. I didn't know any of them—not teachers or guardians, as the grigoris who worked at the school were termed. An eagle-faced woman named Esther seemed to be their leader, and she asked me and Callista into the examining room, with the rest of the grigoris standing out in the hall.

First, Esther took care in examining my feet and hands and Callista's bruises and wounds, and she nodded after looking over each of us. I assumed she was verifying that our injuries had occurred the way we said they had or maybe that we were well enough to be questioned.

We went through all the events again. In the telling, it became much more exciting than the hours of boredom and discomfort I recalled. Then Esther asked us questions. I listened to her carefully before I answered, but Callista could hardly wait to spill everything she knew in a stream of truthfulness.

Though Esther appeared to be paying close attention to what we said, after she had finished asking questions, she left. Before she went out the door, she told us, "I am leaving a guard in the front yard and in the back. We have changed the passwords on the front gate." She didn't say anything about the invisible back gate, so I didn't, either. And she didn't offer to let us know the passwords so we could leave and return as we chose.

We were prisoners.

Callista spent the rest of the day looking downcast. Though she didn't discuss her bad mood, I figured it was because Tom didn't come in to help that day. Neither did Peter, though I didn't get upset about it. Much.

I had a lot to think about. When I had a free moment, I went to the chapel. The two bodies there had disappeared. Perhaps they would be ingredients in some potion or herb mixture I used in the future. The guesthouse was visible but shut up tighter than a drum. I could only assume the shriveled remains of Rosa and Gwen Manley had been removed.

When I could be sure I wasn't interrupted, I got out the photographs that had been in the woman's suitcase, and I looked at them again. I didn't learn anything new.

I did worry about whether the old man would make an appearance. Could he come onto the school grounds? I wandered over to check the front gate. It was secured, not only with magic but with an iron lock. As Esther had promised, there was one bored grigori wandering across at the front of the school, another behind it.

I remembered the power rolling off Mr. Dominguez (I didn't even know his first name). Judging by its overwhelming strength, the old man could open the gate with a twitch of his finger. Or he might be able to see the back gate, the one only the full-fledged grigoris knew about.

I wondered if the grigoris who'd cleaned up the guesthouse had also taken custody of Madame Rostova. Or had she given them some plausible story about coming upon the bodies? But figuring and knowing were two different things, and I thought it would be courteous if they would inform me about what was happening. I felt that very strongly. In fact, I was getting pretty angry about it.

By lunchtime, I was *very* angry about it.

I went to the telephone in the infirmary office and looked up Molly Foster's home number in the school directory.

"Yes, Felicia?" she said when she answered, which impressed the hell out of me.

"Miss Foster, I wondered if you could tell me what's been done about Madame Rostova?" I asked.

"Young woman, that's absolutely none of your business," Miss Foster said. "If it was your business, I would have told you. When you need to know, you will know."

I hung up, really pissed off. I'd been put in my place quite firmly. I sulked for hours, since I'd been demoted from promising student with an inside track to scullery maid.

By midafternoon, Callista, who'd brightened, sat me down for a "come to Jesus" moment.

"You've been a great help to me," she said. "But you're making the milk sour with that scowl. Two of the kids who were getting better soiled their sheets. I don't know what's upset you, but it's leaking all over. Please take a walk or a nap or go to the grocery store for us. Wear a mask against the flu. And put a scarf over your hair, too.

When you come back, take a bath and wash all over, and wash your clothes. We're about to get a grip on this illness, and I don't want it starting back up. I've told the grigori on gate duty to let you out and back in."

It was true we needed groceries. Also, I felt guilty that my bad mood had spread all over the place. But in truth, I was a little anxious about setting my feet outside the school grounds.

When the theatrical healer Talbot Lackland arrived to help Callista for a while, I ran out of excuses to stay within the gates.

So I found the wagon the school cook usually took to the market, covered up all my hair and my lower face as Callista had told me, and went to the store two blocks away, the one the school usually patronized. We had an account there, so I didn't need to carry money with me. Callista had given me a list, of course. When I saw how picked-over the store shelves and bins were, I hoped I could get even a fraction of what she'd asked for.

There was some fresh fruit, and I got it all. I found some yeast. We would have to make our own bread, but there was plenty of flour in the main school kitchen. There was one box of eggs, and I took it seconds ahead of an older woman who glared at me. *Too bad!*

There was some cabbage, so I got two heads, and six potatoes. There was milk! I got a gallon. Butter, too. And cheese. (At least the truck from the dairy was still running.) There were two oxtails on the meat shelves, all by their lonesome, and I bought them. I could always make more soup. The kids might get sick of it, but they should be glad to have food at all. I bought some cans of vegetables and soup, as backups. And a giant can of peanut butter and some crackers. I felt really proud of that. I knew we had jelly on the pantry shelves.

When all my goods were weighed and packaged, I charged the groceries to the school. I'd run errands for the cook before, so Mr.

Dudek recognized me despite the hair and face covering. He prided himself on knowing all his customers.

"They got you shopping today, girlie?" he asked. He was a big, broad man with brown hair parted in the middle.

I nodded. "I'm healthy," I reassured him.

"I'd say that's so. You've grown two inches every time I see you. Anyway, I ain't worried. If I haven't caught it yet, I ain't going to." He looked past me and said in a different voice, "What can I do for you, mister? You looking for something special today?"

One of my bad feelings gripped me. I froze. I raised my eyes to Mr. Dudek just as he glanced down. Our gazes met for a moment.

Mr. Dudek made a snap decision. "Come on, girlie, sign for your family!" he barked. "Get a move on!"

God bless him. I nodded humbly, signed with a scribble, and loaded all my items into the cart, keeping my face averted while Mr. Dudek again asked the man behind me what he needed.

"Do you know what has happened at the school?" a heavily accented voice asked. "The gate is locked."

"One of the teachers told me they were going to close until the flu got better," Mr. Dudek said. "I guess all the students went home. Those kids are dangerous. Got no control. I don't let 'em in the store without a teacher to make 'em mind."

While Mr. Dudek rattled on, I pulled the wagon out of the store and plodded off in the wrong direction. I reminded myself to move slowly. I could not look like I was in a hurry.

I turned left, stopped on the corner, and peeked back. The door to the grocery store was still shut. I ran all the way back to the school, the wagon almost flying along behind me. I said the password to the grigori on duty, who unlocked the gate. I fairly leaped through and hurried off to the dormitory building. Once I was inside, I leaned against the door and panted.

"What's happened?" Peter asked.

He was sitting in a chair in the hall. Casual, one ankle on his opposite knee, his cap in one hand.

"He was in the grocery store," I said. "He was there. Mr. Dudek kept him talking while I got away."

Peter caught on right away. "The old man? The one you think might be your grandfather?"

I nodded too fast. And a lot.

"Slow down, your head will fall off," Peter said. "But you had that headscarf on, and that mask?"

I nodded again, in a more controlled way.

"Callista's idea, I guess?"

"Yes, and I'm so glad," I said in an uneven voice. Since my breathing had settled down to more or less normal, I pulled the wagon down to the little kitchen and unloaded its contents onto the shelves and into the little refrigerator. Then I scrubbed my hands and face.

Peter trailed after me.

"What is that?" He'd unwrapped the oxtail.

I explained, and he expressed ridiculous disgust at the idea of eating something's tail. Then I felt better, which I realized had been his goal all along. When my breathing was absolutely normal, I began to chop up things for a thick stew. Peter helped. Before I knew it, I was fine. Or as fine as I was going to get. Everything was unpacked and put away, and the stew was bubbling. I was peeling the oranges so the children wouldn't have to.

"Surely he can't stay in San Diego much longer." I was heaping the peels on an old piece of newspaper while I sat at the little table, and Peter was leaning against the wall. We stared at each other.

"He's invested a lot in tracking you down," Peter said. "He's lost the man and woman who broke in here, and he's lost Rosa . . .

assuming Rosa was one of his. As far as we know, he's on his own now. Maybe he'll give up and go back to Mexico. Or maybe he's waiting for reinforcements."

"But why? Why does he want me so bad? He kept an eye on me, but that didn't . . . all those years, he never tried to steal me from Father. He never got in touch with us." When I really could have used help. Often. No, he wanted me now, when I had enough to eat and a safe place to sleep, and a few friends. When I was in heaven . . . compared to the place I'd grown up.

Callista bustled into the kitchen and stopped dead when she saw us sitting. "And what are you two doing, on your rear ends, not helping? Talbot Lackland at least helped Mr. Van Peebles with a personal problem he was having. Good to have a man around for that."

"I got back from Dudek's and started some soup," I said. I couldn't see any upside to explaining about my grandfather. "Peter helped me unload and chop."

"Where's the bread?"

"Dudek's was out, so I'll have to make some."

"You can make bread?" Callista had obviously not imagined that was within my scope. "Then you'd better get to it. Can you make soda bread, rather than yeast? It'll be much quicker."

I had never heard of soda bread, but as Callista explained it, it seemed to be an Irish thing, so no wonder. Even my mixed heritage didn't include Irish. Callista found a recipe, and I pored over it. I'd have to go to the main kitchen to get the baking soda and the flour.

Peter and I walked over to the school. On the way, I told him that the bodies in the chapel were gone.

"I wonder what Tom did with Madame Rostova," Peter said, chiming in with my own thoughts.

"Me too. But no one's going to tell us." At least, they weren't going to tell *me*.

The school seemed even emptier today, and darker. It had been almost fun, for a little while, seeing everything differently . . . but it had stopped being fun.

Then we heard a footfall on a wooden floor.

Someone else was in the school.

We'd reached the stairs leading up to the classrooms. And there was another floor of classrooms above that. The sound came from the second floor.

We had our shoes on, of course, and our location had to be obvious to anyone with functional ears. And we hadn't been talking quietly. Why would we?

I pointed to the area under the stairs, telling Peter to hide there. But he wanted me to do the hiding and himself to do the confronting.

I got tired of trying to argue silently. I yelled, "Who's up there? No one's supposed to be in the school!"

Peter spared a second to glare at me before he took cover. I stepped back from the foot of the stairs to give him room to maneuver. I didn't want to get caught in the crossfire.

I'd half hoped the intruder would run away, but no such luck. Here came the footsteps of doom, heavy and deliberate. I tried to believe it was Mr. Van Peebles, feeling well enough to do some cleaning, but I couldn't make myself believe that. At the head of the stairs, Master Rostov appeared. I'd never really paid attention to him—he taught the older kids, and he didn't spend any more time on campus than he had to—but now I saw he was burly and sturdy like his wife, and just as determined.

"Where is Madame Rostova?" he said. "I have looked everywhere for her."

"I have no idea, sir," I said carefully. "I haven't seen her today."

"Who's with you?"

"One of the other students," I said, again truthfully. "We were sent to get some baking soda. We need to make some bread for the sick ones."

I was just babbling, trying to make him relax. Master Rostov was as tense as a coiled spring. I took a small step to my left, trying to get out of his direct line of fire.

"Oh, you're going to *make bread*," Rostov said with a nasty sneer. "I'm betting you and the Savarov boy were really going to *make bread*."

My temper picked a bad time to snap. "Yes, we were, asshole," I said.

The man had the gall to look shocked.

Peter began easing out of the shadows under the stairs. Rostov was standing more or less in the middle of the broad staircase. Most likely, he wouldn't see Peter if he glanced down.

However, I'd better distract him. "So have you been a sneak all this time, and we're just now finding it out? Or did you slowly become one?"

"What are you talking about, you little bitch?"

Wow, we'd gone downhill fast. "Your body-thief wife, she was trying to steal a dead woman." If that got him excited and prone to mistakes, I'd be glad. This was mild compared to my father.

Master Rostov had been girding himself to attack me. But now he deflated a bit. "What are you talking about?" There was some slack in his attitude. It wasn't all fire and brimstone.

I took another small step to the side, just in case. "Yesterday we saw her trying to take the body of the woman Rosa," I said. "She was going to take it out of the guesthouse."

Master Rostov's face was blank. His mouth opened and closed twice. He could not decide what question to ask first. I took another little step. Though the odds were going down that he would try to attack me, I wasn't going to relax. If Peter took a step to his right, the angle would be great for him to aim a spell at Master Rostov, and I would not be in the line of fire.

"She didn't come home," Master Rostov said.

Not what I'd expected. But I didn't know how to respond.

"She didn't come home last night. That's never happened in all our ten years of marriage. I called two of her friends, and they hadn't seen her. I called the infirmary to ask Callista if Vera had come over to help—that would have been just like her—but Callista hadn't seen her, either. I didn't know who else to call."

I had no idea what to say. I shook my head sympathetically. At least, I hoped that was how it came across.

"Where do you think Vera is now?" Master Rostov asked me directly. He truly seemed at sea.

I think she's being held for questioning by the grigori council, I thought, but I didn't think it would be a good idea to say that. However, it turned out Master Rostov could read my face.

"You think she's been accused of trying to steal a body?" His voice rose, and we were right back where we had been. "Did you set her up, you little bastard?"

Those were fighting words, and I braced myself for combat. Though I was not a grigori yet, I had all the raw material. Channeling it and controlling it was my problem, not calling it up. I could feel the power churning around inside me now, just asking to be unleashed.

"I don't want to kill you," I said, without meaning to.

"Hah!" Master Rostov actually snorted. "You think you can best me, you little Mexican guttersnipe?" And his hands came up.

"Now would be a good time," I said quietly.

Peter let loose.

I don't know how to say this without sounding snooty. Peter's magic was pretty. It had more style and grace than mine, and it was aimed better. I was a club; Peter was a scalpel. That was exactly what Madame Rostova herself had told me to be!

Peter's spell shimmered in front of me on its way up to hit Master Rostov square in the back of his right shoulder, spinning the man around and thus sending him crashing down the stairs to the floor.

Where he lay awfully still.

"Oh, no." Peter spoke very quietly, as if he were scared Rostov would hear him. "This is bad."

I took a deep breath and went to squat by Master Rostov, who'd ended up on his stomach with his head turned to his left. His right arm was underneath him.

"He's alive," I told Peter, trying not to sound as surprised as I felt.

Peter made a sound that was a lot of things, mostly relieved.

He was beside me in a few seconds, and he placed his fingers carefully against Master Rostov's neck.

"Whew," he said. "Okay. We need to call someone. We can't carry him over to the infirmary. We need a stretcher. And I bet we need a bonesetter."

"For the right arm? Yeah, I think so," I agreed. "Even if we had a stretcher, I don't think you and I could lift him. He's a big man. You need someone stouter than me."

Peter's face was gloomy. "All we need is Tom O'Day walking in on this," he muttered.

The front door of the school opened. "Speak of the devil," I said.

Tom looked at Peter and me, spared a glance for Master Rostov, and said words I hadn't heard since I'd left Mexico. He took a moment to call over to the infirmary and ask if Talbot Lackland could set some bones, and the older grigori had practically skipped into the main hall in his glee. He worked on Master Rostov while Tom took us into the reception room.

Ten minutes later, we'd been raked over coals I hadn't known were heating up. We were irresponsible, reckless, and untrained. (That was especially hurtful to Peter, who had graduated.) It didn't bother me. Tom was right, in my case.

I got tired of being ranted at, justly or not. "It's your fault, Tom," I said.

He stared at me, his mouth hanging open. "What?"

"Your fault. You didn't think to go by the Rostovs' house and tell Master Rostov where his wife was? What had happened? Didn't think that he might get worried about her and come looking?"

Tom stared at me as if I'd grown another head.

"You blame *me*," he said.

"You've just pointed out how awful I am. How could you leave me unattended?"

Tom flushed red. "Most unattended and untrained grigoris don't go around killing people," he growled.

"Peter defended me. Besides, this man isn't dead," I pointed out. "And even if he was, who'd you rather have dead? Me or him?"

Tom gave up.

As if he'd been cued, Felix came in through the open front door, saying, "Why is the door . . ." And then he saw Master Rostov and began asking questions.

We had to explain all over again. Which Peter did. He gave a very concise summary.

Felix and Tom glanced at each other as if to say, *Do you have any more questions?* Neither of them did.

Peter said, "If you two don't need us anymore, we're going to complete the errand that brought us over here."

"Which was?"

"We need to get baking soda to make bread."

"You? You are making bread?"

"I am, with his help," I said, trying to sound competent and dignified. "Also, I had better tell you this." I hesitated, wondering if this was wise—but it was wrong to leave Felix and Tom in ignorance when they were in charge of protecting the school. "When I was in Dudek's getting groceries for the school, an old Mexican came in asking how to get into the school. As in, why the gates are locked."

Tom was all attention. "How did you learn this?"

"I was there, not wearing my uniform."

"Did Dudek tell him anything important?"

"No. Mr. Dudek was a champion."

Tom nodded vaguely, not as if he was thinking of giving Mr. Dudek a medal but as if that was information he didn't need to attend to. "Did the old man tell Dudek who he was?"

All of a sudden, I faced the fact that I'd made a terrible mistake. I'd only shared my shameful secret with Peter, because I'd thought it had been mine to keep. I understood now that it clearly affected the school. I looked up at Peter and let him see how sorry I was that I had to share.

"No, the old man was too aristocratic to tell Dudek his name. But I know who he is. Maybe." I was hedging, but I'd been sure ever since I saw the pictures.

"Then tell us," Tom said, his patience at an end.

"It's my grandfather." I stared straight at Tom, not letting my gaze fall or waver.

"Your grandfather? Your mother's father?" Felix said slowly. Of course, it had to be, since my other grandfather had been Rasputin.

I nodded.

"What's his name?"

"I don't know his first name. But the bellboy called him Mr. Dominguez."

You would have thought I'd given Felix and Tom an electric shock. They were looking at me as if I'd suddenly turned into a huge snake.

CHAPTER SEVENTEEN

Dominguez. From Ciudad Juárez. You're sure you don't know his first name?" Felix was giving me the cold stare now, the one he reserved for people who had to tell him the truth. Or else.

I was not afraid. I straightened my shoulders.

"I don't know," I said.

"I believe," Peter said, clearing his throat a bit, "that his first name is Francisco. I happened to glance at the hotel register."

I didn't know whether to hit Peter or hug him. He hadn't shared that with me the day we'd gone to the hotel, but there was really no reason he should have. I'd been upset enough. The news wouldn't have had the effect on me that it had on Felix and Tom.

Felix's mouth had fallen open. "*Francisco Dominguez* is your grandfather?"

"I'm not a hundred percent sure this old man is him. I only saw him once before, when I was really little."

"He was the one who came to the door, looked at you, and left."

Felix had a good memory.

"Yes."

"And you think this old man who's asking questions about the school is him?"

"Maybe." *For sure.*

Felix nodded, not like he was happy with my answer but because he could see how that would be.

I thought we might be through with this conversation, but Tom said, "The woman called Rosa, who was killed in the guesthouse. Her English had an accent. Maybe Mexican."

I nodded.

"Do you think she came here with your grandfather? Do you know who your grandfather is?" He meant besides knowing his name.

"He was a rich Mexican who lived in Ciudad Juárez," I said, irritated. "I told you that."

"You don't know who the Dominguezes are?"

"No," I said. "How could I?"

"Your father should have told you."

"Well, as I think I've made clear," I said, and my voice was getting loud, and I couldn't stop it, "my father didn't tell me much of anything unless he was drunk."

Peter put his arm around me. It was a bold move in front of Felix and Tom, but he did it. I felt better and calmer.

"If you think Rostov is safe, we should go sit in the reception room," Felix said, and without further ado (or even glancing at Master Rostov), we trailed into the reception room.

Tom sat behind the desk, where he felt most at home, and Felix took the little chair against the wall, though he shifted it. There was a single chair and a loveseat remaining. We took the loveseat.

"Francisco Dominguez, the head of the Dominguez family, comes from a long line of witches," Felix explained. "He's at least the fifth generation. He has a tremendous reputation. If people want to employ him, they have to make an appointment six months in advance. All his children are powerful, too." Felix shook his head. "You're from a nest of serpents," he said gravely. Felix was looking at me as if he'd never seen me before. Something strange was going through his head.

When I didn't turn into a peacock or a cloud of smoke, Felix looked at Tom, trying to get him to share in Felix's amazement. "One of the *Dominguez sisters* was her mother. Maria Rosa, Isabella, Marina, or Bernarda."

Tom was not as awestruck as Felix, but he seemed impressed.

I didn't want to turn to see how Peter was handling this information. I wondered if he would blurt out our adventure at the Claiborne. I wondered if I would.

"Marina was my mother," I said, shutting my mouth tight after I'd said it.

There was a lot of silence in the reception room.

"My father never told me anything about the Dominguezes in particular," I said, just to speak, to stop all the looking and wondering. "He did tell me that grigoris weren't popular in Mexico, which was why he went to Texoma and New America to make money."

Felix nodded. "Witches are much more a part of the Mexican culture. The church frowns on them, but most humble people and many wealthy people believe in their power and give them respect."

"Father believed all magic was pulled up from the same well. 'Some people just use different buckets,' he said."

"Do you remember this because you knew he had a reason for telling you?" Felix said, taking his time with the phrasing.

I shook my head. "I remember it because that day was one of the few when he was sober and paid me some attention." I hated being pathetic.

There was a long silence. After all, what could they say, when I was a whiny, whimpery sort of girl?

"So," Tom said, and my head snapped up at the tone of his voice.

"What have you and young Peter been up to that you don't want us to know about?"

Well, dammit.

Peter and I looked at each other, and I saw the question in his face. We had a whole conversation in a few seconds. Peter was willing to abide by my decision because it was my life we were talking about. He was willing to take the consequences.

I had forced all this on him by talking him into going with me on our excursion to the hotel.

"It was my idea," I said, switching my attention to Felix and Tom.

"I have no doubt of that," Tom said, dry as toast.

It's been my observation that very few men want to look as though a woman had told them what to do. My brother-in-law, Eli, had been the exception, not because my sister bossed him around but because they seemed to hold decisions in common. Given the nature of their father, that trait could only have been passed along to Peter by Veronika, their mother, because Peter was the same way. His eyebrows asked me if we were going to talk or not, and my slight nod said we were.

"We searched the bodies in the chapel," Peter said, as calmly as if this were an everyday activity.

After Tom and Felix had absorbed this, I said, "We found a receipt for the Claiborne Hotel."

Felix's face froze. Tom turned red.

"Where was this receipt?" Felix said, so calmly that I knew he was very upset. Angry? Fired up? I couldn't tell.

"The man's rear pants pocket, folded into a tiny square," Peter said.

He had tucked the receipt into his own pocket. He fished it out now, unfolded it, and laid it on the desk. All the fold lines stood out sharply.

The two grigoris stared at the slip of paper.

"Well," Felix said at last, "we missed that, Tom."

"Yes."

"Maybe it was put on the body later by someone who wanted us to find it?" I said. (Though that didn't seem likely.)

From the narrow-eyed looks I got, they didn't want anyone to try to make them feel better.

"So you two . . . ?" Tom said.

"Went to the hotel," Peter said, as if the answer was obvious.

"How did you get there?" Felix seemed appalled.

"We rode the streetcar, and we walked." Peter dared them to say we had no right.

Felix sat back in his chair, trying to look relaxed and calm, and Tom did the same.

"Felicia, you left the school without telling anyone? How did that come to pass? No, wait. Tell us what happened that day," Felix said.

Since he asked so nicely, we did. Sneaking out of the dead grigoris' hotel room was especially exciting in the retelling, since we knew we had gotten out undetected.

There was a long silence when we'd finished.

"You didn't get caught," Felix said. "And you did find out some useful things."

He was so clearly trying to find bright spots in an otherwise cloudy sky. And I thought we'd done so well! I looked up at Peter, and I could tell he felt the same way.

"Maybe you haven't thought this through," said Tom in an absolutely deadly voice.

Uh-oh. Something bad was coming, courtesy of Tom. How could I ever have liked him?

"Tom," Felix said warningly.

"If this is all true, you killed *your aunt and uncle* in the attack on the dormitory. But you say you didn't kill Rosa and her sidekick Gwen?"

Peter surged to his feet. "How can you be so unjust? What are you thinking, Tom? Felicia fought back against people attacking the school. She defended us from people who clearly didn't care who died. As for Rosa, who killed her? Not Felicia! Not me! And why was she left in the guesthouse alone with the body of the Manley woman? What if Felicia's grandfather is looking for Rosa?"

"Why did Madame Rostova go over there?" I said, since we were asking questions. "How did she get in?"

"You've asked a lot of good questions," Felix said calmly. He made a point of not looking at Tom. "I only know the answer to one of them. Both David Rostov and Vera Rostova had the spell to enter the guesthouse. Both of them were trusted members of the council that watches over the school. We don't know that Vera was guilty of anything. For all we know, she came to the guesthouse to check on Rosa's well-being and found her dead just as you did, Felicia."

"I don't think David looking for his wife means he was necessarily a traitor, either," Tom said.

They—especially Tom—were trying to make me feel guilty and bad, when all I had done was right.

"To hell with you both," I said, and went to the kitchen to get the baking soda.

Peter did not come with me. On my return trip to the dormitory, I didn't see a soul.

Peter had stuck by me longer than I thought he would. There was that.

I spent my afternoon making the soda bread, three round loaves. Callista came in after I'd gotten them in the oven. She cast a cold eye around the kitchen, said I'd gotten enough flour on the floor to make another loaf, and went back to bustling around for her patients.

I forgave her, because she was right. I had gotten a lot of flour strewn around, and it was my job to clean it up. That filled up the time until the bread was ready.

I felt proud as I pulled the loaves from the oven. I had to tap them to be sure they were done. When I did, they sounded hollow, like they ought to. I let them cool for a few minutes, then tipped them onto a cooling rack.

I just wanted to be by myself and keep busy.

As I slumped on the stool next to the kitchen table, I realized it had been a while since I'd seen Callista. Or heard from the sick little ones or Mr. Van Peebles.

In fact, the infirmary area had been quiet for at least half an hour. Only the noise of yours truly banging around in the little kitchen had broken the silence, now that I reflected.

I had to search the floor.

With great reluctance, I went into the first sickroom, which held two sleeping girls. They were breathing better, and they didn't feel hot.

In the next room, two boys lay, also sleeping, and they were better, too.

In the next room, I found Callista lying on a bed, quietly snoring. She was fully dressed. I decided she was exhausted, not ill. She didn't move when I put the back of my hand to her forehead. It was cool enough.

Mr. Van Peebles was snoring more loudly. He needed a shave.

For lack of anything better to do, I returned to the kitchen. Something was off, but I couldn't put my finger on it. It was odd that all the people had fallen asleep at the same time. But it wasn't out of the question. However, I started looking over my shoulder. The silence was creepy, and I didn't trust it at all.

I threw some rice into the soup to give it bulk. I cut a slice of bread to eat with it when it had simmered for a while, and I had a great meal. It was nice to be alone.

Well, it was at least all right.

But someone should have woken up by now.

When my grandfather stepped into the kitchen, I wasn't totally taken by surprise. I'd heard footsteps, and they'd had a significant off-balance sound, though they were much lighter than they should have been.

For lack of a better idea, I got my grandfather a bowl of soup and a slice of bread (and a spoon and a napkin) and put them in front of him, along with a glass of water.

Francisco Dominguez looked like he needed a good meal. The curves from his nose to his mouth were so deep they looked carved, and his skin was dull. He looked as though he were going to pass away very soon. You gain a grandfather, you lose a grandfather.

He looked at the food in front of him, then at me. He did not touch it.

So we just did some more staring. Finally, he pulled a creased photo from his pocket and showed it to me.

"Mother," I said, remembering her the instant I saw her face. My heart flooded with feelings I couldn't even put a name to. I hadn't been sure when I saw the picture from the suitcase, but now I knew her.

The old man nodded. "Marina," he said, his voice remote, almost echoing. "My oldest daughter."

"Can I keep this picture?" It was a test question. I still had the one that had been in the woman's suitcase. I was beginning to have suspicions.

"No," he said, putting it back in his pocket and drawing out another. "You are not worthy. This is the one you should look at." His voice changed. It was darker and deeper.

I should have been scared out of my wits all along. But I hadn't been at all frightened, until this moment. He moved the picture across the table, with one finger pinning it to the surface.

There were—I counted quickly—four women and a young man in the picture. I recognized all the faces but one.

"They are missing because of you," my grandfather said, and now he was a witch, and he wasn't old but seasoned. His voice had a sort of echo in it. He was getting stronger the longer we talked. Not good.

"Because of *you*," I said, and meant it. "Who's missing?" I looked at the faces again. My mother, Maria Rosa, Bernarda, Diego. "Isabella?" She was the one I hadn't encountered yet.

The fury in his face was very real, though I didn't believe he was furious.

I kept on talking while I looked at him intently. "You brought them here to the Holy Russian Empire. You sicced 'em on me. Did you expect a school where grigoris teach and grigoris learn would lack defenses? And my mother didn't die because of me. She died from a fever, and my father couldn't afford to take her to a hospital or call a doctor. You wouldn't help."

I kind of made up that last part. It was what my father had always told me, but he didn't always tell stories the way they'd actually happened. But I was willing to bet it was the truth.

"Do you believe what you're saying?" He seemed . . . incredulous, that was the word.

"I do. I was managing okay without you and your family, and I'll keep on managing. The time to help was long ago, when I didn't have enough to eat or clothes to wear or a school to go to. When my father kept spelling me smaller to keep me the same size so I would be safe."

My grandfather closed his eyes for a moment. "So that's why I wasn't sure it could be you," he murmured.

That explained a lot. Someone had been talking to him. Someone had been reporting to him. Madame Rostova?

"Did you ever think about just coming to the school and asking to talk to me?"

The eyes, surrounded by deep, wrinkled lids, opened. "You know, I did think of that," he said. I couldn't tell if he was being sarcastic, or not. "But I knew they would never let you go, not when you had the cursed blood from your father."

"We never got to find out, did we?" I swallowed hard. "And now people are dead."

"Have your grigoris captured my children?"

Grandfather wasn't certain that Bernarda and Diego were dead. He wasn't sure about Rosa, either. I could tell he thought it was likely, but to him, it was unbelievable. Literally.

"What do you think? The two who came in here blasting were ready to kill everyone in here. All the souls in this building were sick children or people taking care of the sick. And me, because I'd been hurt escaping from the two goons Rosa hired."

"Maria Rosa had to confess to me that you had escaped. It almost killed her when she found me at the hotel. She had been so proud of getting here first to capture you, ahead of her brother and sisters." From my grandfather's point of view, the whole incident was about his daughter. He looked at me broodingly. "Everything was a contest with Maria Rosa. She wanted to be my best and brightest daughter more than anything. She made up the crazy plan of kidnapping you all on her own, thinking she would present you to me like a gift, outdo her sisters and her brother."

I didn't have to defend myself for killing someone who'd attacked me, but in this case, I was innocent. "She is dead. Though I didn't kill her," I added, to be on the safe side.

"I know Maria Rosa is dead," my grandfather said, surprised at my stupidity. "I had her killed. She had been captured, and she had failed."

With that odd echo, it was hard to tell if he was indifferent or eerily calm about the death of his daughter. I was horrified. It took all my wits to sit there until I could say, "So . . . you got Madame Rostova to kill her?"

"Vera Rostova would do anything for money," my grandfather said with contempt. "Rosa herself knew I wouldn't try to get her back since she had failed me."

I had to bite my lip. "I don't know how she would have justified kidnapping me," I said.

There was something I hadn't learned yet, some piece of information that would explain this sudden rush of grab-the-Felicia.

"I'm sure Maria Rosa would have told you that your real blood family wanted to get to know you."

"Which you had plenty of years to do after my mother died."

Francisco Dominguez really wasn't used to being confronted. He scowled at me. I scowled back. Sometimes the truth hurt, right?

"What do you really want?" I asked. Bottom line.

"I will explain," my grandfather said smoothly.

I knew I wasn't going to like this. But I wouldn't have liked anything other than *I realize I made a terrible mistake, and I want to spend the rest of my life making it up to you.* That wasn't what he said at all, of course.

"There is another family, almost equal in stature to ours in the world of magic in Mexico," my grandfather said. "The Ruizes."

I waited.

"The Ruizes have a grandson who is eighteen. Paco is his name. He is the heir of the family."

I could already tell where this was going. *God almighty!* But I didn't stop the old man.

"My daughters are too old for him, Diego is the wrong sex,

and none of my Mexican granddaughters will be of age for at least five years," my grandfather said. "But when I remembered you, I thought you would be fifteen now, maybe a little older."

Everyone seemed to want me to breed, regardless of who or what I wanted.

"Do the Ruizes know I'm mixed blood?" I had to ask.

His mouth screwed up in distaste.

"Yes, they know your heritage. I would not lie."

Oh, no, he'd arrange to take me away from a place where I'd finally found safety. He'd marry me off to someone I'd never met, someone who might well despise me. But he wouldn't *lie*.

"The Ruiz matriarch, Altagracia, told me she sees the blood of the mongrel Rasputin as an interesting asset, a way of keeping our bloodlines from being too stagnant."

He meant to hurt me, saying that. He was sneering.

Actually, I thought that was pretty smart of Altagracia Ruiz. What a pretty name! Maybe she would be a sweet mother-in-law, the kind who would tell me that I was just like a daughter to her. And Paco sounded friendly, too. He might be even handsomer than Tom and as nice to me as Peter. While I was thinking about the Ruizes, maybe my grandfather would like to give me a hug? I caught myself getting up to go around the table and embrace him.

And that wrenched me out of the sweet, dreamy spell he'd sneaked out.

I leaned over the table and slapped him, hard. I felt some resistance, but it was not really Francisco Dominguez's body I was smacking—it was some kind of magical avatar.

However, it pissed him off plenty.

I was willing to bet no one had given Francisco Dominguez a slap since he was a toddler. Rage flashed across his face. He would never forgive me for it, so I was glad I had done it.

"You asshole," I said, to cement the deal. "You tried to snow me under with a spell."

"How could it not work?" he asked, mostly asking himself, since he was genuinely puzzled.

I started to tell him I was strong, but in the nick of time, I realized that was dangling bait in front of a bear. I might catch the bear, but I'd surely regret it.

"The teachers are protecting me," I said, making that up on the spot. "And now I need you to leave."

"You have to come with me," my grandfather said, as if there were no possibility of my refusing.

As if I were already walking out the door with him. Which I stood up to do. *No, no, no!* I sat down. And held on to the seat of the wooden chair with both hands.

He pulled and pulled with his mind—while his image sat calmly in the other chair—but I would not let go. I could tell he was gearing up to try loosening my hands so my grip would slip.

"I'm beginning to think we should keep you," he said, to distract me. "Inbreeding is nasty, but as you say, you are half-Russian. Diego might be willing. We might not end up with an idiot."

If he thought the idea of screwing my uncle would weaken my will, he had misjudged me. He really didn't know Diego and Bernarda were dead. He'd kill me if he knew. If he could, in this disembodied state? Well, I didn't want to test him.

I wanted to scream and wake up the dormitory, but how would that help me? None of them was strong enough to help me, and they might well die along with me.

I could see from my grandfather's expression that he was determined to get me out of the dormitory. Since he wasn't really there, I couldn't imagine what his plan was, but it was sure to be a humdinger.

I was not going to leave this place with this old man.

A wind started up in the room. I saw the liquid in the stew pot begin to heave as tiny waves formed on the surface. I was glad I'd cleaned up the flour, or I would have been blinded.

The noise of the wind increased until it was practically howling past me. My grandfather was trying to blow me off the chair, but I. Would. Not. Budge.

"What the fuck is going on here?" Tom O'Day yelled from the doorway.

He would have to figure it out. I could not think of anything else but the struggle for the chair. If I let go, it would be the end of me.

Tom wasn't strong enough by himself. But maybe he could give me an edge. I shook all over with the effort of holding on, and my hands were hurting so badly . . . *nonononono!*

A kitchen knife flew past my ear. Tom was throwing it at the old man . . . the image of the old man. Image or not, my grandfather took his attention away from me for a moment to bat the knife aside with a wave of his hand. It was like he knew it couldn't hurt him, but he couldn't stop trying to prevent it from touching him.

I hoped Tom would throw another one.

As if he'd heard my thoughts, Tom picked up my vegetable-chopping knife. It was sharp, too, and it passed through my grand-father's ear. Ears bleed so much, don't they? Not his. However, he winced. *Okay!*

"Need a second!" I shrieked, praying Tom understood me, and it seemed he did.

"One, two, *three!*" he yelled, and on one, I stood. On two, I grabbed the back of the sturdy chair, and on three, I swung it at my grandfather with all my strength.

And it passed right through him to shatter against the wall.

"You're not really here," I snarled.

"I would not have believed this if I hadn't seen it," Tom said.

My grandfather was still sitting in the chair, not bleeding, but his form was fading and wobbly. "You are a stupid girl," he spat. "You always will be."

And then what remained of his image got up and walked out, right through Tom. Tom threw up. I guess my grandfather was still asserting his power.

I sat down on the floor because I couldn't stand any longer, and I stared at the spot where the image of my grandfather had been sitting.

CHAPTER EIGHTEEN

When Tom finally succeeded in rousing the children and Callista, they were very hungry, so it was good I'd made the stew and bread.

I don't know what Tom told Callista, but she didn't appear in the kitchen until after we'd cleaned up—in my case, for the second time. I'd broken a dish or two when I'd swung the chair. There were splinters and bits of crockery everywhere.

At least the exercise helped my hands recover. My fingers flexed freely by the time I was done. I couldn't believe I had lifted the chair and swung it with so much force. I felt proud of myself, for sure.

I stood in the middle of the little kitchen looking blankly at the clean wall, still damp where I'd sponged off the marks the chair had left.

I had tried to kill my grandfather. Only the fact that he hadn't actually been there had saved his life, which seemed kind of silly. I wondered how long it would be before he tried to grab me or kill me again.

Then I remembered the sound of the fountain, which had represented security and safety to the child I'd been. I remembered the desperation in my father's face and the cold eyes of my grandfather as he looked at me and found me . . . trash.

I didn't feel quite so bad after that.

I went up to my room and showered. It had been days since I'd been up the stairs, and I could still smell my roommate's scent in the air. I wondered how she was faring, but I found I wasn't too worried. Anna would survive, one way or another. After my body was clean, I faced another problem. My new clothes were due for a wash. I didn't want to wear my remaining clean uniform, the only thing hanging in my closet after these days of disruption.

I looked in Anna's closet and found she'd left her uniforms here. Of course, she wouldn't wear them at home. Also, she'd left a well-worn skirt and sweater. I would wear those, I decided. I almost smiled when I imagined her reaction. Anna was shorter and bustier than me, but when I put on the clothes, I didn't look too bad.

I stood in the mirror and gave it some real attention. I had grown in the past few days.

It was hard not to be a bit anxious, but I figured it was the exercise of my magic. In the past week, I'd used it every day. Strengthening myself seemed to have pushed the rest of my father's spell away.

My boobs were a little bigger, too.

I felt like a stranger in my own body.

And just as I thought that, I had a strange feeling down below. A fluid, trickly feeling. I stared down as if I could see through my clothes, frightened. All of a sudden, I knew what this must be. Delight rose inside me like a blooming flower.

Oh, thank goodness! Every other girl my age (and many younger) had experienced this, except me. At least I knew what to do. I rushed into the bathroom and raided the cabinet for the supplies I needed. As I fixed myself up, I wondered if the new state of my body had caused (or intensified) my attack on my grandfather.

I was a woman! If I'd remained in Mexico, I'd be ready to marry. My grandfather's wedding plans for me would be put into action.

And I thought of the slow boy, Ruslan, another Rasputin descendent, the one the tsar's advisers wanted me to "breed with."

They could go to hell. I was not ready to marry anyone, much less someone I hadn't chosen. My sister was crazy in love with Eli. You could tell, even though Lizbeth wasn't exactly free with her emotions. That was what I wanted.

I beamed at myself in the mirror.

"Are you up there?" Peter called from the landing.

"On my way down!" I felt positively giddy.

Peter certainly hadn't expected to find me cheerful. He was surprised (but pleased) when I hugged him.

"My mother sent me over," he said. "Not that I needed to be sent. I wanted to see you."

"You've talked to Tom?"

"Yes. I'm so glad you weren't hurt. That must have been scary. But you were strong enough to defeat him!" Peter looked impressed and maybe a little uneasy. "Are you . . . all right with that?"

"I had some bad moments," I admitted. "But yes, I'm glad I stretched my power and learned more about what I can do."

"I wonder how many people he brought with him."

An idea popped into my head. "We need to send a telegram to Eli and Lizbeth."

Peter's eyes widened. "You think the Dominguez family might . . . ?"

"Even if it seems real unlikely, we have to warn them. Do you know how to send a telegram?"

"I've never done it, but how hard can it be? You go to the telegraph company, you give them money."

So on top of an exciting morning and early afternoon, we now had an excursion. Peter remembered seeing a telegraph office near the bus stop where he got off when he came to the school. He had

had permission to come and go from the school. The grigori on duty didn't know me from Adam, so Peter was able to leave with me in tow without much fuss. We walked three blocks. It was another pleasant day, cool and sunny. Peter had searched his pockets to make sure he'd have enough cash.

"Were you hurt in the fight?" Peter asked out of the blue.

"Not really," I said. "My hands and muscles got pulled from lifting the chair. How come?"

Peter flushed red. "I smell blood. Air wizard, you know."

"Oh." I had to control my own blushing. "Well. That's just . . . you know. I'm a woman now."

"Ooooh. Well, with sisters, I figured that might be it."

And we just kept on walking. It was okay after a moment. The embarrassment had worn off. I found myself telling Peter why my grandfather had come to find me, about him wanting to wed me to Paco Ruiz. Peter turned red all over again.

"That son of a bitch," he muttered, to my surprise. "Giving you away like you were a prize filly."

"Exactly," I said, happy he understood. "Exactly!"

We had a long discussion about what our telegram should say. When you know other people are going to be seeing your message, it really makes you think twice. *Eyes open for strangers. Had hostile family visit from Grandpa. Miss you,* was our final version. It cost a quarter to send.

"That doesn't sound too alarming," Peter said. "But it's sure to put Eli and Lizbeth on the alert."

We left the telegraph office feeling we'd done our best and headed back to the school.

"I wondered if you'd like to spend a couple of days at our house," Peter said. "That was where you were going when this all started days ago. I think it's obvious you aren't going to come down with the influenza, and it might be better for the school if you weren't there."

That hurt. "If you're saying I'm a liability . . . ," I began, and then didn't know where to go with the rest of the sentence.

"I'm saying I think your family may try again to get into the school. Maybe this time, your grandfather will come in person. A change of scenery will do you good."

I'd been sure that, sooner or later, I'd experience the aftermath of the struggle with my grandfather, and despite the reinvigorating effect of the shower and the clean clothes and the walk, the reaction hit me then. My steps slowed, and I looked around desperately for a place to sit. We were passing a bus stop at the moment, and I sagged down onto the bench with a sigh of relief. The man already there shrank away from me. Maybe he thought I had the influenza.

Peter said, "Are you all right? Did I say that wrong?"

"Maybe you said that wrong." I took some deep breaths.

The man on the end of the bench got up and moved. Peter took his seat.

"Do you think I brought this on the school?" I said, when I could rely on my voice.

"No, your family did," Peter said. "They could have come to talk to you, explained, found out how you felt about their ideas for your future. Instead, they decided to kidnap you first and explain later."

"But you think the school might not be safe because of me."

"Again, that's their fault. But if there are other Dominguezes in San Diego, or on their way, they won't come to the school if you're not there."

"Peter, better they come to the school than your home."

"That's a good point. But I don't believe there are any more Dominguezes—wow, that's awkward to say—in San Diego. I think we've taken care of them all. I think you'll be perfectly safe."

I had thought I was perfectly safe to begin with, on my way to Peter's house in Felix's car. It seemed like a month ago, rather than days. San Diego had felt so blissful after Ciudad Juárez. The school was like heaven! Food, a bed, order, routine, learning. I had thought if the worst thing I had to watch out for was Anna's disrespect, I had been living the good life. I'd resumed growing.

And then my family had tried to reclaim me.

Peter reached over to take my hand, and I let him. It felt comforting.

"Wherever I go, I bring something bad with me," I said.

"That wasn't what I meant." He was really intent, very sincere. "None of this was your fault. I hate that I made you feel this way."

Peter's misery pierced a hole in mine. I squeezed his hand back.

"I don't know why I'm so blue," I said. "I feel very, very . . ." There wasn't a word for how I felt.

Peter bent close to me. "It's because it's your time of the month," he whispered.

"Really?" I felt stupid having a boy explain it to me, but how else was I going to learn? "That happens?"

"Believe me, I have two sisters and a mother. I know."

"Are you and I supposed to be talking about this subject?"

Anna, for example, would rather have died than have this conversation.

"No rules for us," Peter said.

That sounded good. "Okay."

"So can you walk now?"

"I think so. Let's call the school from your house. That way, no one can stop me."

We caught the next bus, which let us out at a stop a few blocks from Peter's family's house, north and west of the school.

The Savarov house had been severely damaged during the

attack by those who wanted to topple Alexei's regime. I was relieved to see it restored to its former serenity. It was a two-story home on a good-sized lot, with a garage in back and a rose garden in front. There used to be a fountain, but it must have been demolished in the fighting.

We'd showed them what was what. It had been one of the most exciting days of my life. I had learned a lot about myself.

I felt like a very different person from that girl as Peter and I walked up to the front door.

Peter's mother was in the parlor, or living room or whatever they called it. She'd been reading a magazine. I could read the name of it, *Life*. The picture on the cover was of a woman in a very fancy black evening dress. Veronika was surprised to see me but not startled.

"Felicia, you've grown so! I barely recognized you!" She stood up and gave me a quick hug. "Let me call the girls," she said, going to the foot of the stairs. "They had a fitting with the dressmaker, for the wedding clothes."

Alice and Lucy came down in a clatter, giving their brother a casual hello and me a more enthusiastic one. Alice and I were about the same age; she was sixteen, and I was fifteen—and now I looked it. Lucy was eighteen, a pleasant-looking girl with brown hair and eyes. She had a very nice smile.

If the girls got out much, they wouldn't have been so excited about seeing me. Peter was the man of the hour for bringing me home, and when they heard I was hoping to stay a couple of days, they were really pleased.

Mrs. Savarova sent Alice to tell the maid there would be five for dinner, while Peter called the school to tell Callista where I would be.

Veronika said, "But you haven't any luggage!"

"Peter kind of kidnapped me," I said.

"Peter! You should have given the poor girl enough time to get her toothbrush!" Veronika shook her head, but she wasn't really put out at him. When Veronika got really mad, she got cold.

"And I'm out of clothes," I said, figuring I might as well expose my full unreadiness.

"I'm sure we can do something about that." She looked from me to Alice, who was slighter and shorter than her big sister. "My gosh, Felicia, but you've grown! You're just about Alice's size!"

"I'll be glad to share," Alice said immediately.

So all my problems were solved—at least for the moment.

The new maid was a fortyish Irish immigrant named Maggie O'Clanahan. I'd never met an Irish person, and I would have liked to talk to her about her life there and her life here. However, Mrs. O'Clanahan had tight lips and a forbidding way about her. I would have thought she'd be a sour cook, but she wasn't. The roast beef and potatoes and carrots were really good, especially after days of soup or stew at the school. And the dessert (an apple pie) was heavenly. I would fill out in no time if I lived on Mrs. O'Clanahan's cooking.

After dinner, we all carried our own dishes to the kitchen to pile by the sink. The maid would take care of them in the morning. She was now on her way home to serve her husband his supper, Veronika explained. I could tell Veronika was not used to having help who did this, but at least the Irishwoman wasn't a spy like the Savarovs' last maid. (Lizbeth had killed that maid, by the way.)

"How did you find her?" I asked.

We had adjourned to the parlor. Peter was playing checkers with Lucy, and Alice was reading. Veronika had resumed reading her magazine but seemed willing to lay it down when I asked her the question.

"We didn't know if we'd get many applicants or not, because we didn't want to go through the Russian bureau that sent us Natalya."

"Mama advertised in the newspaper," Alice said, before return-ing to her book.

"And we had more than twenty applicants!"

"That must have been a good advertisement," I said.

"So many people are still out of work, even with all the construc-tion going on."

Veronika looked sad. Most of the construction was on North Island, where the tsar had established his residence, and though lots were quite limited, members of the court were trying to cluster close. The Savarovs would never have a home there. On the other hand . . .

"How is Captain McMurtry?" I asked, just as the doorbell rang.

"You may get to ask him yourself," Veronika said, trying to dampen her broad smile.

For a mother who'd had four children—Veronika must be in her early forties—she was all aglow. Peter shook his head as he went to answer the door, but he was smiling. I wondered if it felt weird to see your mother all excited about a man, but considering what a jerk her husband had been, Veronika deserved happiness.

Ford McMurtry was in civilian clothes, a casual shirt and a car-digan. I'd only seen him in uniform, and that was many months ago. He looked like a different man, less stern and serious. After he'd said hello to the others and kissed Veronika on the cheek, he looked at me. I could tell he didn't know who I was.

"I'm Felicia," I said, and his eyes widened.

"Oh, my God. Did they give you growing pills at that school?"

"More like I stopped taking the shrinking pills," I said.

"You look like a teenager now," McMurtry marveled. "Doesn't she, Veronika?"

I tried to look pleasant, but he could stop this any old time, and I'd be glad.

"She *is* a teenager," Peter said, making a visible effort to smile.

He stepped away from the checkers table to stand shoulder to shoulder with me.

Veronika's smiled dimmed a little as she took this in.

And the doorbell rang again.

The Savarovs gave each other anxious looks. They weren't expecting anyone else. Captain McMurtry took it upon himself to answer the door.

"Oh, hello," we heard him say, and then Felix came into the room.

We were all relieved. Lucy smiled like the sun. Felix kissed her on the cheek. There was a lot of that going around. Alice looked a bit envious, maybe hoping for the day when someone would come to the front door to kiss *her*.

"There you are," Felix said to me, disapproval written all over his face. "I've been looking for you."

"Peter invited me to come stay."

"And you didn't think to tell Callista? Or Tom?"

"Peter called Callista. It was a spur-of-the-moment decision," I said, making sure he could hear the coldness. Felix was not the boss of me, and he was not my chaperone, either. "The kids seemed better, so I thought she could do without me."

Felix glared at me, but since he was not helping Callista, he was just as much at fault as I was.

The telephone rang.

"Well, my goodness," Veronika said mildly, but I could tell she was perturbed as she went out into the hall to answer it.

We were all rudely silent as we listened to her answer.

"Hello? Hello? Yes, operator, I'll hold. Yes, that's fine."

A pause.

"Eli, is that you? Where are you, son?"

Pause.

"Oh, yes, is Lizbeth there? She is? Is everything all right?"

Pause.

"What a strange coincidence! She's here!"

I went out into the hall.

"Yes, right here," Veronika said, turning around and seeing me standing right behind her. "Yes, I'll put her on. But you have to talk to me again before you hang up."

I put the phone to my ear. "Hello?" I said cautiously. The line crackled and popped a bit.

"Sister," said Lizbeth. "I got your telegram. Who's after you?"

"I killed most of my aunts and my uncle," I said. "My grandfather's still alive. He tried to kill me."

There was a moment of silence. Lizbeth said, "Do you need me to come? I was going to come to the wedding anyhow, but I can come now."

"I think I just have one aunt left. They're all witches, tell Eli. Dominguezes from Ciudad Juárez. "

"Why did it come to killing? I guess he wasn't going to treat you like a princess?"

"More like a brood mare," I said. "Their big rivals, the Ruizes, have a single son around my age. Paco. I was the only Dominguez girl the right age to take him on."

My sister said something really unprintable. She doesn't often do that, not nearly as often as I do.

"I know we can't keep talking, and Eli's mom wants to speak to him again. So you'd better put him on," I said.

This was going to cost Lizbeth a lot of money. Judging by the faint noises in the background, my sister was calling from the hotel her stepfather owned.

"You write me a letter with everything in it," Lizbeth said. "Tell me to come if you need me. You know I will."

"I know," I said brusquely. "All right, I'm handing the phone to Eli's mom."

Which I did.

It shouldn't be so hard to say "I love you."

But it was.

CHAPTER NINETEEN

Two days went by at the Savarov house, two days of peace and rest.

After the first day, I didn't know what to do with myself. I had never been so idle in my life. Mrs. O'Clanahan did the cooking, most of the cleaning, and the dishes, though the Savarov women—and Peter—dusted and changed the sheets in their bedrooms.

I discovered that before Eli had left home—after he'd graduated from the Rasputin School—the girls had shared a large room, and Peter and Eli each had a narrow box for themselves. Veronika had the largest bedroom, of course.

Veronika had been in a quandary when I'd come to stay. She decided to put me in the large room with Lucy, which held twin beds. Though she was too nice to say so, Veronika was ensuring that I wouldn't be alone to be visited in the night by Peter. I was both insulted and flattered.

Alice was not happy at Lucy's getting my company instead of her, but she managed to smile when she brought me a nightgown and a dressing gown and a set of clothes for the next day. I gave her a hug in thanks, which was a new thing for me.

It was easy to get to sleep the first night, but the second night, Lucy felt like talking. Of course, she talked about the wedding, which would be small, and about going to live in Felix's house. She seemed excited and pleased about everything.

There seemed to be a lot of things I would have expected that didn't feature in her conversation. But there was no polite way for me to ask her about them. I was astounded when she brought them up herself.

"I've wanted to talk to you about this," Lucy said, "because I think you'll understand. I believe you know that Felix isn't really interested in women."

I nodded, warning myself to be cautious. I cleared my throat. "Yes, I do."

"Well, then . . . I want to tell you something I can't tell my mother or my little sister. I am not interested in anything."

It took me a minute to digest this. I wasn't sure I understood. "You mean you don't want to have physical relations with men *or* women?" I had never heard of such a thing.

"That's right. And since I must marry, and Felix can't marry who he wants, it seems we are suited for each other."

So they'd be living together as friends. Pals. Buddies. Lucy wasn't asking for my approval but for my understanding.

"Then I hope you're both happy," I said, trying to sound like I was sure that would happen.

Then Lucy threw a bomb at me. "Would you be my attendant?" she asked shyly. "You're a friend of Felix's and a friend of mine, so it would be perfect."

I told her she'd have to explain to me what that would entail, and she talked and talked, and I finally agreed so I could get to sleep. But I was smiling.

When I woke the second morning, Lucy had already left the room, and her bed was made. I took a quick bath and dressed. I was getting clothed by a lot of people—not that they necessarily knew it, in the case of Anna—and I found I enjoyed it. It was much nicer to have people give you clothes than to beg your sister for money to buy them. At least, I thought so.

Of course, you had to wear what you were given. Alice had loaned me a dress of orange and amber plaid.

I gave myself a once-over in the mirror, shuddered, and set to brushing my hair, a task that took quite a while. Every day, my hair was thicker, and since it had never been cut, it was very long. I went downstairs as soon as I'd gotten my hair in order, because I could smell bacon from my bedroom. Veronika, Alice, and Lucy were all seated and eating.

"I hope you slept well," Veronika said.

"Yes, ma'am," I said. "That's such a comfortable bed. I'm sorry I'm late. I must have been more tired than I knew. A chime wakes us up at the school."

Lucy said, "We're hurrying a little this morning since the seamstress is coming back for another fitting. Mother, I asked Felicia to be an attendant at the wedding, and she said yes!"

Veronika was clearly startled. She recovered quickly. "Oh, that's wonderful! Thanks, Felicia."

Peter came into the dining room and flopped into the chair beside me. He pointed at the coffee pot, and I lifted it from the trivet and eased it over his way. He poured a cup and took a sip, and I returned the pot to its place.

His mother gave me a narrow-eyed look, but Peter was oblivious.

Veronika had been going through the mail, and now she resumed. She paused halfway through the little stack, and then she handed a letter to Peter. Everything at the table stopped.

As Peter looked at the envelope, I could see the letter was from the Grigori Assignment Committee. I wasn't sure what that was. Given the reaction of all the Savarovs, this was a very important moment.

Peter tore it open. I waited with as much suspense as the others while he looked at it. After he'd had time to read it twice, he laid the letter on the table.

"I've been assigned to guardian duty. Two days a week at the airport," he said. "Two days and two nights a week at the school."

I could see his mother didn't know how to respond. Peter wasn't giving her enough reaction.

"You'll be the target of every underclass girl at the school," I said. "Just like Tom O'Day." I grinned at him.

"Tom will go on to better things," Peter said with a shrug.

Okay, that was a clue. This was not Peter's dream assignment. I could understand his being downcast about the airport. Air grigoris could prevent plane crashes, but how often would that happen? Peter would have to stand ready at every landing just in case something went wrong. It wasn't a job offered to the top five people in a class. And the lobby duty at the school, though it was more interesting, was again not a brain-strain.

"And you will go on to better things, too," Lucy said loyally.

"When do you start work?" Veronika asked. She was a practical woman.

"When the school reopens."

"There's no uniform or anything?" Alice asked. She sounded hopeful.

"No, I just show up with my vest." Peter made himself smile at his little sister. "I'll be like a human watchdog."

"This should help you develop your power," Lucy said firmly. "It's exercise every day."

"Of course," Peter said, nodding. But still no enthusiasm.

"At least I will get to say hello on your school days," I said, scraping the bottom of the barrel of reassurance.

"That's true." Peter actually brightened.

I happened to glance at Veronika just then and caught her looking at me with very different eyes in a frozen face. She'd been struck with the knowledge that her son looked at me like a man looks at a woman. Oh, golly. Veronika probably thought losing Eli to my stepsister was enough.

There was not a thing I could say that would ease her mind.

Captain McMurtry stopped by on his way to work—just to beam at Veronika, apparently.

Peter was quiet while his mother's beau was there. I wouldn't like to say Peter was sulking, but he was certainly not smiling or eager to share his news with the captain. He made his excuses to leave the room soon after Captain McMurtry agreed to sit down to a cup of coffee.

"What's gnawing at Peter?" McMurtry asked after Peter had gone upstairs.

Mrs. O'Clanahan came to tell Lucy and Alice that the seamstress had returned for their fitting. After a meaningful look from Veronika, the girls left. She tried to give me a signal, too, but I pretended to be oblivious and ate some more bacon and poured some more juice.

"Ford, Peter seems depressed at his assignment," Veronika began, handing the captain Peter's letter. "Truthfully, I was beginning to be afraid he wouldn't receive one, what with all the . . . you know."

Captain McMurtry covered her hand with his and hitched his chair closer. "Let's be practical," he said, while I commandeered the paper and pretended to read it. "Peter wasn't at the top of his class, and he has to start somewhere. At least he'll get a solid foundation and make some friends."

Veronika began to look more cheerful.

"All he has to do is smile to be more friendly than Tom," I said. "That won't be a stretch for Peter."

"Peter is very personable," McMurtry agreed.

The captain left for the palace—he was an aide to the tsarina—and I got up to go to Lucy's room, since that seemed to be the order of the day.

Veronika said, "I'd like to talk for a moment, Felicia."

I couldn't very well tell my hostess I didn't have the time. I slumped back in my chair.

"You've been very good to me," I said through clenched teeth. I wanted to get this over with. "If you're about to point out that Peter should try to get engaged to some girl of an old Russian family to return you to favor with the tsar, you're talking to the wrong person. It's Peter you need to tell."

For what seemed like an eternity, Veronika Savarova looked at me, her eyes meeting mine directly. It was awful. "Are you engaged to Peter?" she asked.

"No, I'm not. I'm only fifteen or so, and I'm not ready to get engaged to anyone." Why was everyone trying to raffle me off?

Veronika gave me the Look again. "You're right. I do need to talk to Peter. I had no idea you two were attached." She was silent for a moment, probably running over her speech in her head. "Felicia, you know I'm fond of your sister. I think Lizbeth and Eli are well matched." Veronika gave me a poor attempt at a smile.

I had been trying hard to be fair, to anticipate what Veronika might feel. But I was running out of sympathy, and that meant I was getting angry.

"But that's not what you want for Peter. A match with a girl like me." Though it was hard to imagine there were any more girls like me, come to think of it.

"You're a brave person," she said, with a lot of hesitating while she picked the right word. "But that's not all Peter needs."

"Why not? Just so I know." I could feel my face and voice

harden. Veronika would have been too scared to have this discussion with my sister. It must be my age that let her imagine she could tell me my inadequacies.

"You're a killer like your sister. Peter needs someone gentler."

It was like getting hit with a hammer. I had a hard time drawing breath and keeping my face straight. Unfortunately, Veronika kept on talking.

"Someone softer. And he doesn't need to be intimately involved with . . . anyone."

I had not ever anticipated being engaged to Peter Savarov (or anyone else) until this moment. Much less had I imagined having sex with Peter! Now I felt like following him upstairs and going on one knee to ask for his hand or shoving him onto the bed and hopping on him, out of sheer contrariness. I made myself breathe in and out steadily.

After a few breaths, my more reasonable side could see Veronika's point, even if I violently disagreed with her.

I reminded myself that the woman had been good to my sister and to me. At this very moment, I was a guest in her home.

On the other hand, and there always is one, Peter was an adult.

I took a deep, deep breath. In and out. Apparently, I was going to be reasonable.

"Then *you* tell Peter about how we'd better not get engaged or have sex. He is a man. And he knows who I am."

This time, I did rise and leave the room. I think I flew up the stairs, since I didn't remember going up later. Lucy and Alice were in Veronika's dressing room with the seamstress. I caught a glimpse of them through the half-open door. But I couldn't talk to them right now.

Peter's bedroom door was closed, which was good. I could not face him, either.

Since Mrs. O'Clanahan had washed the clothes I'd arrived in, I put them back on, leaving Alice's dress on the bed, laid out neatly. Quietly—but not sneaking!—I left the Savarovs' house.

Veronika was not in sight on the ground floor. Maybe she actually was having the suggested talk with Peter? But I was betting she was not. I opened the front door and walked out.

I knew it wasn't right or polite to leave without talking to (at the very least) Peter, but I was too angry. I feared I would cry, and that would be horrible.

As I strode along, hoping I could remember the long route to the school, I replayed Veronika's words over and over. Her son needed someone kinder and gentler than me. I was a killer.

I tried to think things through.

Some of the things Veronika had said were true. Lizbeth had certainly killed people, and so had I. Lizbeth was bound to kill people. It was part of her job. The way you avoided being killed by Lizbeth was not to attack her. She did not track people down to kill them for sport. Right? And neither did I. Unless my own life or the life of someone I cared about was threatened, I wasn't going to kill anyone.

So we got a pass on that, I figured.

Also, I knew for a fact that Eli could kill people in agonizing ways, and he had. There again, that had been in defense of his own or Lizbeth's life and in pursuance of the tsar's goals. So, excusable, at least to me. It seemed incredible to me that Veronika didn't realize that.

Also, I knew from my sister that Peter had tried to kill someone—his father—but in the end, Lizbeth had done the deed. However, Peter had had it in his head and in his heart to kill. Another pass on that.

So take that, Veronika. Your sons are no better than me and my sister. I began to calm down a little.

I could put this whole prejudice of Veronika's down to igno-rance. She didn't know her own sons as well as I did. She wanted something for both of them that would ultimately lead to their deaths, in fact. If you put it that way, we were actually *good* for the Savarov brothers.

I tried to think of other things to add to my improved mood. Hey, my feet were completely healed. I was going to have to walk all the way back to the school, so healed feet were a good thing. My hands were improved, too, though a bit scabby and bruised.

It would have been handy if I'd been thief enough to steal the money for the bus, though. Hadn't occurred to me until this moment. My feet would not feel so good by the time I got back to the school.

Just then, I heard someone running behind me. I did not turn to look. I knew who it was.

Peter swerved around in front of me, and I stopped. I didn't have a choice.

"What did she say?" he asked.

His color was high, and his eyes were wide. He opened his arms and wrapped me in them, pulling me to him, right there on the street, in public. I had my answer about Peter's feelings, but I didn't know if I felt the same.

"Peter," I said in my calmest voice.

It was nice being hugged, and awkward at the same time. I put my own arms around him briefly to show I appreciated his fervor, and then I pushed back slightly. He let go. But he took a grip on my upper arms. As I looked up at him, I knew he was sweet on me. But was I as sweet on him? If it hadn't been for his mom, I might not have realized that was in the mix.

That was kind of funny.

"What did she say?" Peter asked again.

"Let's walk and talk," I said.

Peter took my hand, and we walked. We'd done that before. Now it felt comfortable.

I began, "It turns out your mom wasn't thrilled with Eli marrying a killer, as she put it. She could see it was going to happen, so she accepted it. Eli was older, for one thing. But when she decided you were, ah, tending to like me that way . . . she didn't want you to be attached to a killer also."

"That's what she called you?" Peter was jumping into the deep end of anger.

"Peter, it's true."

"What else were you supposed to do?" Peter said. He waved his free hand. "Stand around and be killed?"

I was pleased. Peter was following my reasoning.

"That's what I thought," I said. "Your mother's got to know you and Eli are capable of wiping out people." (I had seen Eli kill dozens of people and be quite happy about it, while I had been dropping bombs on them from the roof of the Savarov house.) "Maybe her real objection is that Lizbeth and I are low-class killers, and you and Eli are high-class."

Peter was quiet while we walked about a block. He said, "You may be right."

Of course I was.

"Mother was brought up as an aristocrat and married to a nobleman when she was seventeen. Even on the boats, there was a difference."

The motley flotilla that had left Russia with the tsar had limped around the world for years seeking a safe haven. Children had been brought up on the boats, marriages had taken place, alliances had been formed and broken. Nicholas and Alexandra had still been alive then, and their son (now Tsar) Alexei, a teenager, had been kept alive by Rasputin's blood.

Though Peter was born noble and I was born very low, I had almost certainly been in the presence of the tsar more often than Peter. When it came to blood, that of a child of one of Rasputin's bastards trumped that of a noble.

That made me feel a little sad. Yes, me. The evil low-born killer.

"We should have a talk," I said.

Peter groaned. "What about? My friends have all told me that when a girl says she needs to talk, it means she wants to either get more serious or break up."

"Not this girl. It means I want to talk."

Peter looked relieved. "That's good. What about?"

"Do you like me like a boyfriend?" I wanted to pin this down.

He stopped short. "Since I've defended you to my mother and I'm holding your hand in public, yes. I thought you'd know that."

"How long have you felt this way?"

"Since you grew. The past month or two, I guess. It would have been weird if I'd liked you that way when you looked like a child."

We agreed on that.

"And you said you thought you were fifteen. That's not a bad age for a man of over nineteen to be dating." He looked at me uncertainly. "Do you think the same way?"

"I think the same way," I said, though I couldn't say I had a policy.

"How do you feel?" he asked in return. "You were glad I was there when we went to your grandfather's hotel, and you're holding my hand right back. Do you think of me as your boyfriend? I know you had a crush on Tom."

"Well, all the girls do. They see him in the lobby all the time, and he's gruff and tough."

"I'm not?" Peter was smiling when he said this, which was fortunate.

"You're not a man of mystery like Tom. But I see that as a plus." I smiled back at my boyfriend. "If we are important to each other, how will your mother react? She's definitely not for this relationship."

"Mother has to let us live our lives," Peter said. "She lived for us when Father was so cruel to her and then protected us from my stepbrothers after his death. She stood up to all that for our sakes. I hope that Captain McMurtry will offer her happiness."

"He should propose." After all, they weren't getting any younger.

"My mother is forty-one. Do you think Ford is that old?"

"He might not be. But they can still get married."

"It's usual, though, isn't it? For the man to be older?"

"I think that's just so he can offer the woman a home to come to," I said.

I had no idea how old my mother had been when she'd eloped with my father. I also didn't know how old he'd been when he died. I wondered if Marina, my mom, had imagined that her father would forgive her and make room for her and her husband in the big house with the fountain. I wondered if I could find out; but now I'd killed a lot of my mother's family, and my grandfather hated me, so I'd probably never know.

Well. Dammit. I shook my head. Was it really that important? Couldn't be.

I was only Lizbeth's life away from being alone in the world. I had to make my own path. Though now, it seemed, I had an attachment.

CHAPTER TWENTY

Things had changed at the school in the two days I'd been gone.

One of the children had died, a girl I had hardly known. She'd taken a sudden turn for the worse and was gone before anything could be done for her. The others had all gotten better, including the janitor, who was up and working a couple of hours each day.

Callista had had time to bathe and wash her hair because she'd had help with the children. Tom O'Day had begun staying at the school so he could be on hand, which was why Callista was smiling as she went about her work. Another grigori, Sinead Mallet, had come over to help. She had a heavy Irish accent that was really pretty, though it made her hard to understand. But she could sing like a bird. The children loved it. So did we all.

Felix came by to check up on me. He'd found out about my visit to the Savarovs from Lucy, and he gave me a very dry look when he brought up Veronika. He didn't like his future mother-in-law worth a damn, but that was Felix. He was much more interested in my grandfather's visit to the school. Francisco Dominguez was not at the Claiborne any longer, but that didn't mean he wasn't in San Diego. Felix wasn't sure Francisco would have to be physically close to send his avatar to visit with me, but he thought the closer the better. "A couple of miles at the most," he said. It was strange to see Felix subdued by the idea of someone else's power.

Felix also reported that this wave of the influenza had been the shortest one of the past few years. He said, "Maybe that means it's over."

"For this year?"

"Forever."

I couldn't imagine that. The Spanish influenza had been around as long as I could remember, taking a huge death toll every time it showed up. I'd never gotten it; neither had my father. My mother had died of a fever, but my father had always been vague about which one. I didn't think it was the influenza.

Maybe I couldn't catch it.

Wouldn't that be wonderful?

Felix and I were sitting in the small kitchen. He'd eaten the rest of our bread, toasted, but since he'd brought us a new loaf, that was okay. He reported that the grocery stores were receiving shipments now. He'd also picked up some chickens and some green beans, to Callista's pleasure. I could hear her down the hall, talking to one of the children. Sinead was outside hanging out the wash, which was never-ending. I'd finally gotten my own laundry done, which was a relief.

Felix got up to leave, but he hesitated in the doorway. "Are you going to be able to put up with Veronika for the duration of the wedding? I hear you're going to be Lucy's attendant. Along with Alice."

"I don't want to upset Lucy by backing out," I said. "And I want to be there for the wedding because you're my friend. Veronika and I have some time to repair our relationship." I was positively saint-like.

"You care for Peter?" Felix put a lot of emphasis on *care*.

"I'm happy when I hold his hand," I said. "But as far as, you know, having more contact with him?" I waggled my eyebrows at Felix, who actually almost smiled. "I'm not ready for that."

"Good, since you barely look old enough."

"I'm old enough."

Felix turned red. "I am standing in for your sister and Eli since they aren't here," he said stiffly. "Please, wait as long as you can before you decide to do more than hold hands. No matter what you do to prevent pregnancy, it may not work."

It was killing Felix to talk about this. He must really love Eli to put himself through the wringer of having the Talk with me.

"You know what's interesting?" I asked.

He shook his head.

"I've just been in combat with Mexican witches and killed some of them. And yet I get the big talk about being intimate with Peter Savarov."

Felix's face cleared, and he laughed. "Maybe because the deaths are a done deal, and Peter has yet to be settled."

"I did talk to Lizbeth, you know."

"I know. I got a letter from Eli. They wanted me to take up the Peter issue with you, and now I can let them know I did it in person. My conscience is clear."

"Peter's grown up a lot in the past few weeks," I said in Peter's defense.

"He has. But you don't need to grow up with him, at least in that way. Give us older ones time to catch our breath, please! Just yesterday, you were a real child, and now you're gaining height like a weed."

"You could at least say a flower!"

"Let's wait to see how you turn out."

"Oh, thanks so much."

Felix bowed and took my hand, kissing it lightly on the back.

"Good luck with this situation," he said. "If you want to know, Lucy and Alice are appalled that their mother said something that offended you so much you left without saying good-bye. I think they'd be quite willing to let you ravish their brother, if only you'll return to be in the wedding."

I laughed, which was what Felix deserved, and watched him walk to the main gate and let himself out.

I had another visitor later that day after we'd cleared up after supper. For the first time, all the invalids had eaten at the table. I carried my plate off to sit on the stairs for lack of room. It was my turn to wash the dishes. Afterward, I walked out to Rasputin's tomb for a quiet spell. It was my favorite peaceful spot.

There was a bench on the side of the tomb that faced the school, and it was where I often sat.

For the first time, I told myself this was the tomb of my other grandfather. I'd never gotten to meet him, never thought of him as a person rather than a historic figure. From all accounts, he'd been one of those people who were called "larger than life." I had quite a pair of grandfathers.

At least I'd had no hand in this one's death. Grigori Rasputin had been murdered, poisoned by people who hated his influence over the tsarevitch—who at that point was a grown man by most standards and (though no one knew it) about to become tsar, because Nicholas had begun fading at Alexandra's death and was ready to join her.

Everything I had learned about Rasputin the legendary grigori and Rasputin the bawdy religious man passed through my mind. He must have been difficult to deal with and exasperating. But Rasputin certainly had the power, and he'd certainly wanted to protect other people who had it. Thanks to him, magicians, witches, wizards— whatever you wanted to call them—had a place in society and had been permitted to practice their arts openly, to benefit the public.

I was thinking so hard that I didn't notice Ford McMurtry until he sat by me.

"Now what?" I said, exasperated. "Another scolding? Another warning?"

"No," Ford McMurtry said.

He was easy on the eyes, and for the first time, I wondered if he and Veronika would have children. Wasn't she too old? I didn't know.

"Veronika has sent me as an ambassador. She believes she handled this business badly, and she is sorry for that."

This business, my ass. "I would have thought better of her if she'd come to tell me that herself."

I could see the captain was shocked. Why he didn't feel I had the right to criticize Veronika in return I could not imagine. I had not grown up in a way that automatically assigned respect to elders. Not with my father in charge.

"She was not brought up to apologize to anyone, especially a child," McMurtry said stiffly.

"But that was her point, that I'm not a child. I also wonder why she chose to have her opening conversation with me instead of Peter." I was really getting close to the edge.

"Pride, mostly," the captain said. "Think of this. Your sister rescued Eli when his own mother could not. Your sister won his heart and took him away. It wasn't Lizbeth's fault that Eli had to leave San Diego. But the effect is the same. Eli left with Lizbeth, and now Veronika can't see him and doesn't have his judgment to consult or his shoulder to lean on or his company to enjoy."

Poor, poor Veronika. Her son was alive and had married a wonderful, brave woman who would be faithful until her death. He had been rescued from jail by this brave woman and had dodged execution because of this woman, and Veronika and her daughters had been saved from degradation and rape by this woman. *Boo hoo hoo.* I clamped my lips to keep this inside.

Maybe the captain was getting some atmosphere from me, just as I got from him. "I know that makes her sound ungrateful," he said.

I clamped harder.

"She loves Peter, too."

"That was never in question," I said, biting each word out.

What the hell? I finally grew, finally started looking my real age, acquired a boyfriend—good-looking, nice manners—and then his mom stomps all over me. I found a family, and they tried to kidnap me or kill me. But I rerouted those thoughts back to the boyfriend.

I said, "Peter is a clever, quick-thinking man. He's done a lot of maturing in the past few months. You'd think the last thing Veronika would want to do is run him off by criticizing the girl he likes. And imply—to me! to my face!—that I was seducing Peter under her roof. It didn't even cross my mind!" I had to force the last sentence out between clenched teeth.

And that was the truth. Peter had never even hinted about me sneaking into his room during the night I'd stayed with the Savarovs, and I would have rejected the idea if he had.

McMurtry had reached his limit. "I have told you already that she's sorry for the things she said. What more do you want?"

"I figure there's something she wants. Otherwise, why send you?"

For the first time, the captain looked taken aback. "Huh," he said thoughtfully. "As it happens, Veronika is upset because Peter is threatening to move into the Residence down the street."

"He'll be just that much closer to me, and we all know what a femme fatale I am. Or if she's scared because there won't be a man in the house, why don't you pop the question?"

Now I'd been just as rude as Veronika. I shot off the bench and stomped my way back to the covered walkway and into the dormitory. When I looked out a window a couple of minutes later, Captain McMurtry was still sitting on the bench.

I was pretty damn sick of Veronika Savarova and her problems.

In the next two days, all of us who were in residence cleaned the school. Callista explained that the germs (which I didn't really understand) were clinging to things that the infected kids had touched, and those germs might infect others if they weren't scrubbed off. Though that idea was mysterious to me, cleaning was something I knew how to do. Even Peter showed up to help. He said since there was no door for him to watch, he would do this instead.

I was glad to see him, though I didn't know exactly how to act around him. Peter seemed to feel the same way. At first, this was awkward. But gradually, we got more comfortable keeping company. The grigori guards admitted Peter without asking for the password.

The teachers began to trickle back to straighten their classrooms and catch up with their preparation work. They joined in the cleaning with varying degrees of vigor. Expecting to deal with influenza illnesses and deaths but no more, they were shocked and angry to hear what had happened in the school in their absence. The death of Miss Priddy made them all even angrier. I thought that was a little strange, since no one had liked her, but I remembered being angry about her death myself for about a minute.

There was a lot of whispering about the Rostovs' absence. Felix told me in private that Master Rostov had confessed to killing Rosa at the behest of Francisco Dominguez.

"Rostov got sick when he looked at the body and ran away," Felix said scornfully. "Vera Rostova didn't know what he'd done, but she also couldn't find him. She guessed her husband had killed Rosa when she found her dead. She decided to hide the corpse. But you two were there."

Felix said they were now both in a secret grigori jail, not the one where the city put magical prisoners but a proper jail.

No one seemed to know that the school had been attacked because of me. I could only be grateful for that.

I didn't talk about it, Peter didn't talk about it, and I believed the only ones who knew the whole story were Felix and Tom O'Day. If Tom had told Callista, she didn't hint about it in my presence. That was exactly what I wanted.

It wasn't that I would have lied about it if anyone had asked me. I just didn't want to talk about my family.

The school began to fill back up with students. A few didn't return, either because they'd died or been ill or because their parents didn't want them to go away again.

Anna came back after another week, more beautiful than ever. She'd had her fourteenth birthday while she was at home.

She hinted heavily that she'd become the object of a rich young man's attention while she was in Redding. It was only her age that held him back from a proposal, she said. It took my roommate a day or two to realize Peter now lived in the Residence down the block. It took another day for Anna to realize that the relationship between Peter and me had changed in nature.

Anna had a lot to say about that, but I ignored it all. At first, I had been as fascinated with Anna as I would have been with a bright parrot. But now I could see there was no substance under all that lovely plumage. I had many more things to think about. By the way, I had tucked Anna's discarded outfit, now clean, in the back of her wardrobe.

I was preoccupied by something much more important.

I had forgotten all the teachers coming into my infirmary room and staring after the abduction, in the press of so many events that had happened afterward. One morning, Madame Semyonova handed me a note to let me know I had a long-postponed meeting with the faculty scheduled for the evening.

Now that I was scheduled to face their inquiry, I couldn't guess what would happen. I figured the outcome could go one of two ways. They'd train me as a grigori, or I'd be barred from exercising my magic.

Peter said, "Either they're impressed by your strength and power and they want to make sure you know what you're doing, regardless of your being a blood donor to the tsar, or they're outraged by the action of the family you didn't know you had and how that family harmed the school."

That was so close to the way I'd figured it that I had nothing to add. But after a moment, I did think of one thing. "None of this explains everything that happened," I said. "Someone must have told my grandfather where I was."

"Maybe someone survived the massacre at the train station," Peter said. He'd been thinking about that, too. "They'd know who Eli was. And that means they'd know where he'd be taking you."

My sister had only spoken of that day to me once, and then it had been in very clipped terms. At the Ciudad Juárez train station, she'd had to take a stand with the elderly and lethal grigori Klementina so that Eli could escape with me. She wanted me to live and be fed and to have a place to stay. Since she expected to die, that place would be the Rasputin School.

Lizbeth and Klementina had to kill all the grigoris who were trying to stop Eli and me. Those grigoris didn't want the tsar to have the resource of my blood; they were recruits to the cause of Grand Duke Alexander.

Lizbeth and Klementina had killed and killed, each in her own way, but Klementina had received a lethal blast of magic. Her dying gift to Lizbeth had been a spell of invisibility—the same gift that had helped me escape my kidnappers. If it hadn't been for that, Lizbeth would probably still be in a Mexican jail.

"I'll write Lizbeth a letter," I told Peter. "Ask if there's any way that could have happened."

"I'll take it to the mailbox," Peter offered.

He was sitting at the desk that had been Tom's domain during his stint of monitoring visitors to the school. Tom had always read, and Peter usually had a book to hand. While Tom had read books about magical practice and history, Peter liked fiction. I recommended *Red Harvest* and dug up the tattered copy I'd read in the infirmary.

But Peter was very vigilant. Since the school had reopened and the front gate was unlocked during the day, there'd been a certain percentage of crazy people wandering in. Peter had handled them well, so far. I'd never thought of desk duty at the school as a dangerous job, but it certainly was no peaceful one these days.

Just as I returned from my room to hand the letter to Peter, the front door opened, and a woman with ragged clothes and dark, tangled hair staggered in. Peter stood and was out from behind the desk in an instant. I was to his left, and I took a step back so I'd be out of his way. But I saw her eyes, and though she launched into a crazy song, complete with hand movements, I knew she wasn't a person from the streets.

Peter's fingers went into a pocket of his grigori vest.

She saw him reaching. Her hand gestures became formal. Magic! I took two running steps and jumped on her.

Like so many people trained in magic, the woman hadn't expected a physical attack.

She hit the floor with me on top of her. Peter pounced on her, and I helped him flip her over. He pulled her hands back and slapped on the handcuffs they'd given him to mark his office.

I rolled to my feet and moved away to let him handle the intruder. The woman yowled and growled and kicked.

Most of the returned students were in the dormitory building, but a few had been in the classrooms to fetch their books. A handful of boys and girls gathered in the hall to peer out at the handcuffed woman.

Madame Semyonova's voice preceded her. "What is the rule when someone breaks into the school?"

Everyone scattered instantly to hide and prepare to defend their territory.

Madame really is wonderful, I thought. Then my eyes met hers. I realized that "students" included me. I hurried away with the others. I didn't like it, though.

It was hard for me to choke down food that evening in the refectory. Anna and one of her friends had decided to sit with me and pester me with questions about what had happened after their families had taken them away. I had reached my last nerve when I rose to take my tray to the window.

I stopped at one of the bathrooms to make sure my uniform was straight and unstained, and then I went to the teacher's lounge, up the first flight of stairs.

Ordinarily, the door was shut. The lounge was where teachers spent their unscheduled time during the school day. There were tables for grading papers and planning lessons, armchairs for reading, and a small library. Students knew not to disturb teachers when they were in the lounge unless there was a dire emergency.

This evening, the door was open, and the room was packed. Every teacher I knew (and a few I didn't) had crowded in to discuss my future.

Since there was one chair left and it was at one end of the room, I knew where I should sit. Looked like I was going to be interrogated. Again.

At this moment, I desperately wished I had a friend with me. And then my eyes met Felix's. Why was Felix there? He didn't have any official position at the school, and yet there he was. I felt maybe one of my muscles relax.

Naturally, Madame Semyonova was sitting front and center. For the first time in a couple of weeks, I really looked at her.

"Madame, are you well?" I asked.

She sighed, and it moved her whole body. "I'm well enough. It's you we're concerned with tonight."

"I'm sorry about Miss Priddy," I said.

"We'll talk about that." She turned her head so slowly I could almost hear the muscles in her neck creak. "Is everyone here? John, have you taken roll?"

John turned out to be Master Franklin. "Madame, every living teacher is here," he said.

Did the dead teachers ever attend meetings? But my attention snapped back to Madame, whose face was very serious. Well, more serious. Madame had never laughed in my hearing.

"Felicia," Madame said. "You have practiced difficult—and drastic—magic, though you are not a grigori student. Please explain this to us."

That was not such a frightening question. I explained about my father and his haphazard teaching method.

There was silence.

"Any questions for Felicia?" Madame Semyonova asked.

"One," Madame Lubinova said. "Felicia, where was your mother all this time?"

"I believe I told you my mother died when I was very young," I said, as respectfully as I could. "As far as I know, she died of a fever."

"And your father never remarried?"

"No, ma'am." Though he'd had women, before and after my mother, some who did not consent and some who did.

"And how did your father die?"

"He was killed while he was on a trip with my uncle. I don't know how. My uncle wouldn't talk about it."

"And your uncle subsequently died also?"

I nodded. "Paulina killed him," I said.

There was a silence I could only called shocked. This was new information to the teachers. That was weird. Eli had known about it; I'd told him.

"Paulina Coopersmith?" Master Franklin said, when no one else spoke.

"Yes, sir. Eli's partner. She died, too. When they came to get me, in Ciudad Juárez."

"We believed she had died in the battle at the railroad station," Madame Semyonova said.

Oh, shit. I'd blundered. But Eli had never filled me in on the story he'd told to explain Paulina's death. I hadn't known he hadn't told the truth.

"No, her body was inhabited by . . . something not her," I said. "We all thought the thing was dead, after my sister shot her. But the thing came to life again when Uncle tried to drag it outside, and it bit him."

"What happened after that?" Felix said. It was the first time he'd spoken.

"Uncle told me to cut off its head with a shovel, so I did."

There was a lot more silence.

"And then what happened?" Madame Semyonova asked, but reluctantly.

"He said to leave because he would change into what she was," I said.

This seemed like a book I was reading or a movie I was watching, because it had happened so long ago. In a different country.

"And did you?" she asked.

"Yes, I did. I went to the train station to find Lizbeth and Eli."

"And you encountered many enemies."

"Lizbeth and the old grigori—excuse me, Klementina—killed them all," I said. "So Eli could bring me here."

"You spoke Spanish and English at home?" Master Franklin said.

It was the last question I expected. I answered him in Spanish. "Yes, sir. My father wanted me to learn English since he had to speak it when he traveled, but we spoke Spanish in the community, and we spoke Russian in our house. I'm good with languages."

"*Sí*," he agreed. "*Muy bien*."

The last time I'd spoken Spanish was in our home in Ciudad Juárez, when Eli and Lizbeth had come to talk to my uncle. Well, my uncle had grabbed Eli and forced him to come to our home, and Lizbeth had tracked me down and made me lead her there. I didn't know if she had loved Eli even then, but I figured she had.

I was lost in remembering for a moment. I only returned to the room full of people staring at me when Madame Semyonova said, "We have all noticed how good you are at languages and how keen you are at your studies. Now we must speak of what's occurred recently."

I nodded, trying to get focused on the trouble I was in *right now*. Because this wasn't about assigning me to the appropriate class. At least, it was *not only* about giving me the right ranking for my true age and ability.

"Just tell us what has happened to you, starting the day Felix was taking you to eat dinner with the Savarov family."

I told them about the abduction, my escape, my meeting with

Rosa at Gwen Manley's shop, getting back to the campus with the protection of the grigoris. It seemed like a long time ago now.

"And then the school closed," Madame said quietly.

"And Cyril died," I said sadly.

A few teachers whispered among themselves. Either they hadn't known Cyril was dead or they had forgotten which child he was.

"You were in the infirmary," Madame said, her harsh voice almost inaudible.

"Because my feet were so cut up."

"And Peter was coming in to see you."

"Yes, we're in-laws."

"And friends," Felix murmured.

"Yes, we're friends." That was as good a word as any.

"Miss Priddy was here helping, and Callista was in charge of the infirmary. Since Mrs. Benton had left. And then I heard screaming." I closed my eyes for a second. "I got out of bed," I said. "And I went into the hall. There were two of them, a youngish woman and a man, and they were blasting away at everyone they could see. Miss Priddy hit the wall. There was blood. And then Peter came out of the bathroom; I guess he'd heard the screaming, too. And though he got off a shot, they knocked him down right away. I saw him fall, and I thought next they might go into another room where the sick kids were. So I hit them."

"Not with your hands. With a spell."

"I guess so. I don't really know that many spells. Since I'm not classified as a grigori, I haven't learned any here. But I hit them with my will, I guess you'd say."

"With what result?"

"I killed them."

"Did you intend that to happen?"

Though Madame didn't sound judgy, that question really bothered me.

"I intended for them to stop hurting our people," I said sharply. "And they did."

"There is more for us to talk about later," Madame said to the teachers. "But for now, that will do. Instructors at the Rasputin School for Grigoris, do you agree this girl, Felicia Karkarova, has the ability and right to be trained as a grigori? And that Felix and his ilk have a unique interest in watching over her development?"

Wait, what? What did Felix have to do with my situation?

Madame pointed to Master Franklin, as if to say, *You first*.

"I agree," Master Franklin said.

I hadn't seen Callista at the back of the room, but it was her voice that said, "I agree," second.

Only two teachers disagreed: a British woman, Helen Burkhill-Rogers, and an ancient Russian man, Evgeny Turgenev. Neither had ever taught me or even spoken to me, so I didn't take it personally, though I was sure they meant it that way. They disliked the very idea of me.

"Felicia Karkarova is now a grigori in training," Madame said. "She is also a hero of the school. In our absence, she prevented many deaths."

Miss Burkhill-Rogers couldn't keep silent. "But how do we know it wasn't her very presence that caused the attack?"

It was an intelligent question, and I dreaded the answer.

"When Felicia came to us, she was an orphan who appeared to be about ten years old. Now Felicia is a young woman of fifteen—she thinks—with only a half sister for a family. It simply does not follow that she is the cause of anything."

I couldn't believe what I was hearing.

Madame Semyonova wasn't going to tell everyone about my heritage.

I didn't know if that was wise or not. I did know it might spare me a great deal of pain and shunning. I was grateful. I closed my eyes for a moment, bathing in the sense of acceptance, the prospect of future learning. I would be a real grigori. Perhaps I wouldn't have to be a blood whore for the tsar! No matter what a privilege everyone told me it was, I could tell they pitied me and found the idea repulsive.

When I opened my eyes, all the teachers were gone except Madame and Felix.

"Thank you," I said. "Thank you."

"You know this will not excuse you from helping the tsar."

I nodded. *It won't now*, I thought. *But maybe later?*

"I have been asking questions among the oldest of us. You may not know this, but your mother was half-Russian," Madame Semyonova said, to my amazement. "She was the daughter of Francisco Dominguez by his first wife, a Russian grigori, Irina Drozdova."

"But that's your last name," I said, looking at Felix. To say I was stunned would be understating it.

"I had to be sure, child. I wrote some family members to verify what I suspected. Irina was my aunt," Felix said. "My mother's sister."

I felt all at sea. "How did Irina Drozdova meet my grandfather?" I couldn't imagine how someone from the flotilla would have met up with a witch living in the interior of Mexico. I said as much.

"Their meeting predated the Revolution and the escape of Tsar Nicholas," Madame Semyonova said.

Of course, it must have.

"There's a social gathering every third year. It's held in different places. In 1906—at least, I think it was in 1906—it was held in Ireland. Among us, it's called the Wizards' Ball. Rasputin had not organized the grigoris then and let them out of the shadows—that only happened a few years ago. But the magic didn't come from nowhere. There were always families in Russia with a strong and secret magical background, and families from Mexico, where the practice was termed witchcraft, and families from the British Isles who called themselves wizards. A few families from other countries, China and America, for the most part . . . but they had to be very cautious."

Felix looked grim, but then, he almost always did.

"So they had a *dance*?"

"Yes, but there were several days of fellowship, meals, exchanges of information, parties." Madame sounded nostalgic.

I wondered if she'd met her husband at one of these balls.

"However," she continued, with reluctance, "the most important purpose of the Wizards' Ball was the arrangement of marriages. Families would send pictures and biographies of their children, those who were in the right age range, so the other groups could consider the benefits of the possible alliance in advance."

"Benefits?"

"So no one line would become inbred. So the talent would continue to be passed down. That year, your grandfather Francisco met Irina. They didn't speak the same language, but they were marriageable ages, from separate bloodlines, both strong practitioners. They liked the look of each other well enough. Their families agreed to join forces."

Just like that! It sounded horrible.

"Your grandmother Irina bore your mother Marina and her sister, Isabella. After having those two children, Irina died. I don't know what ailed her," Madame said, to forestall my question. "Your grandfather Francisco remarried after less than a year, a distant cousin of his from a Bolivian family. This second wife had three children, a boy and two girls."

"Those must have been amazing parties," I said, ignoring a thought that was niggling at the back of my brain. I was trying to imagine getting dressed up, knowing you might meet the person you would marry, and being all thrilled at every approach of someone who might be an eligible match. It would be fun for a night. Maybe.

Madame Semyonova nodded. "I remember," she said heavily. "So long ago. Felix, you may have heard next year the ball will be here. In San Diego! Our oldest class will go! I suppose they will play that modern music, and everyone will throw themselves about like monkeys."

"It's not really the time to talk about the Wizards' Ball, though I'd be glad to do that later, Madame. It's time to talk about why Felicia's grandfather picked now to abduct her. And what the remains of his family will do when they learn what has happened. And what it means that Felicia is so powerful."

It seemed obvious to me, now that I knew about the Wizards' Ball. "My grandfather picked now because he thought that I'd be old enough for a husband next year. Since he wanted it to be this Paco Ruiz guy, he thought he'd jump the gun before I could pick someone else."

I'd surprised Felix. "Yes," he said. "I think you're right."

"I can do my own arranging, though?"

"Yes," Madame said with great conviction. "Getting to know someone is far better than getting married to a man you've danced with a few times."

Grandmother Irina had been fearless, or maybe just rash. Maybe her parents had been domineering, and she'd wanted to escape. Or possibly Francisco Dominguez had been very handsome? He must have seemed exotic to a Russian girl from a grigori family.

My mother had followed that pattern in eloping with my father. I would *not* do the same, I vowed to myself on the spot. Then I realized the most important point Felix was making.

"So we're related, Felix. You're my cousin?" It seemed too good to be true.

"I'm your cousin." Felix didn't sound excited, but he sounded sure.

"I have a cousin *and* a half sister," I said, feeling rich.

Madame Semyonova nodded. "You do indeed. And Felix is going to be responsible for your training in the magic that we suspect is your strong suit."

CHAPTER TWENTY-ONE

Oh. Really?" I was stalling while a lot of thoughts ran through my mind.

Felix was respected but unpopular. I'd longed to be accepted into the world of the Rasputin School. Now I'd gotten my greatest wish—to be trained as a grigori, like the other children—only to have the acceptance part hanging in the balance.

"So . . . death magic," I said, when neither of them spoke.

Felix nodded. "But death magic has another side. What you take away you can give. I'll teach you so-called resurrection magic, too. Very hard to accomplish unless you have the death part." He smiled.

I was fond of Felix, but that was a little scary.

"What category does this fall under?" I asked.

Felix looked blank.

"Earth, fire, air, water?"

Madame Semyonova decided she'd been silent long enough. "It can fall under all of these," she said. "You can have an affinity for any of those elements and still deal in death and resurrection. They are all tied to the life cycle."

That made sense to me. "All right, then," I said. "Grigori classes from now on, special instruction from Felix. And the tsar will still need my blood."

Felix and Madame both nodded.

Getting special instruction from Felix Drozdov would be impossible to hide from the other students. I would be the girl everyone was afraid of, rather than the girl who had to give her blood to the tsar and beg for clothes and uniforms.

Put that way, being a death-magic specialist didn't seem so bad. I'd rather have fear than pity any day.

Madame said, "You'll have your new schedule tomorrow."

My only problem the rest of the evening was getting ready for bed without answering any of Anna's questions. I lay awake after our light was out, wondering what I was in for. I fell asleep with no answers.

Since Madame always did what she said she was going to, I wasn't at all surprised to find a folded typed sheet had been slid under our door during the night. Anna was curious, of course. She snatched the paper from my hand and immediately shrieked and dropped it. It wafted around on a gust of air before it landed on the floor.

I was just as surprised as Anna, but I acted as though I weren't.

"Don't touch my things," I said.

Anna's eyes were wide as she looked from the paper to me. "That was spelled!" she blurted finally.

"In a school that trains grigoris, that surprises you?"

Anna frowned. "No one else's paperwork is spelled."

I raised my eyebrows. *So? Mine is.*

We got ready for breakfast in what I could only think of as a thoughtful silence.

Anna's cluster of cronies was all twittery with my new status, and I didn't want to answer questions.

After months of establishing my foothold in the group, I decided to break away for my own peace of mind. Breakfast was often the only meal everyone attended, and I had my choice of groups to sit with. The best choice was with the other pariahs. I should have chosen them when I'd come to the school.

I smiled and slid onto the bench beside Henry Chen and across from Fenolla Gregory. Fenolla's father was English, and her mother was from the Sudan. Fenolla herself was a toasty tan shade, and her features were delicate. She was widely reported to be crazy. All I knew about Henry Chen, who looked to be about my age, was that he'd started at the Rasputin School a month ago, he had mixed blood, and no one ever sat with him except Fenolla. He was very surprised when I swung my legs over the bench.

"I'm Felicia Karkarova," I said, stirring brown sugar into my oatmeal.

"Henry Chen," he replied. No accent, at least not that I could tell from two words.

"I'm an orphan, half Mexican, half Russian. You?"

"Found on a doorstep. Half Chinese, half Caucasian."

"And you, Fenolla?" I said politely.

She shrugged. "Crazy," she said.

Henry wore glasses, and his hair was black and straight and slicked back. His skin was darker than mine, perhaps lighter than Fenolla's.

Fenolla looked like an elf. Her features were fine and thin, and her cheekbones were high. Last month, she had cut all her hair off. It was shorter than Peter's and intensely curled.

"How did you two come to be here?" I said, looking from one of them to the other. I didn't know what else to talk about.

"You don't let any grass grow under you," Henry said. He didn't seem to deem that a great quality. "I was left on the doorstep of the Chinese Christian Church, and Mrs. Delbert took me to a Chinese family she knew who wanted a male child. Since I was half white, the Chens wanted a son very badly indeed."

"I lived with my father and uncle in a Mexican slum," I said. That was my contribution to the weird-people pot. Why had I not done this before? It was so much better than trying to fit in with Anna and her friends.

"Interesting," Fenolla said in her light voice. "I was found under a cabbage leaf."

Henry and I laughed. Fenolla did not.

"How come you're sitting with us today?" Henry asked. He wasn't letting grass grow, either.

"I'm starting a new course of study after I showed I had some talent," I explained. "It's going to be a bit different from anyone else's. So instead of being accepted here on sufferance because I give blood to the tsar, I'm going to be able to become a full-fledged grigori. But with some unpleasant abilities."

"My adopted parents found me making my toys float around my head," Henry told me.

"I made my sister's cat walk on its hind legs and talk," Fenolla said.

"Damn." I was impressed.

Henry smiled, just a little. "You?"

"I killed the grigoris who tried to take over the school while it was closed."

"Ah." That was all Henry said.

"Well done, you!" Fenolla told me.

This was the most interesting conversation I'd had since I'd come to the school. I found it a relief.

The first class I had was Foundations of Magic. Fenolla went to another room, but Henry went into Foundations. Like me, he was old for the class, which was a requirement for grigoris. We got some curious glances. Henry let them roll off. I tried to do the same.

It was wonderful to be in a true grigori class and to belong there, no matter how basic. The others were farther along than I was, naturally. I would have to study hard to catch up.

I didn't know the teacher, Mr. Gaspar, but I recognized him from the meeting the night before. When the class was over and we were leaving for our next class, he kept me back.

"Young lady, I will give you the same chance I give every other student but no extra slack," Mr. Gaspar said.

His graying mustache wiggled when he talked. I didn't like his smell: cigarettes and wet wool and dogs. It was an effort to keep my face calm and respectful.

I couldn't afford to alienate a teacher, especially so early in my new courses. Important to remember. No matter what a deadly opponent I would be when I was trained, I couldn't offend teachers and get away with it. *Nor should I even think about doing that*, I told myself hastily.

The day continued, dragging along. It wasn't the march of triumph I had pictured. I'd gotten what I wanted, but not everyone was glad about that. More practically, some of the students had to switch desks and rows since I was still short for my age and had to sit in front.

By four o'clock, I was tired, and my feelings were all at ragged ends. Some teachers had been pleasant, some had been matter-of-fact, and some, like Mr. Gaspar, were prepared to be my enemies. Some of the students were pleased at my change in status, and others didn't seem to notice. But there was talk, I could tell from the sidelong glances and the little clusters of kids who stared at me as I went past. And since I'd sat with the odd students instead of with Anna's coterie, those girls were buzzing like agitated bees.

When I left my last class, I was still holding my head up, but inside I was feeling battered. Peter was waiting for me. I had to stop myself from throwing my arms around him.

All the students had two free hours until six o'clock. Some strolled outside, some went to their rooms to start studying, and some worked on special projects or went to tutorials.

I dropped off my books in my room and went outside with Peter. I noticed Henry sitting on one of the benches around Rasputin's tomb. I steered Peter over there and introduced them. Peter was polite, and Henry seemed glad to talk to another male. Peter's mom knew Delia Reinbold, a volunteer at the Chinese Christian Church, where Henry had been found on the doorstep. Veronika Savarova was hardly my favorite person at the moment, but it was good to see Henry and Peter establish a connection. Henry made ending the conversation easier by excusing himself to start his homework. Fenolla did not appear.

Peter asked me how the first day of classes had gone. I hardly knew where to start. I didn't dwell on the bad facets of the day. I told him about my connection with Felix.

After a moment of surprise, Peter said, "I'm glad you have more family." That made it easier to smile at him.

I asked him how guard duty had gone today.

"Nothing happened," Peter said with some relief. "Only one visitor, and he was a legitimate relative of one of the students."

"What happened to the crazy woman you handcuffed?"

"She calmed down very quickly," Peter said, shaking his head. "Said she'd taken too much of her medicine, and it had made her feel not herself. We sent her on her way with a warning."

I thought of how she'd looked at me for a moment, as if she was shocked. Her true self coming back?

We sat on the bench Henry had vacated and enjoyed being in the sunshine. I can't speak for Peter, but I was happy to be there.

At lunchtime, I had gotten a letter from Lizbeth, but I hadn't had a chance to read it. I pulled it out now.

I took a deep breath and opened the letter. I wasn't going to read it out loud in case Lizbeth told me something Peter shouldn't hear.

"They've gotten a lot more work," I said. "That's good! The idea of having a real grigori on the gun team is catching on." Lizbeth had been a gunnie since she was sixteen or seventeen, not much older than me.

"Seems like Eli made an avalanche of sand fall on a team of gunmen on their last job," I told Peter, who looked excited . . . and then glum. "Why the sad face?" I asked. "You should be glad they've found a good way for your brother to make a living."

"I am glad," Peter said, though he didn't look it. "It just seems a far cry from sitting in the lobby of the school trying to catch crazy people who want to do crazy things. And that's on an exciting shift. At the airport, I watch planes come in and go out."

"I'm sure Eli had to put in his time doing the same kind of thing," I said, maybe without much conviction. Peter was not a baby I had to soothe.

"As you say. All grigoris have to start somewhere and work their way up." Peter had his *determined to be brave* face on.

I nodded. I appreciated the effort.

"How are the wedding preparations going?" I asked, to brighten the atmosphere.

"Alice and Lucy want you to come to the house to try on your dress," Peter said. "I do, too."

"I'll be glad to come when your mom can welcome me. It's her house. I won't go where I'm not welcome."

"Of course," Peter said promptly. "If we have to, Lucy can meet you at the dressmaker's shop."

I closed my eyes for a moment and plunged in. "I don't think your mother would mind me being there if we didn't have a . . ." I floundered.

"Personal relationship?" Peter suggested.

I nodded.

"But we can't say that, can we?" Peter looked in another direction so he wouldn't be staring at my face.

"No," I admitted. "We can't."

His shoulders relaxed, and he looked very relieved. "That's what I told her."

"I guess after Lizbeth, I'm the straw that broke the camel's back."

Eli's stance as head of the family had been lost before he'd joined up with Lizbeth, though, due to many circumstances. And Lucy was determined to marry Felix, so she might as well have vanished from Russian society already.

Veronika must believe her family had a chance to recoup its position through Peter. And if Peter fell through, somehow Alice would have to do something brilliant, a great marriage.

I did not understand this way of thinking.

"I don't understand my mother," Peter said, as if he'd read my thoughts. "We're in a new country, with new chances. In the old country, our—the aristocratic—way of doing things caused us to get thrown out, leaving behind all the wealth and privilege that made us . . . well, aristocrats. Now we have the opportunity to rebuild. Why hobble ourselves with the past?"

"And yet your mother doesn't seem like that kind of person," I said. "She seems kind and practical and . . ."

"And she loves us more than anything. Maybe that's it. She wants what our family used to have for our benefit. I don't think she's missed going to court, but maybe I just don't understand her. Mother's been so happy since Captain McMurtry started calling. I can't help but think she'd be even happier if she forgot about the past and thought of the future."

"You think that's possible to do?" I shook my head. "I wish I could forget the day my grandfather refused to help us. Or the day at the train station, with bodies falling everywhere. Eli and I waiting to see Lizbeth fall among them. He was screaming at her."

"My brother was screaming? Why?" Peter could not believe it.

"Because he thought Lizbeth was sacrificing herself for our chance to escape," I said.

"Was she?"

I nodded. "Exactly what she was doing."

"Lizbeth is one of a kind."

"Most people would add, 'Thank God.'" I smiled, though I'm sure it was a little crooked.

CHAPTER TWENTY-TWO

Felix had a mouse in his hand. I had looked at it for five minutes. It was in no way a special mouse. Its whiskers wiggled, its bare tail twitched, and it was very small.

"Kill it," Felix said.

He'd been amazingly patient so far. I couldn't count on that lasting.

"Before, when I did this, I had something to protect. I was very angry," I pointed out.

"That is exactly the reason you need to practice your control," Felix said. "You know how most death bringers learn they have the ability? When their little sister throws a toy and hits them in the head, and they have a flare of anger at her. Or when their dog nips them, and they react. And then it's all tears and guilt."

I killed the mouse. It rolled over, its tiny pink feet in the air, and lay still.

"Now," Felix said, "tell me how you did that."

Felix was going to wait forever, until I gave him a reply.

"I took its life away," I said. Even to my own ears, I sounded sullen.

"How?"

"I reached in and grabbed it."

That wasn't a very good explanation for what had been an entirely intuitive process, but Felix nodded.

"I understand," he said. "But you need to be more specific. Pretend you're explaining this to someone who can't do it."

I thought. (I tried to think briskly.) "So, when I look, I see the life inside the mouse. It's like a ball of light."

Felix waited.

"It glows orange and yellow," I said.

How much detail did he want? But Felix didn't say anything, and he was still holding the damn mouse, so I continued.

"What I do is reach inside the mouse and grab the ball and yank it out. And the living thing has no life at all. I have it instead."

"How do you feel after you do that?" Felix's face was expressionless.

"I feel stronger."

"How much stronger?"

He wasn't going to let up. This seemed almost dirty, this exposing of a secret process.

"Every death makes me stronger. Even the mouse's." I sounded even more sullen.

"Is it a glorious feeling?" Felix sounded almost sad.

"Yes." I squeezed the admission out. "But it goes away."

"Can you remember that? That the glorious feeling only lasts a second?"

"And the death lasts forever. So far, I have managed to remember that. I hope you do, too," I said, daring greatly.

Felix's black eyebrows flew up. I thought he was going to launch right into me. I had a flash of fear.

But Felix seemed to get himself calmed down before he spoke. "Now you understand why all of us who can do this, we must *master* it. I had to kill one grigori who could not—or didn't want to—keep control over his appetite for that moment of acquisition."

Acquisition was a word I'd never heard spoken out loud, but I understood what it meant.

I'd taken the mouse's life into myself. The glow was glorious. If taking a life felt that amazing for, say, an hour, I was not sure I could have resisted. But it only lasted a second. I could resist that.

"It gets harder," Felix said.

Not a big surprise.

"It will be a struggle your whole life. The more you use your ability, the more you will want to."

"So it's great to be us, and it's awful to be us."

"That sums it up pretty well."

"Can this talent be passed on from parent to child?"

"It can, but sometimes it just happens. Do you think your father ever had this ability?"

I shook my head. "He would have told me." Especially when he'd been drinking. "So we're going to keep killing things? Bigger and bigger things?" I hated the idea of killing cats, then dogs, then . . . donkeys?

"No. You've already killed people, but through weapons. Not this very personal seizing of life. What finally made you able to take the mouse?"

"I thought of it eating our food."

"That's quite good." Felix almost smiled.

"Maybe I have to see whatever I'm trying to kill as a direct threat to my own life or the lives of those I care about."

"That's good." Felix nodded to himself a couple of times. "You'll do. We need to keep practicing, or the teachers here won't believe that you have mastered the skill. They'll always be scared of you or distrust you."

"Is that so bad?"

Felix shrugged. "Depends on what you want out of your life."

I thought about it. "I wanted to be secure. To not have to worry about food and a safe place to sleep. I have those things now."

"So now you're setting new goals."

"Yes. Now I want to be very good at whatever it is I can do, and I want to have a good relationship with someone, like my sister has."

"And you think you'll find that with Peter?"

"I don't know. Do you? Think you'll find something like that with Lucy?"

Felix looked worn out, for just a second. "No, I don't think so, but it's the best I can do. Lucy and I will at least be free from the judgment of others, and we will take care of each other."

"Since you want only men and Lucy doesn't want at all."

He nodded.

The theory of saving each other was a good one, but I didn't know if it could work out as they planned. I figured I'd poked enough in Felix's business, and it was time to return to the teaching. I killed a cricket, another mouse. Then Felix wanted me to try the cat that had decided to live in the hedge around the backyard, but I refused. An anonymous mouse was hard enough. Killing Kitty would be like killing one of my classmates.

"So it's easier to kill people than a cat," Felix said, sarcastic and cold and mean.

"*Some* people," I said.

After a second, he laughed.

I didn't.

After our third lesson, I asked Felix when we would get to the resurrection part.

"When you're much stronger," he said. He paused. "I don't know if you knew this, but Eli and your sister brought me back once. After we got away from that damn town in Dixie."

"They did? How?"

"Eli applied his power and used her, too. He channeled through her. She has about that much ability." Felix held his thumb about two inches away from his forefinger. "But it was enough."

"Can you tell me what it was like?"

Felix shivered. I thought he wouldn't answer. But finally, he said, "It was like being in a cloud of thick gray fog. I couldn't hear anything, couldn't see anything, but I kept trying to feel my way through."

"Why did you keep moving?"

"I kept thinking I'd find a way out. I'd come to the end of it. Or I'd hear something, find someone else."

"But you didn't."

"I never did. Until I was back in my body. Eli was almost unconscious, and your sister had fainted."

I wondered if Lizbeth had known what Eli was doing. I wondered if she would have agreed to sap herself to bring back Felix. I wondered why Eli had endangered his own life and Lizbeth's to save Felix.

I wasn't going to get answers anytime soon.

By the fifth session with Felix, I could kill anything he brought me very quickly. The quicker I did it, the sooner I could bring them back to life, if he let me. Since I had already proved I could kill real people pretty damn quickly, I couldn't see the point of all this. Felix kept muttering something about consistency. To which I said, "I've never tried to kill something and failed." To which he muttered some more.

My classes were going well, and it was very exciting to be learning things I'd never thought I'd get to study. My grades were good. I was diligent in practicing my magic and doing my homework. I finished all the required reading. And by the way, you wouldn't think a book about magic could be dull, but one or two managed. I read them anyway. I sat with Henry and Fenolla in the refectory and sometimes strolled around the grounds with them. We made up memory games or were entertained by Fenolla's bizarre imagination.

I saw Peter whenever he had door duty. When someone else had relieved him and I had free time, we'd walk together. But Peter did get permission to take me to the dressmaker's for my fitting for a bridesmaid's dress. I could not go off the grounds with him by myself until I was seventeen, since we weren't related.

Truthfully, I didn't mind the restrictions. My body wanted to get closer to Peter, but my body would just have to shut up and obey me. For one thing, even if we could have found a place to be more intimate, I was determined not to indulge myself far enough to get pregnant. Neither of us knew the magic to prevent that.

It was hard to interpret how Peter felt. His body wanted mine, but his bigger brain knew he wasn't ready to commit to me as a wife, and that was what his brain insisted was the right offer to make. I was tempted to tell him to go to a whorehouse and find some girl, but I couldn't bring myself to embarrass him that much. Also, I disappointed myself by finding it made me angry to picture Peter with anyone else.

This was unhelpful and impractical.

To my surprise, our little trio of misfits got a new member: Katerina Swindoll.

Every girl in the school swooned over her older brother, Mikhail Swindoll, who was in college at the University of New Russia. He came with Katerina's parents to visit, at least once every two weeks.

That was what made me suspicious.

Katerina was swamped with overtures of friendship from the older girls (and a boy or two) at the Rasputin School. Mikhail was perfect: from a grigori-friendly family (but not a grigori), very hand-some, and apparently quite well-to-do.

"Why does she want to be with us?" Fenolla asked one afternoon.

"That's what I was asking myself." There was no point in pre-tending we were popular.

Henry said, "I have no idea why Katerina is keeping our com-pany. There must be a secret flaw in her we don't know about yet."

Fenolla and I looked at each other and nodded.

"What does 'well-to-do' mean?" I asked.

"It means that the Swindolls have enough to eat and drink and more clothes than they need to wear for every day, and a house to live in. And money left over for extra stuff."

"But Mikhail and Katerina have parents and food and clothes and an education," I said. "If that doesn't mean rich, what does?"

"They have a moderate amount of money," Henry said stiffly. "You can tell."

"I can't," I said.

"Yes, I can see that."

Henry could be a stick-in-the-mud sometimes. This was one of those times.

In the refectory, one of the seventeen-year-old boys called Henry "Henry Half-Chink." Before I thought about it, I was standing in front of Henry. "You want to say that again?" I asked.

The refectory was crowded, but all of a sudden, it was silent. The boy I was challenging was Nikolai Turashenko, and he was supposed to be a very strong earth grigori. He was also a bully and an asshole. Since I was beneath Nikolai's notice, our paths hadn't really crossed until now.

"Are you trying to get in my way?" Nikolai said, and he simply couldn't believe it.

"I am in your way," I said.

Henry muttered something behind me, but I couldn't spare any extra attention. I needed to keep my focus on this kid in front of me. If he spoke the word, I'd be at the bottom of an avalanche.

I was counting on Nikolai having better sense than that. I was also counting on his not knowing if I had better sense or not.

"You going to let a girl defend you?" Nikolai jeered, I suppose at Henry.

"She seems very capable," Henry said.

His voice was so calm and sure that I immediately felt more confident.

I'd kept my eyes fixed on Nikolai's, and I hadn't blinked. He was waiting for the smallest waver, the least flinch. I wasn't giving him any.

I don't know what would have happened if Master Franklin hadn't happened in to get another cup of tea. Possibly, there wasn't any "happened" to it. Possibly, he had "trouble" antennae, and they'd begun twitching.

"Mr. Turashenko," Master Franklin said mildly, "what on earth are you doing?"

Nikolai jerked as if he'd been stung by something. "Sir," he said after a moment.

"'Sir' is not an answer, Mr. Turashenko."

"I was . . . nothing, sir."

"Then you won't mind doing nothing elsewhere."

"Ah . . . no, sir."

Nikolai hesitated.

"Now what?" Master Franklin said, his voice cold.

"I don't want to turn my back on her, sir."

"By 'her' you mean Felicia Karkarova?"

Nikolai nodded several times, as though he just couldn't stop.

"Then, Miss Karkarova, if you would be so kind?"

Immediately, I turned my back on Nikolai and sat down on the bench.

"Now that you are safe, Mr. Turashenko, you may proceed."

That was one thing I wished Master Franklin had not said. It underlined what was already written in bold. I was not afraid of Nikolai Turashenko, and he was afraid of me.

CHAPTER TWENTY-THREE

There was a lot of buzz about the "showdown" in the refectory for two days. When war didn't break out, it faded.

I didn't relax.

I had dealt a blow to Nikolai's pride. Unwittingly or not, Master Franklin had fanned the flames. Nothing to be done about that now. But I had to watch my back from now on until the end of the school term. Bullies can't bear to be shown up, especially if they're physically stronger than the person doing the showing. Unless I underestimated his intelligence, Nikolai was going to screw himself up to the boiling point. Then he would explode.

Henry was not happy with me, either. I'd realized he wouldn't be.

Fenolla, whose first allegiance was to Henry, was also not happy with me. In fact, she turned cold. Katerina thought the whole brouhaha was ridiculous, but she agreed with me in principle, she said. I wasn't sure what that meant.

Suddenly, it all seemed like too much: the reading, the studying, the classes, the eyes of all the students upon me to see what would happen next.

I was scowling and sullen the next week, especially after Peter said he'd sleep outside my room if that would help.

"That would help ruin my reputation," I said. "Nothing else."

I'd hurt his feelings, and I knew it, and that made me feel worse.

"Sorry," I snarled. "I know you mean to help, and it's good of you. But I have to do this myself."

Peter tried to look like I'd eased his mind, but he couldn't manage it.

My roommate, Anna, found me alone, practicing a spell that attracted birds. I was behind the school with about ten little birds on my arms. I had no idea what they were—wrens or something. She stayed back so she wouldn't scare them away.

"Good job," she said. "Listen. I know we're not really friends, but you need to hear me out."

"All right," I said in a very calm voice. I didn't want the birds to fly away. "What's the point of this spell, do you know? I can't imagine why I'd use it."

"If you were hungry, you would," Anna said. "I'd think you, of all people, would appreciate that. You've told me several times how bad you had it in Mexico."

Anna was right. How many times could I have used this in my hungry childhood? I could have caught many fat pigeons.

"It doesn't take much to forget," I said quietly. "Once upon a time, I would have been glad to know this."

"Hear me out," Anna repeated.

"I'm listening."

"Henry Chen is older than he looks."

My arms were beginning to tire. It wasn't the weight of the birds, it was the extended position. I'd been trying to get as many to land as possible, without thinking what standing like this would mean in the long run. I made that kind of mistake often. Inexperience, Felix said.

I started to ask Anna what she meant, but that would have been a stupid, inexperienced question. She meant Henry Chen was older than I thought.

"How did you find out?" I asked instead.

"I went through his wallet."

That did surprise me. "How come?" I said.

"Because I saw him meeting a stranger outside the school gates yesterday."

"How?" I said again, trying to ignore the way my arms were beginning to tremble.

I was going to lose the damn birds! I'd kept them on my arms for a good three minutes. That exceeded the guidelines of the lesson. I should call it quits.

"I was upstairs in the dormitory between classes. I had forgotten my psychometry book. I looked out the window. I saw them."

"What was the stranger like?"

"This will surprise you. It was a pretty woman. Not Chinese, either."

It took everything I had not to flap my arms, I was that surprised. "That does not make one bit of sense." Henry with an adult girlfriend?

"I know. I couldn't believe it, either. But I had to tell you. After I saw that, I stole his wallet."

"You *what*?" There, that was a stupid question. I had heard her clearly. "I'm sorry," I said hastily. "How did you do that?"

"I held his coat while he was practicing bird-calling, like you are. He didn't want them to make a mess on his coat. You're going to have to scrub that blouse."

Another thing I hadn't foreseen. She was right.

I said, "So you went through his wallet?"

"He turned around because a falcon was coming in to land on his shoulder," Anna said. "I told him he'd better watch so it wouldn't land on top of his head."

"What did you see?" That was a good question. (A falcon? That made me envious.)

"He has a driver's license. It says he's twenty."

I lowered my arms a bit. The birds could take off anytime now. They'd served their purpose. They seemed to want to stay on me. I had to resist the urge to flap my elbows and shriek.

"Twenty." I closed my eyes and undid the spell that had called the birds to me. One by one, the little things began to take off. Most of them flew into the tree and stayed there. Surely they should have gone about their ways?

"And a woman!" Anna reminded me.

"They were just talking, I guess?"

"Yes. Didn't talk that long."

"I need to do some thinking."

"I agree." Anna turned to go back inside, then paused. "I like you," she said, to my astonishment. "And I understand why you . . . made friends with Henry and Fenolla and Katerina. But I feel like someone's going to get killed." Anna was sincere.

"I understand. Thanks for telling me about Henry."

She went back into the building.

It took me three more minutes to disperse the birds.

I didn't want them to die because they'd answered my summons.

The next day, I ate breakfast and lunch with Henry, Fenolla, and Katerina as usual. I kept wanting to stare at Henry, search his face for signs of his true age. I had to control myself. I made all kinds of stories up in my head about why Henry would pretend to be younger than he was. Was it really any big thing, this deception? I, too, had seemed younger than I was, though no one would mistake me any longer for a ten-year-old.

Nikolai muttered to his friends and scowled at me, maybe still hoping to frighten me into submission. Even his friends thought he was acting like an idiot.

While I pondered what to do, I wondered what Lizbeth would tell me. I heard her voice loud and clear: *Tell Felix.*

So that afternoon, as we took a break halfway through Felix's tutorial, I did.

Felix didn't say anything after I'd finished. His eyes were fixed on me, making me feel mighty uncomfortable—but I knew he wasn't really seeing me. He was going through the narrative, trying to make sense of it.

"When did Henry start classes here?" he asked.

"After we reopened from the influenza," I said.

"When did Fenolla start?"

"Last school year. And Katerina came this fall."

"Did either of them make overtures to you?"

Had they? "No. I did, to them."

"Why?"

"Because they were oddballs." *Like me.*

Felix nodded. "Keep on going as you've been. I'll see what I can find out."

We didn't have much of a lesson after that. We were both preoccupied. After he left, I sat and thought. It seemed like all I did was "keep on going." Just continuing on the same path did not mean making progress in any real sense.

I struggled with my Poor Pitiful Pearl mood. I had felt grateful to be in San Diego until the influenza outbreak. I'd begun to take safety and food for granted, which disgusted me. Then the Dominguezes had started trying to abduct me or kill me. Then my own power had surged out.

Now I had my own boyfriend and three miscellaneous friends, and at least one of them was an imposter with an unknown purpose.

I needed to get back to basics. When I was on my way back

to my dorm room, I passed red-haired Callista, and she gave me a warm smile.

"I miss having your help in the infirmary," she said.

Madame Semyonova stopped Callista to discuss needed supplies for the infirmary, and the two women pulled me into the discussion to ask me how their stock had held out during the school closing.

I felt a bit better after that. I ran into Peter, who was on his way back to the grigori dormitory for his evening meal, and he tugged me into a spot where we couldn't be seen and kissed me. This was a rare event, and it made all kinds of crazy feelings break loose.

All in all, I was in a better mood when I went into the refectory for dinner and sat with my three pals. I slid onto the bench beside Katerina, facing Henry and Fenolla. Katerina was excited about her parents' visit during the upcoming weekend and looking forward to a gal friend of hers coming with them. I didn't ask about her stunning brother, because the last thing I wanted was for Katerina to think I'd joined his fan club. She got enough of that.

I didn't want to think any of them had become my friend for some nasty reason. The truth was, we were more allies than friends.

The smell of beef stroganoff overlaid every other odor. That was my favorite dish. It felt like a feast day when we got beef.

After a few bites, I felt eyes on my back and twisted in my seat. Nikolai was glaring at me. None of his buddies was on alert, and everything else seemed normal. Across the central aisle to my right, Anna flirted with a boy our age despite her "understanding" with the young man back home in Redding. Madame Semyonova pushed open the door to come in, her cane clacking against the floor.

Someone made a startled noise behind me. I turned to see Nikolai sagging on the bench, his head lying on his friend Harvey's shoulder.

"Hey!" Harvey said. "Sit up!"

He shoved at Nikolai, who flopped backward and slid bone-lessly off the bench. Nikolai made no attempt to stop himself from falling. The thud when his head hit the floor was horrible.

Harvey swung his legs over the bench and stood, shuffling back-ward from the body.

"Madame," he called. "Help!"

Gradually, everyone who'd been speaking shut up, and there was a strange silence in the large room.

With Harvey's assistance, Madame knelt beside Nikolai. All of us were frozen in our places, some with forks halfway to their mouths. The other boys who'd been sitting at the table with Nikolai and Har-vey shrank back, trying to get as far from the scene of the commotion as they could get without actually moving off the benches.

I thought, *Oh, no. No.* Because I could see what had happened, and I knew what was going to happen.

Katerina put her hand on my right shoulder and squeezed. "Be brave," she said.

Across from me, Henry drew in a deep breath. "How could you?" he said, in a voice louder than his usual. "How could you do this in front of everyone?"

If Henry had been less nervous, he'd have let Fenolla speak first. I'd have had some doubt. Now I knew he was the guilty one.

I whispered, "This was not my doing."

"I know that," Katerina said.

"Fenolla?" I said.

But Fenolla didn't speak. Her brown eyes were wide and full of panic.

"They'll all think so," Katerina whispered.

Madame looked up, from face to face, until her eyes met mine. "Felicia," she said, her voice a well of disappointment. "I thought you knew better."

"Madame, I—"

"Don't speak now. The rest of you, leave the room."

I turned to meet Henry's eyes. I put everything into that look. But I didn't say it out loud. They couldn't prosecute me for a look.

I did not look anyone else in the face as the other students filed out of the refectory. I was too angry.

When the door swung shut, Madame said, "Come here, girl."

I did, but my legs felt numb.

"Did you do this?"

"No, ma'am."

Her ancient eyes were like needles, piercing their way through my heart and mind.

"I'm very angry," I warned Madame.

"Why?"

For the first time, I thought Madame had asked a stupid question. "Someone pretended to be my friend and maneuvered for this to happen. Someone wants me branded as a criminal with no self-control. When self-control is all I have."

I could identify the emotion in Madame's face after I finished. It was relief. She said, "Though I had a faint hope you would say you were angry because of the waste of Nikolai's life, I should have known better. However, I am sure you would have done a better job if you had decided to kill Nikolai."

"Yes. Thank you. I would have."

"But we must keep this a secret for now. There must be a trial."

"Why?"

"You can't just *be* innocent. You have to be *seen* to be innocent."

Madame was telling me this all alone. No witnesses. I felt the creeping cold of doubt. What if Madame wanted me to be silent until I was convicted? Then it would be too late. Grigori sentences, I'd heard, were carried out on the spot, unlike human sentences.

"You're asking me to trust you," I said, to give myself a few more seconds.

"I am, Felicia." The blue-veined lids closed over those old brown eyes and opened again.

Just as I thought, *I wish I could talk to Felix about this*, Felix came through the refectory doors like a black tornado. I couldn't help but hold out my hands when I saw him, and he obliged by grasping them in his own. But if I'd expected any vigorous denial of my guilt, I had to think again.

"You idiot," Felix snapped, gripping my hands tightly the whole time. "What have you done?"

"Not a damn thing," I said, able to sound calm since he was so furious.

"Language," Madame said automatically. "Felix, as you can see, Nikolai Turashenko is dead. He and your protégé have been having a feud lately—"

"I'm aware," Felix snapped.

"And of course, she is the main suspect. In fact, I think everyone who was in the refectory believes in her guilt."

"Who did it?" Felix said, looking directly into my eyes.

"I'm not sure."

"Yes, you are. Don't try to keep me in the dark. Or you'll wind up dead." Felix was absolutely sincere.

"Henry Chen," I said. I was proud my voice didn't shake.

"The boy you defended against Nikolai's bullying?" Madame said. Her white brows drew together.

"Yes, ma'am," I said.

"Why would he have done this?"

"I don't have a clue."

Madame opened her mouth, looking scornful.

Felix got in there first. "Don't even start by saying everyone can't be her enemy, because you know good and well that they can be. We've been waiting to see if her grandfather's clan would strike back. We've been speculating that it would be by means of someone unsuspected. And here she stands, all but accused of murder, and who is least suspected? Her friend, the outcast Henry Chen."

Madame's mouth snapped shut as she thought. "Though you're very rude, there's some sense in what you're saying," she admitted. "On the other hand, we can't just announce a heretofore innocent student is a murderer because it simply can't be the obvious suspect."

"What do you suggest?" Felix said, in a more tolerable tone, speaking directly to Madame.

Apparently, I was not going to get to suggest anything. I poked Felix's shoulder with my forefinger. He glared at me.

"Tell Henry he'll be under house arrest starting tomorrow," I said. "That he has tonight to get all his studying and books and assignments together and up to date."

"What basis? For house arrest?"

"Call it protective custody. Time out. Whatever you like. Just make it clear that Henry has only tonight to contact whoever gives him his orders. And have someone watching each of the school telephones."

"So he'll have to go out, if what we suspect is true," Felix said, and nodded approvingly. "Very neat, Felicia."

"But not easy. I can't think of a credible reason to tell Henry he won't be able to go out tomorrow." Madame was scowling again.

I thought hard. "Oh! Tell him that you've planned to have a conference with him at eight tonight, and he should count on its lasting a long time, until lights out."

"That's good," Felix said, nodding.

"So someone very, very sneaky will have to follow him," I said.

If Henry did steal out to contact his mentor, it would mean he was a traitor. If he was a traitor, he would be jumpy and suspicious.

We all frowned at the same time.

"It must be someone he doesn't know at all," I offered. "Someone from the grigori home. No vest."

"Yevdokia," Madame said suddenly. "Yevdokia can be anything. I don't think Henry Chen will know her at all."

"Will she do it?" I said.

"Of course," Madame said. "Yevdokia has a new baby, and she needs the money."

Madame was not sentimental.

"Then that's settled," Felix said. "I'll go to the Residence and have a word with her."

"Can you act normal around Henry?" Madame asked me as she stood to go. She was leaning on her cane more than ever, I noticed.

"Normal? No," I said. "I can't imagine who would expect me to. He accused me of murder."

She glared up at me. I realized that I was now taller than Madame. That was sort of wonderful but scary.

"Now I have to go talk to Henry and tell him about the meeting," she grumbled. "Felicia, you must think of a way to explain the fact that you're still at liberty."

Now she gave me responsibility!

"I'll come up with something," I said. "By the way, you might want to know that Henry is twenty years old. Anna picked his pocket to find his identification, and she told me."

Madame's lips pressed together in an angry line. "He has lied to everyone all along," she said. "I will retrieve his letters of recommendation and ask those who wrote them what they really know about him."

"Anna is a mystery to me," Felix said, and left.

"Why is Felix marrying the Savarov girl?" Madame demanded.

I started to tell Madame it was none of her business, but instead I bit my tongue. Madame was an ally, a crucial one.

"You would have to ask Felix that," I said, doing my best to sound neutral.

"I have, and I got no answer," she retorted. "You know the girl?"

"Yes, I know Lucy."

"What do you think of this?"

"I think it's none of my business."

Madame laughed, though it sounded like more of a bark. "Felix is one of the greatest grigoris we've ever trained," she said. "I fear it will all come to naught if she hasn't a spark of magic in her."

Breeding again.

"Still not my business," I said. "Thanks for believing me, Madame. Have a pleasant day. I'll see you later."

I left as quickly as Felix had.

CHAPTER TWENTY-FOUR

Anna was flabbergasted to see me walk into our room.

So was the boy she was kissing, who couldn't leave fast enough.

Anna made a face at his departing back, but she didn't look really upset. "You didn't get dragged off to prison?" she said.

"No. I'm as surprised as you."

"Why did you do something so stupid?"

Anna seemed more interested than frightened, which said a lot about her sense of self. Anna simply didn't believe I would kill *her*. Other people, yes. That did not seem to bother her.

"I didn't, Anna. You know that, or you'd be a lot more worried sharing a room with me."

She snorted. "What would you do if I moved out? You think everyone wants to room with a girl who's gotten five years older in the past few months?"

I grinned at her. "Maybe Fenolla or Katerina would move in," I said.

After a second, she grinned back.

"Nikolai was an ass," Anna said more soberly. "But I don't believe he should have been killed."

"Me either," I said, though I wasn't sure I cared much. "Maybe he had a heart ailment or some other physical sickness we didn't know about?"

"His family is important." For once, Anna's face was sober. "His father got involved in developing real estate, and they live in Los Angeles. They'll be here any moment. His mother is terrifying. They'll come after you unless someone else is found guilty."

The last thing I needed was someone else wanting vengeance.

"You're taking this awfully calmly," I said.

"I have a test tomorrow," Anna said, gesturing at the book open on her desk. Evidently, it was back to business as usual.

"And I have homework."

Though I sat at my desk and lined up my tasks, concentrating on my work proved impossible. Other students kept sticking their heads in the door to talk to Anna, maybe checking to see if she was still alive. None of them could believe I was walking free. Some of them seemed angry rather than scared. I hoped I didn't get lynched.

Though I sat in front of my basic spells book, my mind wandered off on its own path. I wondered how Peter was reacting, if he'd heard about Nikolai. There were very few telephones at the school—one in Madame's office, one in the infirmary office, one in the reception room, one in the teachers' common room. All of them (except the one in Madame's office) were in more or less public places. If all the telephones were going to be watched in case Henry tried to contact his mentor, I couldn't try to use one to get in touch with Peter.

I resigned myself to patience, which did not come naturally to me. I forced myself to practice some spells. This was not as simple as it sounds. If you got the words right and you felt the magic begin to work, you had to learn to stow that spell into a pinch of sawdust or ash or sage. Something you could put in a pocket. That was why the traditional grigori vest had so many tiny pockets. You had to establish your own order of these substances, the arrangement of them in your pockets, and never vary from that—and never confide your arrangement to another grigori.

Maybe one day I'd understand the need for all this foofaraw. At the moment, I found it ridiculous. If you just aimed your will and focused and your magic was strong, the result would be what you aimed for. Why codify it? But countless grigoris did. Was I different from them? I didn't know. Every time I'd used magic, it had worked, at least in some fashion—and it had worked most strongly when I'd been in dire straits.

I could see it would feel different if you were an earth grigori and wanted to raise a wall of dirt at a construction site. If you were an air grigori and you were hired to help a ship cross the ocean, you would have to coax the wind, not confront it. Every time I tried to make myself concentrate on what herb or powder would best hold my spell for that strong gust of wind, I felt the process was unnatural.

But I had to learn it, or I wouldn't be certified as a grigori.

Now I had successfully distracted myself for five whole minutes.

No one came to drag me outside to lynch me. No one came to tell me Henry Chen had been arrested, either. I didn't hear from Felix or Peter or Madame Semyonova. Nikolai's ghost didn't come through the door to accuse me of murder.

Nothing, nothing, nothing.

Finally, I went to the communal shower room and stood under the hot water, remembering the sheer delight of the first few times I'd used it. (I still didn't take hot water from a showerhead for granted.) I scrubbed my hair and my body, dried off, and put on my nightgown. My hair wrapped in my towel, I trailed back to our room to comb it out bit by bit. Anna had taught me a neat little spell that made it not so tangled, and I thanked her every time I used it. Not out loud, or she'd have gotten cocky.

I was sitting cross-legged on my bed, comb in hand, when there was a knock at the door.

"Come in," called Anna, who had not glanced my way for a long time.

Felix stuck his head in, saw me in my nightgown, and shook his head as if it was exasperating that I should be in my nightclothes at bedtime.

"Felicia, you should come down," he said. "I'll wait outside."

Anna had given an affected little shriek at a man looking into our room at night, but she abandoned that when she saw it was Felix. She handed me my bathrobe, a very utilitarian navy one that I'd inherited from the discarded-clothes box.

"Good luck," she said, and she patted me on the back.

For Anna, that was extraordinary. I felt quite privileged as I slipped out the door to go with Felix.

Felix was not in a question-answering mood. "You'll see in a minute," was all he would say.

"I might almost think you were taking me to be executed," I said, not joking.

"Not this time," Felix said. Finally, he smiled, just slightly.

"If that's supposed to be funny, it isn't."

"Funny? Never."

And Felix spoke no more as we went into the school building and up the stairs to the teachers' common room. Again.

Madame was there, of course. A very tall young woman was seated in one of the chairs, wearing an outdated suit and heels. She looked bored and uncomfortable.

I wasn't sorry to see Fenolla and Katerina come in on my heels. They had both been better friends of Henry's than I had been. They deserved to understand what was happening.

And there in a wooden chair sat Henry Chen, bleeding from the nose and handcuffed. All three of us sat opposite him and stared. I was trying to see the traitor under the friend. It was shocking to see Henry bleeding. He had always had such dignity and composure. I didn't know what Fenolla and Katerina thought at this moment, and I didn't really want to know. It was hard to live through. Henry did not meet our eyes.

Though Henry had always been hard to read, anyone could see he felt guilty.

I felt sorry for him . . . until I recalled that Henry had accused me of murder.

"Shame on you," I said, my voice shaking. I was torn up inside. I hadn't realized it would hurt so much.

Henry had tears running down his cheeks and no way to wipe them off with the handcuffs on. He was making me sad/mad. That was even worse. I kept my hands at my sides with a huge effort. Hitting a boy who was handcuffed was not admirable. But golly, didn't I want to!

"I'm sorry, Felicia," he said. "So sorry. Fenolla, Katerina . . . I'm sorry."

We did not look at one another. None of us said a word.

"Henry has confessed he was paid to apply to the school," Madame said. She was clearly exhausted, but she was not going to give in to her weariness. "He hasn't yet said by whom."

"I'll bet Henry will tell me," Felix said. For the first time I could remember, Felix smiled broadly.

"Felix, he has to be able to tell the whole school he did it, or everyone will always think it was me," I said. "So will Nikolai's family. I've got enough people hating me. So don't mess him up too much."

"Henry, why did you do that? We gave you nothing but friendship," Fenolla said. She was crying.

"Oh, thanks so much! The outcasts willing to be friends with another outcast! I'm touched." He was ashamed and using scorn to cover it.

"Wasn't that why you came here?" Madame Semyonova said. "To target Felicia? And now you're criticizing these girls because they were kind to you? I thought better of you, Henry Chen."

Henry lost control. "You would hate me no matter what! If I was the emperor's son instead of an illegitimate half-Chinese, you would hate me anyway! Everyone sees my skin and shrinks away! Everyone makes jokes about my skin, my eyes! My father and mother!"

I hadn't observed that, hadn't known it. To this day, I am not sure if that was just the way Henry saw it or if that was the way it really was.

The tall young woman, who must be Yevdokia, stood up and said, "Time to feed the baby. I'll report tomorrow for the school meeting and the trial. Ten o'clock?" She barely waited for Madame's nod before leaving.

I didn't sleep most of the night. I had too many questions.

Some of them got answered at the school assembly the next morning.

In front of the whole school, Yevdokia said that she'd followed Henry from the school to a phone booth, and she had listened to his side of the conversation. She closed her eyes and recited, "Hello? It's Henry. The boy is dead, and she's under suspicion. No, I don't know why they haven't arrested her yet. It's a sure thing. I have to get back to the school before I'm missed."

After which, Henry said, "I am guilty." He was led away by two tough-looking grigoris to stand a formal trial to satisfy the Turashenko family. I was not asked to attend.

So that was the end of Henry's abrupt confession to the school. It did clear my name of the death of Nikolai, true. But after it was over, I was more talked about than before.

That was no wonder, considering the complete lack of details. There were so many loose ends.

Among the unanswered questions: Who paid Henry's school fees, and why? How did Henry's magical talent come to the attention of someone who had the idea of inserting him into the Rasputin School? What would have happened if I had been imprisoned for killing Nikolai? Would Henry simply have continued his studies at the school and then gone on to make a career for himself as one of the few Chinese grigoris?

All these would remain unanswered for the present, since Henry killed himself. He'd been moved to a cell at the grigori Residence until his trial. Every hour, the grigori on guard would look in through the barred window in the door of his cell to make sure all was well. The guard on duty at one o'clock in the afternoon reported Henry was sitting on his cot reading a biography of Rasputin, left in the room by the previous prisoner. At the two o'clock check, he was dead.

It was determined he had stuffed pages from the book down his throat until he had choked and died.

I tried not to think about the solitary determination it took to do such a thing.

That is, if Henry had really done it himself. Even if he'd had an attacker, it would have been horrible but somehow not as much. He would have had someone to fight.

The grigori on duty happened to be Yevdokia, the young woman who had followed Henry when he'd gone out to call his contact. After the one o'clock check, it had been time to feed her baby, and she'd bathed and changed him. She confessed that she'd performed the two o'clock check five minutes late. It would not have made any difference, Felix told me. Henry's body was only a bit cooler than the cell.

There was nothing more to learn, since Henry was dead. I asked Felix if he couldn't raise Henry to ask him questions, and Felix looked at me funny before he told me it was a grotesque idea. I'm sure he was thinking about the expenditure of time, energy, and magic involved in raising Henry's body enough to get it to answer. I couldn't blame Felix for that, but I did want more information than we had. I had no idea who was after me—or, rather, which group was after me—so I had no idea how to protect myself.

Henry's death simply didn't make sense to me. If he hadn't wanted to answer any questions, he would have tried to kill himself before he had to stand up to interrogation by his peers, which must have been extraordinarily painful to a self-contained bundle of resentment like Henry.

Neither Fenolla, Katerina, nor I wanted to discuss the pain that Henry had caused us. We stuck together to keep others from attacking us, but in the days following Henry's death, we took little pleasure in one another's company.

Peter was dreadfully angry with me, as I'd known he would be. I hadn't had a chance to tell him anything before he heard Henry's confession in the refectory. I didn't think his anger was justified, but I'd known it would exist. For days, we didn't see each other apart from chance sightings when he was on duty. I didn't know what to do. I couldn't pretend I didn't see him, but I wasn't about to approach him while he was so miffed. It added to my sadness.

Sadness never lasted long with me. It always transmuted into anger.

Peter had the sense to relent before that happened, but it was a close thing.

Seven days after Henry's death, Peter was waiting at the foot of the stairs when I came down after my last class. He was going off duty. He said all the things I'd expected. Why hadn't I called him?

He'd been so upset when he'd heard from someone what had happened, when he should have been the first to know.

I couldn't argue with any of that. I could only tell him what I'd been thinking: that I hadn't wanted to sound like I was begging for his help and that having him there would have made me feel weaker rather than stronger.

Peter couldn't understand that.

I began to get angry (again) when I had to explain it. Doesn't everyone feel weaker when someone is beaming sympathy their way? Because that means you need sympathy. When what you need is strength and defiance.

Luckily, Peter did understand that . . . after a while.

We walked outside together, and he put his arm around me. It was very comforting, and I enjoyed it a lot. Apparently, when I didn't need protection was when I enjoyed it the most.

CHAPTER TWENTY-FIVE

You have a caller," Master Franklin told me after he'd read a message one of the smallest students had delivered.

I was very surprised. "Thank you," I said, staying where I was. I assumed I'd wait until class was over to go to the lobby.

"You may go now, with your books," Master Franklin said.

"Thank you," I said again, and gathered up my books to leave.

Even when Lizbeth had come to the school unexpectedly, I had been obliged to wait until class was over to see her. And she was my half sister. Who else would visit me?

I tucked my books under my arm. Carrying them against my chest was getting difficult. I was blossoming all over. My uniforms were getting tight again, in different places.

The woman waiting for me in the lobby was a stranger. She stood when I came in and gave me a head-to-toe look. She was blond and smooth and wearing a suit with pearl buttons. Her brimmed hat was tilted on her head. I could not imagine who she was or why she was there. She certainly didn't look like one of my south-of-the-border relatives.

She stuck out her hand. "I'm Harriet Ritter," she said, and her accent was one I'd never heard. "I know your sister Lizbeth. I met her in Dixie."

"I'm glad you lived through it," I said, shaking her hand. "My sister said it was a close thing."

"Too close." Harriet Ritter's face closed down a moment, and I thought she might be thinking about her fellow agent, the man who had been hung from a tree. I could not remember his name.

"I wonder if you'd like to go to lunch with me," Harriet said. "Can you leave your books here?"

It was Peter's shift, and I'd been aware he'd been watching us every second. I didn't blame him a bit. The arrival of Harriet Ritter was a very odd thing.

"Peter," I said, "I'm leaving my books here and going with Miss Ritter for lunch."

"Do you need an escort?" He looked me straight in the eyes.

"I think I'll be fine," I said. "I shouldn't be very late for my next class."

That was a clear signal that I didn't plan on being gone much more than an hour and a half. To my surprise, Peter held out his own hand, and I shook it. I realized he'd put something into my hand and closed it just in time. I slid the little lump into my pocket. Peter had prepared to track me. The fact that he'd gotten this ready ahead of time just in case I needed to be tracked . . . I have to admit, I was touched.

I did not actually deserve Peter.

On the walk to the restaurant, Harriet Ritter told me she lived in Britannia, outside Boston, the capital. Housing prices were too high for her to afford a house closer to the city, and she'd always wanted her own house. I can't imagine why she thought I would be interested in her living arrangements.

When I'd been in Mexico, having only three to a hovel was extravagant.

"Have you seen my sister lately?" I asked. If Miss Ritter wanted to have a meaningless conversation, I could keep up my end.

"I saw her and Eli last month," Harriet said. "They were on a job in the lowest part of Britannia, South Carolina, and I happened to be there, too. Our jobs crossed." She smiled. This seemed to have been a happier meeting than the one in Dixie.

"They don't usually go that far," I said, though I wasn't certain.

"Could be I gave them some recommendations after Dixie," Harriet said.

It wasn't up to me to thank her, but I smiled.

"That Eli needs a lot of keeping busy," she added.

"I don't know what to make of that," I said. If Harriet was implying my sister wasn't keeping Eli content and happy, I was against her.

"No!" Harriet said right away, getting my drift. "You misunderstand. He likes to keep busy. He's used to a faster pace of life than Texoma affords."

"Uh-huh," I said flatly.

At that point, fortunately, we got to the restaurant Harriet had picked, and the hostess seated us with an admiring glance at Harriet's suit. I hadn't been to many restaurants, a great understatement.

"All this food is Italian," Harriet said. "Do you like spaghetti? Or have you ever had lasagna?"

"We have spaghetti at the school sometimes," I said. "It must be cheap to fix. What is lasagna? Or veal parmigiana?"

After Harriet explained the food to me, I picked lasagna. A salad came first, and I was glad to see it. It was fresh and green.

After we were served a basket of bread and Harriet had gotten a glass of wine, I waited. To give her credit, Harriet got right to the point.

"I don't know if you're familiar with my background, but I work for Iron Hand," she began. "It's a continental agency for security and intelligence. We guard and investigate and snoop."

I was thrilled. Iron Hand was always in the newspapers, and some of its operatives were famous. The operative in *Red Harvest* was modeled on an Iron Hand employee, maybe Dashiell Hammett himself. But I kept my demeanor calm and cool.

I could tell Harriet was a little taken aback that I absorbed this without oohing and aahing. But after waiting a moment to see if I had any questions, she continued. "A few months ago, the only bureau we have in Texoma—it's in Dallas—had a visitor from Mexico, a Señorita Rosa Dominguez. I happened to be visiting that day. Our Dallas head invited me into the talk, since the lady looked really rich."

I pulled a piece of bread from the basket and buttered it so I wouldn't blurt out a lot of questions.

"She'd come to hire Iron Hand to track down a missing child. She claimed the little girl had been kidnapped from Ciudad Juárez some months ago and was being kept against her will at what she termed a 'crazy school' somewhere on the Pacific coast. The girl didn't know she was a kinswoman of the Dominguez family. Miss Dominguez made that sound like she was related to God.

"We'd heard rumors about the Dominguez family. Frankly, if we could get in good with them, we figured it would be to our advantage." Harriet looked apologetic. "Hearing the story from their side, it sounded kosher to us."

I didn't know what "kosher" meant, but I could get a sense of it.

"So what happened?" I asked. Harriet had paused to see if I was going to react, but I just wanted to hear the end of the story.

"I didn't know who she meant, since I didn't meet your sister and Eli until after they'd left you here. So I assigned our San Diego operative, Maude Jones, to think of a means to infiltrate the school so we could get an eye on you."

"She put Henry into the school." That explained a lot.

"Eventually. For a month, Maude asked questions of a grigori or two she already knew. A couple of teachers at your school, known to be not exactly upright. The Rostovs. Very indirect questions leading around to your preferences and character."

I waited.

When Harriet knew I wasn't going to ask any questions, she went on. "She learned a lot about you that way. Maude figured if she could find someone you'd stick up for, that would be her way in. She asked in various orphanages, and finally she heard of Henry Chen, who had been abandoned at the Christian Center and adopted by Christian Chinese parents. Henry was known to have grigori abilities and to want to develop them, but his parents didn't have enough money for the school. Henry had already started work at an herb shop and was showing some skill with using herbs, so he seemed like an ideal choice. He looked younger than his years, too."

"I took the bait like a fish," I said, with a lot of disgust.

"And now Henry is dead," Harriet said.

"Not by my hand," I said, with justifiable indignation. "Either Henry killed himself, or there was more than one grigori who had a hand in placing him in the school. The Rostovs are in jail, probably. Or dead themselves."

Harriet glanced away. Her face was tight. She was angry with herself or her "operative" or both.

I pitied her, though she was everything it was good to be: attractive, self-supporting, blond, smart. She lived a life of adventures. But she had to depend on other people. And other people would always let you down.

I felt something shift and harden inside me.

"So why did you bring me out of the school?"

At that moment, our food arrived, and we began eating as if

there wasn't any tension in the air. I hadn't had much Italian food, and it was so good: hot, well seasoned, and lots of flavor. I was surprised to find I was really hungry, and I dug in with a will. Even the salad was good.

"Still growing?" Harriet said, sounding very adult and amused.

"Yes." I chewed and swallowed. "Now that you've told me all this, what does it mean?"

"Mean?"

"Yes. Does Iron Hand intend to follow up somehow? What do you intend to do about me? Has my Mexican family approached you to do anything else?"

So far, what I'd heard had been interesting, but it didn't change anything. Henry was still dead.

Harriet said, "I thought you'd appreciate the information is all. I don't know what your aunt Rosa has planned for her next step in getting you back."

I was surprised. "You're behind the times, Harriet. Rosa doesn't have any plans. She's dead."

"Miss Dominguez is *dead*?" Harriet's eyes were wide.

I nodded as I took another bite.

"How do you know this?" she asked, not exactly doubting me but full of astonishment.

"Someone killed her after she tried to kidnap me." I decided to be honest. "It was her father, my grandfather. Here's what I think." I didn't know this until I said it. "My grandfather found out Rosa was trying to jump to the head of the succession line by getting me first and presenting me to him like a present. Or just maybe she was trying to do me a good turn and save me from him. Either way, he found out, and after Rosa and her buddy were in a sort of jail on our property, he bribed one of the Rostovs to go in and kill her. Master Rostov got there first, I guess."

All of a sudden, she was a very different Harriet Ritter from the smooth woman who'd taken me to lunch. "You wouldn't be joking about any of this, would you, young one?" she said, her lips barely parting on the words.

"I would not be," I agreed. "I'm really not much of a joker."

We were both quiet as Harriet paid for our meal and led the way out of the restaurant.

"I'm not sure my grandfather is still alive," I said. "He sent a sort of image of himself to the school to kill me. Maybe the same teacher told him where I was. And I did the image in, but I suspect he's still alive."

We began strolling back to the Rasputin School.

"If he is dead, I guess his son, Diego, will inherit the leadership of the house."

I almost hated to say anything, but I'd been honest with her so far. "No, he won't."

Her eyes narrowed as she looked at me. "Why not?"

"He's dead. And his sister Bernarda."

Harriet Ritter stopped in her tracks. She took some deep breaths. "Don't tell me you killed them."

I looked away.

"Golly, girl. What's with you?" Harriet was eyeing me in a way that made me really uncomfortable. "You trying to kill off all your kin? Seems to me like you could use some family. The Dominguezes are powerful and rich, good people to have on your side."

"If they hadn't been trying to kidnap me and kill my friends and take away my will with a spell, sure."

"Oh?"

Harriet and I were boulders in a stream as we stood facing each other while people flowed around us on the sidewalk.

"They wanted me so they could marry me off to Paco Ruiz."

I'd managed to surprise her again.

"Are you sure that's a bad idea?" Harriet said. "Because I have seen him, and he is gorgeous. Assuming you like men?"

"I do," I said. "But I don't think that means I dislike women."

"You'll have an interesting life," Harriet said, and gave a short, brisk nod. "Well, as I say, you could do worse than Paco, at least looks-wise."

"I like to do my own picking."

We started walking again.

After a minute or two, I said, "Paco might be a dreamboat, but the way to get me to do something is *not* to tell me I have to or force me. If he'd just come to me and asked . . ."

"Do you really think it would have turned out different?"

"No. Because my grandfather isn't the kind of man used to asking or to accepting an answer that doesn't go his way. I'll tell you what would have made a real difference. If he'd acknowledged me when I was a kid. That would have won me over. Because we needed help, and he turned my father down."

Harriet didn't speak for a moment. Then she said, "I wouldn't have forgiven him, either."

After that, we were easier.

When we got to the school, I had another question. "Do you know anyone else in the family?"

"I'll have to ask our Ciudad Juárez operative. You want a message delivered?"

"Yes. I'm happy where I am. I don't want to marry Paco. I don't even want to meet him, unless he comes here and asks nicely. The Dominguez family would not help me when I needed it the most, and I don't consider myself a family member."

"You want me to tell them you'll kill anyone else who comes after you? That would be waving a red flag."

"No, I don't want any mention of killing. I might be a kid, but I'm not stupid."

"Okay, I'll send you a bill. We charge for everything."

"Of course you do," I said, though it had never occurred to me. "It will be paid." I just wasn't sure how.

Harriet turned to go.

"Wait! What if they kill your operative in retaliation? Will I owe a life?"

Harriet rolled her eyes. "No, that's part of the job."

"Thanks for coming by and telling me all this. And thanks for lunch. It was good."

Now she was biting back a smile. "It was nothing. I'm glad to make your acquaintance. Tell Lizbeth and Eli I said hello. Come to think of it, I won't send you a bill. I owe them for Dixie. They cut my partner down from the hanging tree." Then Harriet did walk away.

I watched her go. Meeting Harriet had explained a lot of things I'd wondered about. I hoped someday we'd have another conversation. She wasn't a grigori, but she was someone I admired.

CHAPTER TWENTY-SIX

After I'd waved to Peter on my way through the lobby and dropped his tracking button on the desk, I hurried to my next class feeling a little numb. I'd gotten some information, I'd given some information, and I had to think about it all. I hoped my wave had conveyed some of that.

I sank into my seat in the Magic and the Law class and heard almost nothing of the lecture.

It was possible no one else would be coming after me. I'd given my grandfather (if he was alive) something to think about. He'd said Altagracia Ruiz had given the green light to my heritage, so the Ruizes at least knew I existed. But the deaths of my aunts and my uncle had to show them I was unwilling. Either way, Altagracia and her son would have to look for a different bride for Paco.

I had another class, and then I had exercise, which was a simple pastime. You walked around the compound wall ten times, and then you ran it ten times. Some people took a longer time, some people took a shorter time. But every lap had to be done, and though there was no one obviously watching, the teacher on duty always knew if we were short on our laps. If it rained, we did jumping jacks in the refectory, which was cramped and unpleasant.

I had spent my entire childhood running, it seemed, and I enjoyed running now. I began to do my exercise run with Anna,

Fenolla, and Katerina—a strange pack. Life without Henry was changing Fenolla and Katerina, and being roommates with me was changing Anna.

Today it was Anna who paced me, and Fenolla and Katerina were right behind us. The day was colder, so we walked with our sweaters on at first. We dropped them in a pile when we began to run.

It felt good to stretch and strain, it felt good to breathe deeply and with discipline. It felt wonderful to know I was quick, that I could outrun most people. I remembered my long dash to get away from the kidnappers and how my feet had hurt and bled. This was so much better! Maybe the value of bad times was to make me appreciate the good times?

I was certainly willing to try to appreciate the good times without the experience of the bad, if I ever got a chance.

Today was not that chance.

As Anna and I rounded the corner of the northeast wall, we ran right into a huge black hole that had appeared just for us. It swallowed us up, and we were gone.

Anna and I shrieked, almost in unison, and then we were in a hotel room holding on to each other. Fenolla and Katerina were missing.

Anna's lower jaw was trembling, and my whole body was doing the same. I didn't know where the hotel room was—that is, in what city. I assumed we were really in a hotel.

Anna straightened up before I did but kept a good hold on my right hand. With her free hand, she straightened up her hair. I could see why. Sitting on the end of the bed was a middle-aged woman with a young man. The woman was dark-haired, brown-skinned, very well dressed. She was wearing a lot of jewelry for daytime. There was a mink stole tossed onto the bed beside her. The young man was the handsomest young man I'd ever seen. His coloring was as dark as the woman's, but his eyes were lighter, and his teeth were showing in a smile. Those teeth were really white and regular. Either he was simply lucky, or he was able to afford a dentist.

"We got two for the price of one," the woman said. She was speaking Spanish.

"Speak for yourself. It took me forever to design that circle and drop it in the right place at the right moment," the young man replied, also in Spanish.

"You could not have done it without eyes on the spot." Her own eyes were going over us as though we were two horses she was evaluating for possible purchase.

"Whose eyes helped you?" I asked, and Anna jumped at hearing me speak Spanish.

"Who are these people?" she asked me in English. "What do they want?"

"I have no idea," I told her. That wasn't true. I did have an idea.

"Are we really here?" Anna said. For once, I thought she was being absolutely sensible.

"I don't see how we could be."

Which made me wonder if we were still running laps at the Rasputin School. If this was what witchcraft was like, I hated it. I wondered briefly if my father had been wrong. The flavor of this magic was different from grigori magic. It stuck to my tongue like licorice.

I hated licorice.

The two on the bed hadn't answered me, but now the young man said to me, "Are you the girl we're after?"

"If you're looking for the granddaughter of Francisco Dominguez, you have found her."

"Too bad. The other girl is prettier," the woman said.

"Are you Altagracia Ruiz and Paco Ruiz?" I asked in turn.

"We are," the young man said. "I'm pleased to meet you."

Paco was more polite than his mother. She'd be the worst mother-in-law ever, I decided. Way worse than Veronika Savarova.

"We've been looking for your grandfather," Altagracia said. "Do you know the truth of the rumors?"

"I might have killed him," I said. "If that's the rumor you heard."

It was nice to see them both look shocked. But I couldn't let it go to my head.

Paco looked at his mother at the same moment she looked at him. "Too rich for our meals," he said. "She would choke us."

"Not what we were looking for," Altagracia replied.

"The other one, she is lovely."

"You can but ask."

Paco addressed us in accented English. "Beautiful blond girl, may I know your name?"

"I am Anna Feodorovna," my roommate said. She'd found her courage and wore it proudly.

"Are you married or affianced, Anna Feodorovna?"

"I am not yet affianced," Anna said, her tone making it clear that such an event was in the process. "And I am a student grigori." She didn't add that she was fourteen.

"Our children would be beautiful," Paco said.

I suspected that to Anna, this sounded romantic. To me, it sounded disgusting. However, Anna was not about to demonstrate that she found Paco handsome.

"My children by anyone will be beautiful," Anna said with certainty.

Paco laughed. "Where are your parents?"

"Redding, to the north. In the Holy Russian Empire," she added, to make sure Paco Ruiz understood.

"Thank you, most beautiful Anna," Paco told her. "I hope to see you again. And now, you two may return to your run."

He and his mother made coordinated hand gestures, which were very strange-looking to me, and then . . . we were running around the school again.

Fenolla and Katerina were screaming their lungs out. When we reappeared, Fenolla fainted, and Katerina hit me.

All the other runners had stopped in an agitated clump and were looking around for us wildly. Anna and I sagged against the wall. We both began laughing. I can't say why, exactly—we were just so glad to be back in a place we recognized.

The oldest student, Susan Foster, came around the building at top speed. She lurched to a halt when she saw us. "You've reappeared," she said, catching her breath. "Good God, what happened to you?"

"We went into a black hole," I told her. "We saw people there."

"Oh, my God," Anna wheezed. "Did that happen? Did you see them, too?"

"Yes, I saw them, too."

We spent the next hour telling Madame Semyonova about our adventure. Fenolla and Katerina verified that we spoke the truth, and so did several other students. Vanishing was not an everyday occurrence, not even at the Rasputin School.

When Madame was sure we weren't harmed and hadn't "brought anything back with us," as she put it (she went over us with a magic spell), she sent us to our rooms for lack of anything better to do.

It was hard to pick up where we'd left off, to go to the refectory for supper and return to our room to study, as if nothing had happened.

After the fifth time Anna exclaimed over the good looks of Paco Ruiz, I said, "You don't know who he really is, or you'd run the other way."

"His family is prominent in witchcraft in Mexico," Anna said. "They are very rich, next to the Dominguez family. Everyone knows that."

She'd stunned me. "No one knows that," I said. Even I, a close relative, hadn't known that. "How come you do?"

Anna flushed red. "My parents researched the best possible marriage for me. Paco Ruiz was on the list as a remote possibility."

I was sure my mouth was hanging open. "Truly?"

"Truly."

"God Almighty, Anna. Don't you feel like they're selling you?"

Anna's lips pressed together in a hard line. All of a sudden, she didn't look so winsome. "I feel like they're trying to find the man who will help my family regain its fortune. I can't do it on my own. I'm not a good enough grigori."

There were a lot of things I wanted to say, but none of them made it past my lips. They were all along the lines of *But don't they care about your happiness?* and *What about your brother?* I kept silent because those were such obvious thoughts they had to have been considered by the family many times.

The last bell rang in the main building. Even from our dormitory room, I could hear the other students spilling out of class.

Anna said, "My brother is simple."

I didn't understand. My face must have said this.

"He's . . . he doesn't have all his wits."

So the burden of pulling up the family rested on Anna's shoulders. That's what she believed. That's what her parents had taught her. I really didn't know what to say.

"Anna, are your parents poor? Are they hungry?"

"No," she said, furious. "Of course not! But they should be living here, at the court, working to get in with the tsar and tsarina. Not running a farm and a logging mill up in Redding."

"Of course, that's worth selling their daughter for, a better house in a nice location."

"You don't understand *anything*!" Anna said, tears making her eyes shine.

Even on his worst day, my father would not have sold me. At least, I didn't think so. Not for a new house or a position at court.

No, on his worst day, my father might have entertained the idea of selling me for a bottle of good whiskey. If someone else had suggested it. Maybe that was why he kept me looking like a child, I thought. The awful thought sort of slid in through the cracks in my armor.

"Maybe I don't," I said. I put my arm around her. "I'm sorry." I thought for a moment. "Paco might not be so bad after his mother dies," I offered.

Suddenly, Anna snickered, the most inelegant sound I'd ever heard her make. That set me off, and we were both laughing by the time one of Anna's friends stuck her head in the door.

Later that evening, when I was showering, I thought over the strange minutes we'd spent in another place. Where had our bodies actually been? Was it possible we had really, physically, been standing in a hotel room?

I had a healthy respect for Mexican witches now. The power of my grandfather, the fear Altagracia and Paco had raised in me—these were great forces. And the magical abduction of Anna and me, so much more elegant and subtle than the grab on the street!

I found myself wondering if I could learn to do the same thing myself.

CHAPTER TWENTY-SEVEN

Of course, I talked to Peter about what had happened, and of course, he got furious that he hadn't been there to prevent it (how he could have done that I have no idea). He was also furious once he understood how ardently Anna admired Paco Ruiz, because I had been exposed to this same handsomeness.

The only person I could discuss the black hole with was Felix. He listened with great attention, asked me several intelligent questions *not* having to do with the looks of Paco, and seemed to be as impressed as I'd been with the ability of the Ruizes.

"It makes me wonder what your grandfather could do in his prime," Felix admitted. "If his was the stronger of the two families, he must have been terrifying."

I nodded. We were practicing again, and I'd brought a frog back to life three times. "It looks older," I said, holding out my hand.

"What do you expect?" Felix peered down at the frog. "I think the process is aging it." He frowned. "Try again."

I concentrated on the frog. This was the second phase of my training, the bringing-back-to-life phase. I disliked it even more than the first phase, the killing. It seemed meaner. But Felix insisted I practice, and it was better to practice on a frog than on a human being. Felix had pointed that out to me several times.

Felix believed you could take away life and give it back without the creature changing at all. That seemed unrealistic. I asked Felix if he'd ever done that to a person, and he muttered something under his breath.

I could only believe that Felix had killed someone, maybe more than one, and everything after that was practicing to perfect his "gift." Our gift. Our talent. One of our talents.

I didn't believe killing and reviving was all I could do. I believed I could do many things I hadn't yet discovered. That I was very strong.

But when I looked at Peter, when he had his arm around me, when we were talking about his life in the Residence (which he termed "interesting") or the classes I was taking, I wondered how the magic that was now pulsing around in me was going to exist with Peter's impulsiveness and moods. Most of the time, Peter was happy, cheerful, upbeat. But sometimes, when he was angry or indignant . . . I didn't fear at all for myself, but I did fear that he would ruin his life with some crazy reaction.

On the other hand, when he kissed me, that didn't matter anymore.

After a couple of weeks, I hadn't heard any word from the Ruizes, which was great. I also hadn't heard anything from the remaining Dominguez family, who still might not know what part I'd played in the deaths of the family members who'd come to San Diego. The teachers were keeping a close eye on me since I'd been promoted. I studied hard and practiced hard.

Anna didn't say much about Paco Ruiz, but she also stopped chattering about the young man back home she'd been so close to being engaged to.

Fenolla broached the subject one day in the refectory. From time to time, she sat with me now, no matter who else was at the table.

"How's that boy doing, the one you were so sweet on?" she asked Anna.

"Oh, he's all right. His father is still talking to my father." Anna didn't sound nearly as enthusiastic as she had at first. "He's not a grigori, doesn't have any of the blood. But he's wealthy."

"How long an engagement would you have?"

"At least two years. I'd have to be sixteen, and my mother would prefer that I be a bit older." Anna shrugged.

"I agree with your mom," I said, though I was sure Anna couldn't care less about my opinion. "Why get engaged so early?"

Fenolla said, "Girls our age are promised all the time, Felicia. At least, in my culture."

I wasn't sure if she meant English or Sudanese, but I thought it might be wrong to ask.

Anna said, "Fenolla speaks the truth. And girls like me and Fenolla are picked up quick."

She knew I hated talk like that. "True, you're quite the catch," I said in a bored voice. "You'll go fast when you're ripe. You'd have to stay in Redding if you marry this boy?"

"Yes," Anna said, in a way I can only describe as sulky. "Though his family is very important there, and they're native-born."

"They are Indians?" Fenolla asked, suddenly interested.

"Oh, God, no! They are first-wave white Californians. They're Barlows. But they are distantly related to the Hearsts."

"But not in line for any of the Hearst money."

"No. They're invited to La Casa Grande once a year, though."

In the first major step toward the tsar becoming emperor of the Holy Russian Empire, William Randolph Hearst had invited the wandering Russian flotilla to land and come to his castle. The tsar had not left this land since then.

Once a year would not be enough for Anna.

Why was I spending time worrying about someone who'd been born with advantages I'd never have? Anna was beautiful, she had a family and a good background, she was being raised in what I considered to be easy circumstances, and she had a small magical talent.

"I'm tired of worrying about you," I said abruptly. "You'll ruin your life with a bad marriage, or you won't. I can't stop you, either way." I took my tray to the window, handed it in, and set off for class.

I'm sure Anna began to plot her vengeance that very moment.

Two days later, Peter said, "Did you do something to upset your roommate?"

"On the contrary," I snapped. "She upset me."

"Because she's looking at you all hurt," Peter said. "And she seems kind of pitiful."

I took a deep breath. "Of course she does," I said, and then did not say another thing. I hoped Peter would take the hint.

He only heeded that warning for a day.

"Fenolla said you were mean to Anna," Peter told me, and his voice was not quite questioning enough.

"Have you been talking about me to other people? I don't know much about having a boyfriend, but it seems to me like that's wrong."

Peter flushed. "Fenolla came to me."

"Of course she did. And why did you believe her?"

"Anna looks so miserable," he said, and shrugged.

"Do I ask you how you get along with the other grigoris at the Residence?"

"No. But I wish you would."

This was getting deeper and deeper. "Why?"

"Because I would know you were interested in me and my life," Peter said.

"Have I ever given you cause to think I wasn't? Do I not listen to everything you say to me?"

Peter hesitated. He was on the brink. "Yes, but you're not listening to me about this."

"It's my business."

"Yes, but—"

"No more 'Yes, but.' Anna became angry with me because I was criticizing her goals. Now she's retaliating in the way she thinks will hurt me back. You do understand that, right?"

"I know she's younger than you and she's hurting."

"Anna has been younger than me for about ten minutes," I said.

Peter flushed again, reminded of how quickly I had grown in the past few months.

"It seems like you haven't been listening to me, either." The pain inside began to blossom. I could feel my own eyes fill with tears, and I was horrified. That was an Anna ploy. "You had better leave," I said. "Go away, Peter. Anna has done her job."

"What do you mean?" He looked genuinely confused.

"Just go."

I lost any patience I'd had. Which hadn't been much, truthfully, because I'd been waiting for something like this for a couple of days. After a long moment, Peter got up and left the room. I wondered if Anna had decided that with Paco too far away and too dangerous and her Redding beau too far away from San Diego geographically, Peter might do in a pinch.

When she came traipsing into our room thirty minutes later, I did not look up from my homework. I did not speak. Truthfully, I did not trust my self-control, and I didn't want to give her any satisfaction whatsoever. I remembered the time I had kissed her, and how nice it had felt, and how strange, too. If I had known her then as I knew her now, I would never have touched her.

"Felicia?" Anna said, after she'd put down her books and taken off her sweater. "Did I see Peter on the stairs?"

"Of course you did," I said, and kept writing.

"Are you all right?"

"Don't you dare ask me," I said, not looking at her. "*Do not dare*."

And she didn't.

CHAPTER TWENTY-EIGHT

Despite the strain of living with a girl I had begun to loathe, I pulled ahead in all my classes. I began to think that the next school year might be better and that I might even earn one of the highly valued single rooms in the attic. An extra set of stairs for privacy? I'd do it.

Or maybe I could room with Katerina, who remained my friend. At least, she didn't try to kill me or betray me. Davis McGregor, an older boy from Scotland, decided to speak to me. Then his girlfriend, Bridget McIntosh, nodded to me in the hall. And after that, a few more of the older kids and a few of the very young ones.

I didn't know why, and I didn't ask questions.

I had two weeks of peace during which no one came after me. I was beginning to think the peace might last. The pain of my estrangement from Peter could not ache forever. Either I'd quit caring or we'd reconcile, but either way, I was not going to appease Anna to bring that about.

Screw her.

Francisco Dominguez did not show up, and apparently the Ruizes had lost interest. In Lizbeth's letters, which came every two weeks, all the news she shared was benign. She and Eli were making good money, she hadn't gotten shot in weeks and weeks, and Eli had been experimenting with dowsing. Given how dry Texoma was, if Eli could find even one well, he'd make good money forever.

My teachers began treating me like just another student.

Then came the telephone call from the palace.

The tsar needed blood.

It was about ten at night when Madame knocked on the door, waking me and Anna. All she said was, "Felicia, you're wanted. Dress at once."

It had been months since the tsar had called for me, and I'd lulled myself into hoping he'd never need me again. I hated giving him my blood. I felt sorry for Alexei. Pitying the tsar was not a good idea. Plus, I could not talk about this to anyone. It made me feel he needed me for some perversion, rather than to stay alive.

There was a car at the curb, and I ran out to it, with Madame watching from the door. Captain McMurtry was driving, which surprised me. He was an aide to the tsarina. As far as I knew, this was not part of his job.

"Felicia," he said. "Good to see you."

"I'm sorry the tsar is ill," I said, trying to be diplomatic.

"Yes, it's the first time in a while," the captain said.

"What happened?" That was not strictly my business, but he might answer.

"Another assassination attempt."

We passed under a streetlight. For the first time, I saw that McMurtry's uniform was stained with blood.

"How many does this make?" I asked. Just in case he felt like answering.

"At least five." The captain sounded exhausted.

The coup attempted by his uncle had been the most serious. Now the would-be assassins were former Americans who didn't believe they should have a king or emperor. Where had they been when the vote had been taken? (Probably outside the polling places after they'd voted, raising signs and yelling, "Death to tyranny!")

"He was wounded?"

"His aide stepped in front of the tsar and took the bullet."

That explained McMurtry's being the errand boy.

"The aide is . . . ?"

"Yes, he's dead."

And that explained the blood.

"So the tsar needs me because . . . ?"

"Because the aide knocked the tsar down to get him out of the path of the bullet, and the tsar landed on his knees."

I nodded. For anyone with hemophilia, joints swelling with blood was a great torment.

Since the captain was answering questions—which the usual driver would not do—I risked another one. "Where is Arkady?" Arkady was one of the last surviving bastards of Rasputin, and he was the tsar's usual blood donor. (It was more seemly for the tsar to take blood from a full-grown man than from a young girl, a view I agreed with.)

"He's been ill," McMurtry said. He was dodging a direct answer.

"Is he still alive?" Maybe the captain would give me a straight answer.

"Oh, yes."

McMurtry didn't sound too confident. But I felt he was telling me the truth. So Arkady was breathing but might not be at any moment.

"Nestor?"

A longer pause this time before he answered. "Nestor seems to be missing."

Then Nestor was definitely missing. You didn't temporarily misplace blood donors.

"Is Ruslan still among us?" I may have sounded a bit sarcastic by then. Ruslan was the boy they wanted me to "breed" with.

"Yes, he is under guard now. Just to keep him safe."

"Is there anyone else remaining?"

"Only you."

"You'd better make sure nothing happens to me."

"I intend to." And that was all Captain McMurtry said until we got to the palace.

I believe the kernel of the palace had formerly been the officers' club on the military base or maybe the commander's house. Or the two combined. It had grown immensely since Tsar Nicholas had decided the promontory was the most defensible place for his residence. When his father died, Alexei was reported to have been not too thrilled with the location, but the work had already gone so far he was not willing to change everything. That would be a huge waste of money and time, and Alexei knew the people (formerly American) would not put up with the lifestyle that had made his father anathema to his own people.

I was not at all surprised when the captain drove around to the side of the palace, to an obscure door. He unlocked it himself, and we went in. The passage was dimly lit, and no one was around. No servants, no courtiers. I'd been snuck in before, but there had always been servants. Always.

The hallways were blank and anonymous, to the point where I wasn't sure I could find my way out without help. We saw two people as we walked, both of whom faced the wall until we had passed. That was new, too.

In a moment, we'd come to halls that were decorated with paintings and thick carpets, and I recognized where I was. There were two guards outside the tsar's door, and the tsarina herself opened it when Captain McMurtry knocked.

I had not seen her in several months, and something interesting had happened in that time. Caroline was visibly pregnant. Well, that was good news! The tsar's aunt, Grand Duchess Xenia, was sitting by the bed, her old age giving her the privilege of sitting even though the tsarina was standing.

Xenia was holding the tsar's hand. He was a good-looking man, but now his face was contorted with pain. I could tell he was putting in a great effort to keep from crying out. Though he was covered with a sheet, I could see his swollen knees through it very easily. They might as well remove it, I thought, because even the light sheet would be causing him pain.

A medical doctor was there with the apparatus for the transfusion. He was a small man with a monocle and a great air of self-importance. A grigori was also standing by, a woman I didn't know. She knew who I was; I could tell from the way her eyes widened. I gave her a nod and went to the chair on the other side of the tsar. I got the privilege of sitting, too, since I was giving the tsar blood. Lucky me.

I had never fainted before, but if he didn't show improvement in a reasonable time and they had to take more blood than usual, I might. I was secondary in this healing drama. I rolled up the arm of my blouse, and the doctor swabbed the skin clean with sharp-smelling alcohol. He did not look at me any more than he would have looked at a footstool. I had seen him every time I'd been in the tsar's room, but I was sure he would not know me if he passed me on the street.

At least, the doctor managed the transfusion neatly. After less than ten minutes, the tsar's restless movements stopped, and his face relaxed. While I sat there, my blood running out of me and into royalty, I felt I was doing something wonderful. Everyone in the room began to look easier. I was alleviating the pain of the highest person in the land, and that was no small achievement.

But I paid for it.

The grigori brought me a glass of cold fruit juice to drink. It was very welcome. The cool, sweet fluid gave me some energy. But soon I began to sag to the side, and though I kept my mouth closed about it, I felt weak and dizzy.

"The girl feels ill, Dr. Bartofsky," the grigori said quietly.

The doctor looked at me with some surprise, as if he'd just noticed I was a mammal. Then he bustled around checking the swelling in the tsar's legs, taking his temperature, checking his pulse. Finally, Dr. Bartofsky nodded. He began the unhooking process. "Five more minutes would be better, but this is the smallest donor we have," he grumbled.

The grigori woman's upper lip lifted in a sneer. "She has given as much as anyone," she muttered. "Show some courtesy."

The doctor looked at her blankly. "What?"

She didn't answer.

"That will be all, doctor," said the tsarina. "Please return in an hour to check on the tsar."

Dr. Bartofsky bowed profoundly. "Of course, Your Imperial Majesty." He straightened and aimed his next bow at Grand Duchess Xenia Alexandrovna. "Your Highness." Xenia inclined her head very slightly. After the doctor bustled out the door, the atmosphere seemed to relax, or maybe that was just me.

The tsarina fell into a chair by Grand Duchess Xenia's, and they both stared at Alexei's face intently. And with love, it seemed to me. Not that I knew much about the look of love.

It didn't seem as though anyone was going to speak. Finally, the grigori said, "Excuse me, Your Imperial Majesty. May the captain take Felicia back to her school?"

Caroline shook herself. "Of course, Zoya. You go, too. Send someone to replace you, just in case."

"Of course, Your Imperial Highness," Zoya murmured.

She helped me stand, and we both stole out of the room as quietly as we could manage. Ford McMurtry opened the door for us and followed us out.

"Well done, Felicia," he said, as we began our trek to the side exit. (At least, I supposed that was where we were going.) "And you, too, Zoya."

I mumbled something. I was asleep on my feet.

Zoya said, "Of course," which might mean anything. She said, "Felicia, I'm Zoya Antonova. I live in the Residence. I'm a fire wizard."

"Pleased to meet you," I said. "Thanks for your help."

"No, thanks for yours. You can actually keep the tsar alive and well. So few of us are privileged to serve this way."

I couldn't be sure if Zoya was trying to impress Ford McMurtry or if she genuinely felt that way. Either way, ugh.

But she had seen to my well-being, so I kept my attitude to myself.

"Just a few more feet," Zoya told me.

It did seem as though the halls had gotten longer and more complicated. At last, I spotted a door at the end, not just another opening. We finally reached the car.

Even Zoya seemed relieved. Once we'd climbed into the backseat, leaving Captain McMurtry to the front, she said, "I'll have to call Felix to wake him. He's so hard to deal with."

"He's my friend."

"Yes, I heard. We all think that's amazing," Zoya told me.

Of course, people would be talking about me, especially other grigoris. (I knew I hadn't earned the position yet, but I would.)

"After all, Felix has never fallen for anyone that we know of," Zoya added. "You're unique."

I was so close to being asleep it took a moment for the meaning of her words to register.

"What? Felix is engaged to Lucy Savarova, not me." And knowing that the man in the front seat—who could hear every word of this—was involved with Lucy's mother (and Peter's) made me deeply chagrined.

It was Zoya's turn to be astonished. "At least she's a little closer to his age. We thought he was robbing the cradle," she said. "But he is a quirky kind of guy, and you're obviously an unusual girl."

"I'm not unusual enough to want to be with a man more than twice my age," I retorted. And my blood cousin, but that was not public knowledge.

She laughed a little but then fell silent, to my relief.

In my weary state, I felt very misunderstood. I was vexed with Peter, hurt and angry. I was relaxed in Felix's company, but if he learned of this popular belief that we were a couple, I didn't think that would last. And I despised Anna, whom I had once had tender feelings for. Not, I had to admit, because I'd ever believed she was a fundamentally good and kind person. Even Veronika Savarova had pushed me away. And Henry had been a traitor.

All the pleasure I felt at alleviating pain washed away.

I trudged to the dormitory from the front gate, wrapped in my own misery.

A figure moved in the deep shadows on the lawn, and instead of attacking, I only stopped and stared.

"Who are you?" I said, feeling I couldn't lift a finger to defend myself.

"It's me," Peter said, stepping out of the darkness into the glow of a streetlight.

"I see you. What do you want?"

"I want to beg your forgiveness," he said, in his emotional Peter style.

"Yeah? What led you to this?"

"Anna. She told me I was a fool, that you had never been anything but honest with her, and that she thought of you as one of the most interesting people she'd ever known."

"Poor, hurt Anna? To whom I was so rude and mean?" I wasn't about to let him off the hook so easily.

"I'm sorry I even believed that a little. Not that you can't be rude and, okay, a little mean, but that you would be devious or sly about it. Anna said she had acted a part, and she was sorry."

"So you believe her now? But you believed her before. Which time do you think she was telling the truth?"

"Oh, for God's sake, give me some mercy." Peter sounded raw and unsure and as miserable as I was.

Maybe that was all I had wanted to hear. I trudged over to him and put my arms around him. He held me, too. It was a very good moment. He kissed me, and I kissed him back.

But then I had to let him go. "I have to go to sleep," I said. "I gave blood tonight, and I . . . am very, very tired."

"Good night, Felicia," Peter said, with the tenderness I'd been missing in his voice.

"Good night."

I still had to climb the stairs to the third floor. By the time I got to our room, I had barely enough energy to drink a glass of water and pull off my clothes. My nightgown felt so soft and comforting. I pulled up my blanket, though it wasn't that cool. It simply felt good.

And I was out until morning, which came all too soon.

"What got into you?" I asked Anna, who was brushing her hair and looking in her mirror.

"What do you mean?" But she knew. Even as she tied a black ribbon in her hair and put on a tiny bit of rouge, she was trying not to meet my eyes. "Sometimes even I can do the right thing," she said, tart-voiced. "Peter is such a sheep!"

I thought of how quick and resourceful he'd been that day at the hotel. "You underestimate him," I said.

"Then he is simply very uneducated in the ways of girls and boys," Anna said, with all the worldly-wise airs of a beautiful and spoiled teenager.

"I'm willing to give you that."

I should have asked more questions, but I was having a hard time waking up. I could have used two more hours of sleep and a big breakfast. Instead, I had to hustle to shower and dress and make it to the refectory to grab a cup of tea with sugar. The oatmeal was all gone, and so were the eggs.

I went to my first class and slipped into my seat. A few eyes went to the bandage on my arm, but of course, no one spoke of it.

Which was fine. I didn't want to talk about it. In fact, I wasn't supposed to. The first time I'd been brought to the tsar's bedside, I'd been sworn to secrecy about the treatments he received, how he looked, who'd been present while I donated my blood, and how much blood I had given the tsar. Any detail at all I was not supposed to let pass my lips.

I could understand that. The tsar lived in more of a glass house than I ever would. I would hate to have the public know my worst failing, my weakest moment. Even my strong moments would never make gossip fodder, to my relief.

It was no surprise that I had a hard time keeping focused in class. The teachers were nice enough not to call on me. Or maybe that was just random. Most teachers at the Rasputin School did not believe in being tender and understanding with the students. There were standards you were supposed to meet, and that was that.

Anyway, I made it through to the class before lunch. I was so hungry. It was impossible to keep my mind on track. I wasn't paying attention to what was going on around me.

I did not know Anna was missing until the bell rang for my class to go to the refectory. I had grabbed up my books when one of the senior boys came to get me. "You are called to Madame's office," he said.

That meant I didn't have time to eat. My stomach gave a sad little growl.

I could hear the sound of weeping as I approached the office.

Fenolla and a girl named Adele Parkhurst, whose family was also from Redding, were crying on a bench outside Madame's open door. This was very worrying. I was even more concerned when Madame beckoned me inside and told me to shut the door behind me.

Madame looked gray and ill and very angry.

I put down my heavy book bag because I couldn't stand holding it any longer and Madame had not asked me to sit.

Madame said, "Felicia, you must tell me the last time you saw Anna."

"I saw her when I woke up this morning," I said. "Of course." What was this about?

"What did she say?"

"She was almost dressed and ready to go. I had slept too late, and I had to hurry to get ready. She was putting a black ribbon in her hair, and she . . . oh, no." *That fucking idiot.*

"What?" Madame prompted.

"She had a carpet bag out at the foot of her bed. I only saw it in passing, and I was in such a hurry to get to breakfast I didn't think much of it."

Madame took a deep breath. "What did you talk about?"

I was damned if I would tell anyone about our conversation about Peter. But he would have to enter into the narrative.

"I had run into Peter outside when I returned from the . . . place where I had to go." With the other girls possibly within hearing, I wasn't going to be more explicit. "We had a good talk, and it seemed we were going to get over our recent difficulties. I mentioned that to Anna. She acted very grown-up and worldly wise—which in some ways she is, I know. And then she left."

"She didn't say she was going on a trip or meeting someone or anything of the sort?"

"Gosh, no! She's gone? You're telling me Anna has left the school? Oh, *no*," I said again.

I remembered Paco Ruiz and the way they'd looked at each other, calculation and appreciation mixed together. I hoped so hard I was wrong! But I didn't think that was likely.

"Have you remembered something, Felicia?"

In a very unsubtle way, I tilted my head toward the door. We could hear the girls whispering to each other right outside.

"Fenolla, Adele, you may go back to your classes now," Madame called.

There was silence outside after a moment.

"My grandfather wanted me to marry Paco Ruiz," I said. "Do you know who that is?"

"His mother is Altagracia. I have met her." Madame didn't sound as though it had been a pleasure.

"That's right. She doesn't like you, either!" I had remembered the note in Altagracia's voice when she'd asked about Madame.

If Madame had looked sharply at me before, she looked at me like she was a knife and I was a cheese now. "You have talked to Altagracia Ruiz?"

"Yes, Madame. When Anna and I vanished for a few minutes. Remember?"

Madame looked as though she was drawing a blank. But she covered hastily. "And why do you associate this with Anna's disappearance?"

I wasn't going to ask her if she remembered again. She didn't. "Because Anna was with me."

Felix came in without knocking and sat to one side of Madame's desk. I repeated everything I'd said for him.

Finally, Felix spoke. "When you saw Peter last night, and you and he reconciled, did you not wonder what had happened to change his opinion?"

"I thought he'd cooled down and seen the error of his thinking," I said. "He said Anna had explained herself."

"You never considered that was out of character for Anna? That she was trying to tidy up because she was planning on leaving and she wanted to set things right?"

"No, of course I didn't think that! I was tired and ill, and I'm still tired and ill. I was only glad Peter and I were okay again. It never occurred to me Anna would do something generous. It also never occurred to me she'd think of doing something as stupid as going to Paco. Especially after we talked about it!" And that was the absolute truth. I could see doubt on Felix's face. "You may not think well of me, Felix, but I would *never* do that," I said bitterly.

"I believe you," said Madame Semyonova.

I was able to shove back the tears somehow. Damned if I would cry in front of Felix and Madame. I stiffened up all over. Back straight, fists clenched. I would have given almost anything to go into the women's room and scream.

"But you talked about it," Madame went on. "Going to Paco? That he seemed to want her?"

"I told her she shouldn't sell herself for her family's bank account." That had been the gist of the discussion, the way I remembered it.

"So you knew it had crossed her mind."

"Anna could see his admiration, and she's used to that. But she had been telling me she was as good as promised to a young man in Redding. So yes, we didn't talk about it directly, but that was the background of our discussion."

"And yet you didn't say anything to me this morning." Madame's eyebrows were almost up to her hairline.

"I did not. There was nothing to tell."

I took a deep, deep breath. I felt very unsteady. For the first time in my life, my head went swimmy, and down to the floor I went. I didn't even have time to feel relieved.

"Tell me again about the magic when Paco and Altagracia talked to you and Anna," Madame said when my eyes opened.

"Water," I said.

We were in the infirmary, and I was lying on a cot. Madame was in a chair by the cot, and Felix was handing me a glass of water. I drained it, and he silently went to get another.

"Have you eaten since last night?" he asked.

I moved my head from side to side. "No breakfast left this morning, because I got up late. I was about to go to lunch. When Madame summoned me."

Madame didn't exactly look ashamed, but she pursed her lips.

"Tell me about the Ruiz magic again," she said instead.

So again I described the portal to the best of my ability. Felix was back before I'd finished.

Madame nodded. "Did you recognize the room?" she asked me.

"Yes," I said, surprising myself. No one had asked me that before. "It looked like a room in the Claiborne, where my grandfather was staying when he was in San Diego."

I hadn't realized that until this moment. As far as I'd been concerned, they could have been in Chicago or Mexico City.

For the first time, Madame looked pleased. "Maybe we can catch them," she said. "Before the girl is ruined, but if not, at least she'd be alive. Felix, go gather the best and meet me here in ten minutes. We'll need cars."

Felix nodded, gave me a dark look, and vanished.

"Do you feel we are blaming you, and you are innocent?" Madame said.

"You *were* blaming me. I *am* innocent," I told her.

Madame seemed to accept that. "I know Anna is no saint," Madame said. "But I knew her grandmother and her mother, and I had hoped Anna would grow out of her vanity and slyness. Her mother was the same, beautiful. Her family regarded her as money in the bank."

I nodded.

"Your grandfather wanted to sell you to the Ruizes in just the same way," Madame remarked.

This wasn't an idle reference.

"You know my grandfather?" This was news to me.

"I danced with him at a ball or two," Madame said. "He was a handsome man in a sort of eagle-ish way."

My imagination could not conjure up any image of Madame at a ball or of a young Francisco Dominguez. I could see his aged face, distorted by pain and rage, all too clearly in my memory. I pushed that picture back, away, out of my head.

Back to Anna.

"I'll go with you," I said.

"No, you won't. I've brought my radio for you to listen to, and a book. You'll stay here and eat and drink and rest. Anna will need able friends when she returns."

There was no arguing with Madame when she spoke in that voice, and I realized she was right. I was listless and sad, not clear-thinking at all. Altagracia would make toast of me. And the book was another Dashiell Hammett.

Madame seemed surprised when I nodded. She said, "I'll have Callista bring you some food and lots of water. Stay here."

"Yes, Madame."

Madame got to her feet and picked up her cane. "I hear the cars in the street," she said, and left to do battle with the Ruizes.

I felt curiously flat when she was gone. There would be a battle, and I would not be there. On the other hand, I was too weak to do a jumping jack just now.

Callista pushed the door open with her hip to deliver a big pitcher of water and a glass. She made another trip to the hall to bring in a tray with bread and meat and fruit and cheese. And a slice of cake! Sweets were rare at the school, and I couldn't imagine where it had come from.

"Tom brought me a cake for my birthday," Callista said, as if she'd read my thoughts. "It's chocolate."

"Tom is very thoughtful," I said. "And so are you."

Now that I was a bit grown, I realized I'd never had a chance with Tom O'Day. He obviously preferred women with more meat on their bones than I'd ever have. Lucky Callista.

Trying not to imagine what might be happening at the hotel, I turned on Madame's radio and listened to music while I slowly ate everything on the tray and drank water until I thought I would pop.

I felt so much better! Now I could use a nap. Despite worrying about the rescue party and Anna, I fell asleep.

Then the bad dream began.

My grandfather stood in front of me. He looked weaker and older and grayer, but it was undeniably Francisco Dominguez. He was delighted to see me.

"I knew it," he said. "You would be too weak after giving your blood to that leech of a tsar to come to find your little friend."

Something in me stirred at that, insisting this wasn't a dream.

How could a dream about a dead man include something that had just happened? My grandfather couldn't know about the tsar or Anna! I struggled to wake up.

"You're dead," I said. It didn't come out very clearly, but he understood. In the dream. Which wasn't a dream, I was sure now.

"You thought you could kill me that easily? Girl, you will never be ready to fill the shoes of someone like me!"

"I don't want to fill your shoes," I said more clearly. "You're awful."

"So are you," my grandfather retorted. "You killed my family!"

"I *am* your family."

"You killed the family I loved," he corrected himself, intending this to hurt.

Actually, it did. I opened my eyes wider. I was almost fully awake. This really was my grandfather, and he really was standing in the infirmary.

"Did you drug me?"

"Your red-haired friend did that. Of course, I helped."

"Why?"

"I told her Madame had called me in to examine you, but she wanted you to rest first. I told her you would resist any sleep aid, so I sprinkled some powder on the cake. I knew you wouldn't taste it with the chocolate."

"You gave her the cake?"

My mind kept getting snagged on the smallest items. But I could not believe Callista or Tom was deceiving me.

"It was a great opportunity," my grandfather said. "I would have put it on the meat if I'd had to, but it would have been more detectable, even to an idiot like you."

"This idiot wounded you pretty damn bad last time I saw you," I reminded him.

"Not only boastful but foul-mouthed," my grandfather said.

"You are my blood," I said, just to make him angry.

I regretted that almost immediately, because his face tightened, and he made some fancy hand gestures. Pain ripped through me, pain so intense that I screamed. He took my voice but not quickly enough.

The door flew open, and Callista ran in. She stopped at the sight of the old man, and several emotions crossed her face at almost the same time: a knee-jerk respect for the elderly doctor she thought he was, worry for me since I was clearly in pain, and caution. Callista settled on caution, which was good but too late.

"Sir," Callista began, her voice calm and just barely polite. "You should leave. Make an appointment if you want to see Felicia or the head of the school." Her left hand went to her vest.

But he was too quick and too ruthless for Callista. He flung out his hands, again with gestures, and she folded to the floor. All her color was gone, and her red hair arced out around her like spilled blood. Callista had never been anything but kind to me, and if I hadn't wanted to kill my grandfather before—I thought I *had* killed him before—I was determined to do it now.

I felt inside myself, to see what power I had. It surged up to meet me, roaring to be set free. Maybe my power was akin to Francisco Dominguez's power since we were kin by blood? Maybe that power was angry because he was trying to destroy me? It was the do-or-die moment.

I came up off the cot in a single leap and wrapped my hands around his neck, squeezing with all my might. I had the body of a teenage girl—not as strong as a teenage boy but maybe stronger than an old man.

We would see.

He threw spells at me. His hands were free. But my grandfather was distracted by the pain and by his shock that he could not shake me off.

The door opened, and a woman stepped in. I had a confused impression: she was pretty, dark, about thirty-five, dressed well, groomed well, and . . . delighted. My grandfather flung out a hand to her and grunted, clearly telling her to help him.

I was nearing the end of my strength.

But in answer to his appeal, the new woman laughed.

As if I weren't choking a man to death in front of her, as if he weren't fighting for his life, the newcomer said, "Pleased to meet you, *sobrina*. Thanks for disposing of Diego and Bernarda. I see you're doing your best to kill Father."

"You! You were the one who helped us," I said, sure this was the young woman who'd talked to my father that day in Ciudad Juárez at the house with the fountain. "I've wondered where you were!"

The distraction cost me another wound, this time on my cheek, as one of my grandfather's magical strikes sliced it open.

I had to concentrate more on holding on, not loosening my grip a fraction of an inch. My hands were aching viciously, and I was bleeding from a dozen wounds.

"Yes, I'm your *tia* Isabella. That was long ago. I never believed I'd get rid of this old man who has ruled my life. But his lust for acquiring you has done him in. You seem to be bleeding quite a bit. Shall I help?"

"Of course," I said from between clenched teeth.

My grandfather was turning a satisfying ashen color, but I was weaker and weaker.

It was harder to choke someone than I'd imagined.

He kicked at me, and we went down to the floor, but I never lost my grip. To my amazement, I could feel the numerous cuts and slices closing up. I'd lost blood and energy, but at least I wasn't going to bleed out. I was hoping Isabella would help me a little more directly. Maybe she didn't feel she could actively take part in killing her own father.

Isabella might not have been confident that I was going to be able to hold on, because she dropped her scarf to the floor.

"Oh, no," she said. "That's too bad! Oops!" She knelt and held the scarf over her father's nose and mouth. "Bad Father," she said. And her voice dropped from its light amusement to something entirely different. "*So bad!*"

That was the bit of help I needed. I got one knee onto his right arm, and the left flailed about with less purpose. I shifted my right knee and finally trapped his left arm, too. He still bucked and rolled from side to side but without actually moving very much. My aunt kept the scarf in place, watching her father intently as he weakened.

"You seem to be prone to choking people," she murmured.

I looked at her more closely. "You were the crazy woman who came into the school! Why did you do that?"

"Just testing the defenses. Getting the layout. As a bonus, I got to see you, *sobrina.*"

Then we were silent.

Finally, when my own strength was almost at an end, I realized my grandfather was not moving any longer.

"Safe?" I asked Aunt Isabella.

"Yes," she breathed. "We are both safe."

Shaking all over, I got myself off the body. With Isabella's help, I was able to stand, though my knees promptly folded, and I collapsed onto the cot. She may not have been as unmoved as she'd been pretending, because she sat beside me. She took my hand.

"Thank you," she said.

"Oh, thank *you*," I said. Which was ridiculous. "How did you come to be here?" *In the nick of time. Suspiciously.*

Isabella looked me square in the eyes. "When you almost killed him through his avatar, he decided he had to have you. You couldn't get the best of him and remain at liberty. He had thought it would be easy to lure you in, since you were untutored and young and half Russian." She pressed her lips together for a moment, then said with some wonder, "And he trusted me all through it, told me every step! And he was sure I would help him in any way possible."

I didn't know what to say. *Why didn't you kill him years ago so I didn't have to?* didn't seem very politic.

"As long as Bernarda and Diego stood by him, there was no way I could survive killing Father. Rosa had made her move, and she died for it, he told me. But Diego and Bernarda? They were stuck to him like leeches. After you killed them and wounded him, he was a goat staked out to attract stronger predators. And he knew it, but he couldn't really believe it. He never doubted that I would help him destroy you." She shook her head. "He never doubted."

It seemed like Isabella was having mixed feelings about that. I didn't know what to say. *Congratulations on being such a good deceiver?* My aunt had preserved her own existence by living a lie for years. I hoped the rest of her life would prove worth it.

Fenolla pushed the door open cautiously, and then she and Katerina came in, their hands at the ready. Other students rushed in, some clutching their spell books, ready to take my side. Aside from my two friends, they all looked very young, the same class I'd been in a few months ago.

Two of them screamed when they saw Callista and the (now) benign-looking old man on the floor and Isabella and me sitting on the cot. I was spattered with blood from my many cuts.

Isabella looked just fine.

The children knelt by Callista, using their little magic to make her feel better. Her color did improve. She was breathing. When I had enough energy to get up, I would go to check on her.

"Children," Isabella said with some distaste. "Well, it is a school. He told us you were in training here, so I hoped you had escaped your father."

"He is dead. My uncle is dead, too."

"Not a large loss," Isabella said, and stood. "It's been wonderful to see you, niece. I must go."

"I hope I see you again sometime," I said. I was surprised to find that I meant that. "You and I are at peace, right? You're not going to try to kill me or kidnap me or marry me to Paco Ruiz?"

Isabella laughed, which was so strange in that bloody room that the children pushed back to the doors, their eyes wide. "I will not kidnap you or try to kill you or try to marry you to Paco. I feel sure I'll see you again."

And Isabella walked out as calmly as she'd walked in, the children parting before her like the Red Sea parted for Moses.

CHAPTER TWENTY-NINE

They drew us out professionally," Madame Semyonova said the next day. "Anna was in the hotel room, safe and sound, though tied up. She was the bait to get me and other strong ones out of the way while Francisco came for you. He knew I wouldn't leave the school if you were in danger. He played me like a fish on a hook."

"Instead, he got landed and filleted," Felix said, sounding almost proud.

"I managed," I said, trying to sound matter-of-fact.

I didn't make it credible: Madame looked at me sideways.

Anna was back in our room, receiving guests like she was a queen. Madame had said I would be well enough to get out of the infirmary ("your second home," she'd called it) and go back to my class schedule after one night. A healer had been called in from the residence, since Callista was not up to par. He worked on my many cuts. Thanks to Isabella, I would not have as many scars as I'd imagined. There would be one on my face, though. I would always be reminded of my grandfather and his attention to me.

Peter sat beside my bed holding my hand, on a break from his lobby duty.

Felix leaned against a wall, scowling at me while Madame sat in the other chair. She had already forgotten some things about the day before. I met Felix's eyes. He knew.

Isabella, Madame's mysterious sources had told her, had boarded a train for Mexico City two hours after she'd left me sitting on the cot. The Ruizes had left their room at the hotel and departed from San Diego before Anna's search party had even arrived at the Claiborne. The Ruizes had left a note for Madame, begging her pardon and Anna's for their "accidental" involvement in Francisco's plot.

It was hard to see how that involvement, which included luring Anna into leaving the school and then imprisoning her, could have been accidental. But rather than start a feud with Mexico's second (now maybe first) most prominent witch family, Madame had accepted the apology at face value as long as the Ruizes never again involved themselves in the school's affairs.

Now Madame's office was full of flowers and boxes of candy, Peter said, as word spread of what had happened. I hadn't known Madame was so well known and respected in the supernatural world. I didn't think any of the students had. It was an interesting revelation.

Peter stood up when Madame had finished asking questions and held out his hand to help me sit up. Since I was truly not a hundred percent restored, I took it. I finally asked the question I'd been dreading.

"Madame, are you sure you want me here at the Rasputin School? I've caused a lot of trouble, though it mostly wasn't my fault."

I didn't know where I would go, but somehow I would manage. I could go live with my half sister in Texoma, though I'd always been a city girl.

"As far as I am concerned," Madame said, "you are the strongest

student this school has ever had. It is our calling to train you to realize your potential and to be a credit to your profession."

"Hear, hear," Felix said unexpectedly.

I jumped a bit.

"And just so you know," Madame continued, "I have had a talk
with Miss Anna, and I think she will be a model student from now
on. Her family has been telephoning every other hour. Mostly to verify that she was not 'ruined' when she was a prisoner."

I opened my mouth, shut it.

"What do you want?" Madame asked. "To see if I verified
Anna's virginity? And if I did, how I did it? Do not ask. Anna is
completely marriage-worthy." And Madame's face looked extra icy
as she said this.

"Of course she is, Madame," I said solemnly. "I am so relieved
for her."

And finally, I left to go back to my dormitory room, with Peter
holding my hand. There just so happened to be quite a lot of students
loitering about the hall outside of the infirmary. By some strange
circumstance, they all happened to be there to look at me. And they
touched me when I passed them on the way to the stairs.

Small hands (and some large ones) reached out hesitantly to
touch my skirt, my free hand, my shoulder. No one grabbed or kept
hold. It was strange, and it was . . . lovely. Like I was a good-luck
charm, instead of the opposite.

We made our way in silence up the stairs. Peter said, "That's
what you should remember."

I knew he was right.